Murder 101

RICHARD BOYER

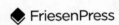 FriesenPress

Suite 300 - 990 Fort St
Victoria, BC, V8V 3K2
Canada

www.friesenpress.com

Copyright © 2021 by Richard Boyer
First Edition — 2021

This is a work of fiction. The characters, organizations, places, books, and actions are products of the author's imagination or used fictitiously.

ISBN
978-1-5255-8451-0 (Hardcover)
978-1-5255-8452-7 (Paperback)
978-1-5255-8453-4 (eBook)

1. FICTION, CRIME

Distributed to the trade by The Ingram Book Company

Honor trumps ambition in the cheeky mystery novel *Murder 101*, wherein a curious professor refuses to be stymied by university bureaucrats.
—*FORWARD CLARION REVIEWS,* 4 OF 5 STARS.

I loved this book! A well written, cleverly plotted, hugely entertaining romp through the (almost literally) backstabbing world of academia. A treat for anyone who's spent any time in a university community. Boyer uses his deep understanding of the pressures and conflicts facing today's academics to create a cast of well-rounded, flesh-and-blood characters.
—E. R. BROWN, EDGAR AND ARTHUR ELLIS AWARD SHORTLISTED AUTHOR OF *ALMOST CRIMINAL.*

Three cheers for the suspicions of Professor Monroe, humanist hero in this comically believable story of malice, murder, and loss on the modern campus. Required reading for all Presidents and administrators.
—JOHN CRAIG, FORMER DEAN, FACULTY OF ARTS AND SOCIAL SCIENCES, SIMON FRASER UNIVERSITY.

Prologue

"Not the best view from here." Monroe swept his hand toward the ski run. "Gets better on the trail."

Peter Eliot lowered his window, turned toward the forest beside the chairlift, and breathed deeply. "The air . . . I need it. Cooped up too long in the office."

A few minutes later, Monroe pulled out his daypack from the trunk. "For the trail. Friuli cheese and a baguette I baked last night."

"Ah, you historians, the art of living. Pour moi, a few apples, humble Spartans, zucchini bread. All store-bought."

Monroe laughed. "It's all good. Look, Peter, the trail has a lot to offer, even for a rock climber like you. St. Mark's lookout is . . . hold it, you're losing something from the side of your pack."

Eliot reached around and zipped the side pocket: "The EpiPen . . . bloody allergies."

Belongings secured, the two men set a companionable pace until the twin peaks of the Lions came in view. Eliot stepped onto a fallen log and looked as if to chart a route up. Moving again, each of them paused occasionally to take in a vista, or check mosses, bark, lichen, fungi, or mushrooms. "Amazing . . . so much life," muttered Eliot, as he poked gently at a log with a beetle emerging from a crack. Above the trail, a raven eyed them.

After an hour or so, the two men reached a steep section at the base of a ridge. The trail became rocky and muddy as they scrambled to the top. "This is it," Monroe said. They stepped onto the granite surface, smoothed by weather and falling away toward the edge of a cliff face above Howe Sound. Silently they viewed blue waters far below that shimmered and rippled in play with wind, currents, and the slanting light of the fall sun. Eventually, Monroe pointed out Bowen, Gambier, Keats, and Passage Islands, and then retreated to lean on a tree and pull out his bread and cheese. He watched as Eliot, in a zone, sucked in the air, chest expanding and contracting, eyes busy, now scanning glaciers of the Tantalus Range, now looking out toward Vancouver Island half hidden in mist, and again turning downward. "Ferry coming . . . an eagle . . . *two* eagles," he said softly.

"Watch the edge," Monroe said.

A few minutes later, hikers arrived and a voice pierced the calm: "Bullet, come here, *now*." An exuberant German Shepherd, ignoring the order, bounded up to Monroe, pushed against him in friendly contact, then turned and raced toward Eliot. The dog skidded on the rock and crashed into Eliot, who fell and started to slide headfirst toward the cliff face.

Monroe sprang to his feet and, with three or four steps and a lunge, got a hand around Eliot's ankle. But his forward momentum pushed them both toward the edge, even as he tried to find a toehold on the rock.

Finally, he felt hands on his legs. "We've got you, sir." It was Bullet's owner. Slowly, she and her friends pulled Monroe and Eliot back from the edge.

Afterward, standing back from the rock, Bullet's owner broke the silence. "Sorry, mister. He's a young dog. . . . I know, supposed to be on a leash." She turned away.

Monroe and Eliot moved away from the others and sat together near the trail. "I thought I was done. How'd you get me so fast?" Eliot asked. Monroe shrugged his shoulders, the left one throbbing from his launch onto the rock. "Maybe something from high school football, wide receiver, short quick routes." He paused. "Quite a long time ago now, don't move as fast as I used to."

"Well, fast enough to rescue this fifty-something. My head was right at the edge. Nice view though"

"Dog owners."

Eliot studied the breadcrumbs and bits of cheese on the ground. "She meant well. That one's a hand full. Liked your baguette." He passed Monroe an apple.

As they started back, Eliot stepped over to Bullet, gave him a pat, and spoke softly to him. The dog wagged his tail.

"You two buddies now?"

"Yeah, told him we'd bring him another baguette next time."

Monroe laughed. On the way down, the two men settled into private solitudes, their plan to discuss university matters dropped.

"A splendid day," Eliot said when Monroe dropped him at his home. "Damn dog. I liked him. Anyway, see you Tuesday. I have some big-picture thoughts—still rough, about restoring collegiality. We'll see what you think."

"Sure." As he drove away, Monroe looked up and again saw a raven (the same one he'd seen earlier?) high in a spruce tree next to Eliot's house.

1

⠶

Tuesday morning Monroe grabbed his briefcase, pulled the door closed, and took the stairs two at a time. At street level, he glanced back and saw James, the neighbour's cat, stalking something near a rose bush. "Leave the birds alone," he muttered as he slipped through the gate and jabbed it closed with his elbow. Warren Kingsley's aged Honda was two steps away and the door groaned as he pulled it open.

"This thing's in pain, Warren. Only needs a little grease."

"Yeah, it's on my list. Something bothering you? You look annoyed."

Monroe took a deep breath. "James was hunting birds in my yard this morning. Cats. They kill a billion birds a year."

"Don't get me started. I saw the same article. Cats, pesticides, climate change. Down three billion birds since 1970. My birding group talks about it all the time."

"Did you go out on the weekend?" Monroe asked.

"Just on my own at Seymour."

"I'd never be able to find that place of yours again," Monroe said. "Damnedest thing, you can walk right by it without noticing it."

"That's the idea. Privacy. I was watching a pair of red-breasted sapsuckers that hang out near my cabin. They're lovely."

"Never seen one."

"They're not uncommon if you know where to look. I also did some class preparation there Sunday. I've got fifty in the intro course and three new grad students. How're your courses going?"

Monroe paused, taking stock. "OK, I guess. A lecture today after lunch and I'm meeting Eliot at 8:30."

"Again. A regular thing, no?"

"Well, winding down. His consultations with faculty till the end of this month. He's trying to put a plan together to improve the culture of this place."

"That would be big," Warren said, his voice dripping with sarcasm, his eyes straight ahead, his hands squeezing the steering wheel. He veered left into Lot B at the eastern edge of the campus, bounced through several potholes, and came to a stop between two older cars. "That's it, carpooling . . . day one. Could be a new routine. Hey, that's Jenson's Volvo on your right. Oldest guy in our department. He used to bird with us, crazy about raptors, but his hearing's shot now and doesn't walk well. Retiring this year."

Monroe didn't know Jensen but wondered if he should be driving. One didn't have much contact with faculty outside one's own department at Northlake. As they neared the quad, Monroe's phone buzzed with an incoming message. "Uh oh, change of plan. Eliot's canceling. Up for a coffee?"

Warren shook his head. "Can't. Gotta get to the lab. Wait, Eliot's over there now, by the admin building and looking our way. See you."

Monroe waved at Eliot and cut across the lawn toward him. "Just saw your message."

"Sorry about the late notice," Eliot said. "Thought I could fit it in. *Wanted* to. But the meeting went on. Librarians . . . they're talkers. Needed to air their concerns. *Concerns*—a polite word but it got heated. Plus I lost some time with an early visitor this morning." His eyes locked onto Monroe's briefcase. "Coming from the parking lot? Where's your bike?"

"Carpooled with Kingsley." Monroe cricked his neck in the direction of the psych building. "Trying to help the stats for the Go-Green."

A grimace passed over Eliot's face. "Not the best name. But it's coming along. The mayor said he'd upgrade bus service to campus."

Monroe looked doubtful. "The mayor's a fast talker. He'll have to corral the council first—they're all over the place. How about later for our meeting? I want to hear what you've pulled together."

"It'll have to wait. Too backed up now. Mildred will be out of the office for a dental appointment so it might mean some extra chaos from phones and drop-ins. Then there's lunch with today's visiting speaker."

"Oh right, the president's lecture series." Monroe wasn't thrilled about the speaker. Essentially the student society had proposed him, the author of a best-selling book, *The Lost City of Z*. Monroe knew that the book dramatizes Colonel

Percy Fawcett's disappearance in the Amazon in 1925 as mysterious, tragic, and somehow heroic. A good story. But he also knew that the historian John Hemmings had shown Fawcett to be reckless and ignorant. *Free speech of course, but let's be clear about what's fact and what's fiction.*

"How about later in the week?" Eliot asked. "Or Whyte Lake on Saturday? I'll bring my notes. And I'll pick your brain about getting a new commuter bike. I'll phone you."

⬛⬛

In The Buzz, the student union run café, Monroe grabbed a coffee and settled into a corner seat. He lapsed into lizard mode as the sun warmed his back and he sucked in the aroma of baking cinnamon buns. Idly counting down as the tower clock bonged ten times, he picked up on a conversation at a nearby table. Mason Kennedy, a Chaucer expert, was holding forth to some attentive grad students. Monroe admired him, a dashing Oscar Wilde type: smart, witty, curious, and always stylish in a bow tie and designer shirt and jacket. A person he'd like to see more of but somehow didn't.

As he shifted in his chair, Monroe picked up the rapid fire of Kennedy's words and wondered if his stutter was real or affected: "And s-s-so they finally figured out that Hastings had a br-br-br-brain tumour and the doctors pre-scribed avastin, which more normally is given for colorectal cancers. Very strong doses reduced it from the size of a golf ball to a m-m-m- marble—but as a side effect, he got a heart attack so it seems to me that . . ." Monroe strained to hear more but Kennedy—*how does he* know *all this?*—had turned away. Poor Hastings, whoever he was. Another person trapped in treatment that prolongs agony. Maybe increases it.

Monroe reluctantly pulled out a stack of essays. Working steadily, he marked seventeen of them before refilling his water. As a reward, he took out a collection of stories by Borges. He flipped through the battered paperback but couldn't settle on one. The Buzz might be the wrong place for Borges. One needed less, well, less *buzz* to savour Borges's disjunctions of substance and style, his made-up citations to scholarly authorities and interpretive schools. *A perfect riff on how we academics fight to the death over ever-narrower subjects or interpre-tive entanglements.*

"Bruce, you old dog." Monroe jumped as a hand clapped him on the shoulder. Jean-Michel Sevene, director of the Kerr Art Gallery on campus, beamed down at him.

"For god's sake," Monroe said. "Where have *you* been? Sit."

"Saw you through the window. Actually on my way to the squash courts. Join me? I've got till 1:30, then a meeting."

Monroe reached across and squeezed his right shoulder, still sore, then checked his watch. "Well, I could, but I don't have my racket."

"I've got an extra. Let's go."

⬛

After squash and quick showers, Monroe and Jean-Michel were walking back toward the quad. "What's your meeting about?" Monroe asked.

"Mrs. Kerr wants to pry a few Emily Carrs out of the Vancouver Art Gallery for a month or so. Good luck. I don't see how we could afford it. Starting with insurance and transport. Then there's our pathetic security system. We'd need a guard 24/7, which couldn't be done without an angel with deep pockets."

"Why not Kerr herself? She's the big patron of the gallery. And being on the board of governors, she has access to Howard Davis. He's loaded, and it's something as chancellor he might step up for."

Jean-Michel shrugged his shoulders. "I know zip about fund—"

"Hold it," Monroe said as he gestured toward the flashing lights of a fire rescue truck and ambulance in front of MacLane Hall. "Something's wrong."

2

Two firemen entered the building. One had an oxygen cylinder, the other held what looked like a defibrillator and a medical bag. Two paramedics were pulling a wheeled stretcher from the rear doors of the ambulance.

Near the entrance Fred Turner from political science looked on as he leaned against a cherry tree. A small crowd stood by as a couple of university security officers kept watch. Must have been a heart attack. But who?

Monroe jumped into step behind the paramedics. At the door he flipped open his wallet and flashed his faculty ID card at a security guard whose nametag said Dobbs. "I'm with these guys. Faculty liaison." Dobbs looked doubtful. "Doing a great job. Keep it up."

At the top of the stairs the paramedics paused, apparently to assess where the firemen had gone. "You guys know your way?" Monroe asked. "Dean of arts is to the right, university president to the left."

"Left then," one of them said, "even if it's pro-forma."

"Pro-forma?"

"We were told the person is already dead. That's why there was no siren. But we got here as fast as we could anyway."

"Who?" Monroe asked with a sense of dread.

"The president." As the two men hurried down the corridor, Monroe sagged against the wall, fighting back a wave of nausea. Eliot dead. How? He had just seen him. What, a couple of hours ago? In full stride, with plans for the university, plans for the weekend: Whyte Lake . . . the future. He gripped the notebook in his pocket with its jottings for tomorrow, for next week, for next spring. *We all have such a book, a bet on our future.*

Monroe walked down the corridor and entered the president's offices. The firemen were in the outer office and had been joined by the paramedics. A doctor from the university clinic stood with Mildred Jones next to her desk.

"I just heard. I take it he's in the inner office."

"Yes," Mildred said softly. "I found him when I returned from my dentist appointment. Phoned 911 and the clinic."

"George Chambers." The doctor reached out his hand. "New to the campus this year. I came right away. Pronounced President Eliot dead and signed the death certificate. It looks like a straightforward case of misadventure, most likely an allergic reaction, although I'm not a pathologist."

Monroe thanked the doctor, peered into Eliot's office, and, without thinking, entered. He looked at an old ice ax mounted on one wall along with a few photos of a younger Eliot with climbing companions, packs mounted on their shoulders, peaks in the background, smiles a little forced as if embarrassed to be passing themselves off as serious alpinists. The usual paraphernalia sat on the desk: a coffee mug, paper clips, a couple of reference books, and a penholder. Eliot's body lay on the floor, scrunched up, his face locked in a grimace. His pant leg was pulled up and there were scratches at the side of his shin. An EpiPen lay next to his leg. Had he been trying to stab himself with the pen? Monroe crouched down for a closer look and studied it for several minutes as he tried to imagine Eliot's last few moments. Slowly, he returned to the outer office, where Mildred and the first responders were still standing around.

"Mildred, I have to go teach a class. Maybe this was an accident but something doesn't seem right. Could you phone the RCMP and tell them the president has died and emergency people have been here? They should have a look at this if they're not already on the way. Ask for Inspector Martino, if he's available. I know him."

Dobbs was still at the doorway when Monroe left the building. "Hey, Dobbs, they need you upstairs till the police arrive. Keep an eye on the president's office and don't let anybody touch anything."

3

Monroe was about eight minutes late. The class seemed happy enough for the slow start but became attentive by the time he reached the podium. "I have an announcement. Peter Eliot, our president, died earlier today. That's why emergency vehicles are in front of MacLane Hall. I don't think Mr. Eliot's death will affect any of you directly. Life will go on. Your courses will proceed. But speaking personally, I feel that the university has suffered a serious loss that may play out in ways we cannot yet anticipate. So let's carry on, as I'm sure Mr. Eliot would have wanted."

After a quiet moment Monroe reached for a piece of chalk and wrote NEW HISTORICISM in block letters. "Working definition, anyone?" He looked around the room. "No? Well let's start with how we know what happened in the past. Start with sources. Diaries, letters, documents of one kind or another. Understood in a *context*: who created the document, when, why, where, and in what situation."

Monroe had ambled to the door and looked through the glass panel at the top. He had heard some commotion in the corridor. Did it have anything to do with the arrival of the police?

He turned back to the class. "Stephen Greenblatt's essay on Sir Thomas More in *Renaissance Self-Fashioning*. Are there any comments on his source?" Angela Delaney raised her hand. "Apparently there was a mix-up. The reserve librarian filed the photocopies under an English course and so it wasn't available until yesterday. By then it was too late with pre-midterm exams this week."

Monroe frowned. "Pre-midterms? That's a new one."

Several other students nodded their heads. Monroe thought he overheard Angela whispering "Turner" to her neighbour. "OK," he said, "you're off the hook. We'll have a short class. But here's a preview. Greenblatt looks at something that at first might seem unimportant or incidental for understanding the broader culture. But he argues that it can fully represent it. Like extracting DNA from a tooth that can reveal all kinds of things about a person. In this case, we'll want to notice how much Greenblatt can extract about Sir Thomas More's society from his memory of a dinner party hosted by Cardinal Wolsey."

Later, standing at his office window, Monroe wondered why the class hadn't shown much concern about Eliot's death. It was quiet now in the quad, although a policeman was stationed at the entrance to MacLane Hall. Dobbs must be still upstairs. He decided to call Margo Johnson, receptionist in the dean of arts office.

After one ring, the dean, Evan Spelt, answered and invited him over for a drink. Monroe accepted the invitation but didn't leave right away. He stood at the window for a while, looking down at the quad and over at MacLane Hall. Then he walked to his bookshelves to scan titles as if one of them might have some answers. He reached for his Montaigne, the *Essays,* and found what he was looking for. Death bothered him, he wrote, not in the abstract but particulars: a shirt, a saddle, or a book left behind. *Or a well-used ice ax,* he thought. He slipped on his jacket and headed out the door.

At the entrance to the administration building, Monroe nodded to the campus policeman. He took his time on the stairs, and turned into the dean's office. In the outer office he waved toward Margo and two other staff members huddled around a table at the back with cups, a teapot, and a plate of biscuits. Spelt's office door was open. "It took you a while." He handed Monroe a scotch.

"Thanks. You know what happened to him?"

"Beats me. Possibly food poisoning."

"From what?"

Spelt shrugged his shoulders. "Maybe bad food caused a heart attack. He threw up, Mildred said. After she found him she came down here. It took Margo a while to calm her down. A sudden death is a shock." Spelt glanced toward the photos in his bookcase.

"But she was able to tell you about finding him."

"Yeah. Apparently everything was normal this morning. He went to a meeting with the librarians before she left for a dentist appointment. When she came back, she found him dead. Too late to do any good, of course. After she sat with Margo for a bit, she asked me if she could go home. No point in her staying."

But she didn't go home right away, Monroe thought, for she had been in the office when he went up there after squash.

"Margo thinks she was in shock," Spelt said. "I told her she should see a doctor. She was pale, she spoke softly I could hardly hear her, her hands were shaking, and she burst into tears a few times. Margo gave her some tea. I don't think she noticed, but I spiked it with some scotch. It seemed to help."

"Then you told her she could go home."

"Yes, although she seemed reluctant. Margo thinks her marriage isn't going too well right now. Anyway by then the emergency people were here and the doctor had certified him as dead. Mildred said something about the police coming, but I don't know who called them or why."

Just then the phone rang. "Dean of arts, Spelt speaking. . . . Oh, hello, Howard." *It's the chancellor,* he mouthed in Monroe's direction. "You got my message, sir?" Spelt walked toward the window. "Yes, terrible. . . . No, I can't speak for the doctor or the emergency people. . . . Yes, I think everybody's still in the building. Except Mildred Jones, his office manager. I told her she could leave. She found the body, was understandably upset. . . . Right now I'm with Bruce Monroe"—Spelt gave a nod toward Monroe—"from the history department, a little moral support. We're waiting now for the police to arrive, apparently they're coming . . . Hmm, don't know sir. I suppose it's routine when someone dies. . . . Right, no longer an emergency."

Spelt paced the floor and fiddled with a book on the shelves behind his desk. "Me . . . are you sure?" A smirk crept onto Spelt's face. "Of course, I'd be honoured, but wouldn't it look better if it were someone from the board of governors or one of the vice presidents? At least short term. After all. Eliot's appointment process was somewhat heated and I was, uh, in the thick of it."

Monroe watched Spelt, his personality in full deferential mode now. Everyone knew that Chancellor Davis had supported him for the presidency and the minister of education had intervened to put Eliot forward. No one knew exactly how the voting had gone with the board of governors, but it had apparently involved some last-minute shifts. Now Davis was getting his man after all.

"Yes, of course, sir. I've always been grateful for your confidence. . . . Yes, sir,

I understand." He smiled. "Of course, temporary until it is not. Count on me to do my best. It's definitely a crisis, but also, if you will, a fresh start and no time to lose. . . . Pardon? . . . Certainly, I'll speak to Mildred Jones tomorrow. I assume she'll be in." In a soft voice, he added, "She'd better be," then returned to a normal volume. "Mildred will be important for the transition. Professor Drummond can take over my duties in this office." As if half expecting her to enter on cue, Spelt glanced toward a door on the far side of the general office with the sign "Professor Lucile Drummond, Associate Dean" on it. "She's in a meeting now. . . . Oh, of course. I'll ask her. I'm sure she'll be fine with it. Good luck with the press. Goodbye, sir."

Monroe, meanwhile, had strolled toward Spelt's bookcase, which displayed a few books, a small Inuit carving, and a lot of photos. Most were of Spelt's daughter Chiara. In almost all, she was holding her cello. A couple of years ago a local music critic had declared her a child prodigy. The article was framed and tucked in with the photos. That was roughly when Spelt began telling anyone who would listen about Chiara, especially after she was invited to play the Elgar cello concerto with the Seattle Symphony. At the edge of this collection, there were a couple of photos in which a much younger Chiara posed with a taller, slightly older version of herself who was holding a violin. Who was she? A sister? In another, the two girls were standing with an elderly gentleman who had a shock of grey hair and a winning smile, a look that reminded Monroe of Spelt, although this man was taller and had broader shoulders. Interesting that there were no photos of Spelt's wife, whom Monroe had not seen at any university events for several years.

"Nice photos," Monroe said. "Chiara's looking so grown up. In the more recent shots, I mean. Is that your dad with her on the right? Who's the other girl?"

Spelt hesitated, a look of sadness clouding his eyes. "She is—*was*—Chiara's sister. Leda was the really—" His voice broke and he paused before continuing. "Really gifted one. Lost her to leukemia the year before I came to Northlake. The girls are with my father in that photo. Since then he's deteriorated, has memory problems that accelerated when my mother died two years ago."

Monroe shook his head. "I had no idea. I'm sorry to hear about your loss."

Spelt nodded but looked rueful. "You don't get over it."

After a moment of silence, Monroe said, "By the way, who will notify Eliot's wife and family?"

"You got me," Spelt said. "Probably the chancellor. Or the police. If Eliot had children, they must be grown up. No one knew him that well."

"*I* was getting to know him," Monroe said. "He was a good man."

Spelt eyed Monroe, as if caught by surprise.

4

Still in the dean's offices, Monroe stood with Spelt in front of a large window overlooking the quad. A dark sedan pulled up and Jim Martino got out. He moved fluidly as in their football days, though possibly with a hint of stiffness from too much time at the desk. A uniformed officer in a Sikh turban followed. Jim looked around and up as if securing a scene. A second car, a white VW Golf, pulled in behind the sedan and a woman emerged.

Spelt cocked his head toward the door. "Let's give them five minutes. Then go see what's what."

Stepping into his new role, Monroe thought. The *president.* "Likely they'll need more than five. I know the inspector, by the way. A friend all the way back to high school, survivors of geometry with Mr. Bonaguidi and mates on the football team."

Spelt didn't respond. He was suddenly busy with his phone. He didn't look up until Luce Drummond entered the office. "Evan, I just heard . . ." Noting Monroe's presence, she stopped. And smiled a greeting.

Spelt waved her in. She walked over and stood next to Monroe. "I just heard," she repeated. She intertwined her arm with Monroe's. "Long time no see, professor." *A bit too long,* he thought.

"In the Centre for Dialogue building, we didn't get the word," Luce continued. "Might as well be camped on a rock in Haida Gwaii."

Monroe smiled. "Or birding with Warren Kingsley at his North Shore cabin."

Spelt paused, perhaps surprised to hear about the cabin, then continued without conviction. "At least no distractions at the Centre," he said.

"I think we'd like one now," Luce said. "To avoid the elephant in the room, err, down the corridor."

Spelt nodded. "Well, here's something,. Howard . . . our chancellor has already conferred with the board of governors and they've asked me to stand in as acting president and you as acting dean."

Luce at first didn't respond but nodded. "Of course, it's an emergency. I'll do it for a week or two as I've done before. Why make it that official?"

"It's not for a week or two. It'll be the rest of this year at least. The institution needs to show that key positions are all covered. The chancellor said the keyword is continuity. 'Still moving forward' is a phrase he used. In a press release he'll probably say something about filling the now vacant position of university president."

"Indeed." Luce paused as if thinking. "They should strike the search committee right away."

Spelt didn't respond. "By the way," Monroe said, "who will notify Eliot's wife and family?"

"You got me," Spelt said. "Probably the chancellor. Or the police. If they have children they must be grown up. No one knew him that well."

"He conferred with a lot of us," Monroe said. "Was putting together a plan for his term as president. Now where are we?"

A beat of silence passed.

"It's been almost fifteen minutes," Spelt said. "Shall we get it over with and make an appearance? I know you don't want to hang around here all afternoon."

"Definitely not," Monroe said. "I'm just going to say hello to Jim. Coming, Luce?"

"No, thanks. Seems ghoulish if you ask me. I'll keep myself busy here."

Monroe gave Luce a wave as he followed Spelt out the door. Ghoulish? Not exactly. He felt a need to revisit the scene just to come to terms with what happened. It seemed so unreal. He thought back to his initial opposition to Eliot's appointment. An outsider, political appointee, and all that. Then he met him and they hit it off right away. Eliot was modest, curious, eager to learn, smart. He knew how to listen and had a sense of humour. Monroe smiled, thinking back at Eliot's promise to bring that crazy dog another baguette next time. But he didn't get a next time. What could have happened? Heart attack, stroke, a seizure of some kind? As he moved along the corridor, Monroe noticed that a lot of the office doors were open as people stood around looking disoriented. "Everyone's in shock," he said.

"What's that?" Spelt asked.

"Mumbling to myself," Monroe said. "The office doors are open, but nobody working. Everyone's in limbo."

Evan glanced sideways. "Hmm, I suppose." His eyes went back to his phone. *Maybe checking the appointments calendar*, Monroe thought. *Beginning to reinvent himself as president.*

The constable with the turban, arms crossed in front of him, stood in the doorway to the presidential suite. Monroe watched Spelt square his shoulders and stand as tall as he could as he approached him. "I'm *Doctor* Evan Spelt, the new acting president; this is Professor Monroe. We would like to speak to the inspector."

The constable looked unimpressed and took a few extra seconds to give Spelt the look. "Well, now, *Doctor* Spale, *Inspector* Martino is pretty busy right now. But wait here and I'll tell him."

"The name is *Spelt, S-P—*"

But the constable had already turned his back and was paying no attention. From the inner office, they heard only the words "professor" and "president" until Jim Martino's voice boomed out in annoyance. "What in the hell do they want? We're busy. Tell them . . . oh, all right, I'm coming."

Martino emerged from the inner office in disposable crime-scene overalls. He was carrying a clipboard with some notes. As soon as he saw Monroe, his face lit up. "Well, I'll be damned . . . as long as it's *this* professor. Where in the hell have you been hiding out? Haven't seen you since the picnic in July." Jim and Monroe embraced and he then turned toward Spelt, hand extended. "Hi, there. And you are the president? Jim Martino."

Spelt shook Jim's hand. "Evan Spelt. Yes. Acting president."

By now the constable had resumed his post at the door and Monroe could read his nametag: Constable R. Singh. Jim glanced over at him. "Thanks, Ravi." He looked back at Monroe and Spelt. "I guess you can come in, but stay in the outer office. Lois—Dr. Mendoza, the pathologist—is having a look at the body. Good of her to come. Straight from a hike on the Trans-Canada near Squamish."

"Right," Spelt said "And when you're finished, I'll like to get a clean-up crew in here and move in."

Jim turned his head quickly. "Not so fast. This may take some time. I'll let you know."

"And there are the books, papers, and Eliot's personal stuff to clean out," Spelt added.

"I'm afraid you must be hard of hearing, Mr. President. I said *don't* rush us. We'll let you know when we're finished."

"Do you suspect something?" Monroe asked.

"Anything's possible. I've only been here a few minutes. I'm waiting to hear from Mendoza."

Spelt crossed his arms and frowned. "Well, surely this was a heart attack or something ordinary. I'd like to get on with running the university as soon as possible."

"Look, Dr. Spitz, or whatever your name is. We just got here and now you're telling us to get lost. Well, for the third time I'm telling *you* to hold your horses. Mind your own business while we get on with ours. You can be president in *this* office only when we tell you we're finished."

"The name's Spelt, S-P-E-L-T. I'll let you get on with it then." He looked at Monroe. "I need to phone the chancellor. You coming?"

"No, I'll be heading back to my office."

Spelt stalked out, brushing by Constable Singh without a glance.

Jim watched him march away. "Testy little guy, isn't he? Odd name. Sounds like one of the loaves you can buy at the Nelson Cove bakery."

Monroe smiled. "Yeah, at Spurling's. Well, probably anxious to prove himself. I'm glad you're taking the time to figure out what happened."

"We'll take as much as we need. Pretty clear that it was quick and violent. A lot of pain because of the way his body is twisted. My first thought was that he was poisoned."

Monroe took a few seconds to process the point. "You think?"

"We'll rely on our experts to decide." Jim walked a few steps toward Eliot's office and called out: "Lois, when you can break for a minute, could you come out?"

Lois appeared wearing rubber gloves and crime-scene overalls belted at the waist. They fit snugly and she looked good, almost stylish. She smiled as she pushed back some wayward strands of shiny black hair. Monroe had a reflex to reach out to help but thought better of it. She noticed and made eye contact as Jim made the introductions.

"What do you think so far?" Jim asked.

"Well, only an educated guess without an autopsy and lab reports. I'm pretty sure he died from suffocation. His neck is badly swollen and I'd bet his upper airways were squeezed shut from swelling. Blood pressure likely dropped quickly and he could have lost consciousness quickly or become dizzy and disoriented. There's an EpiPen on the floor next to the body. Looks like he was trying to jab himself, but the pen is damaged as if he became uncoordinated and jabbed it into the floor or the side of the desk. His face is swollen, red, and blotchy with hives. Classic indicators of allergic reaction. The way he is scrunched up suggests gastrointestinal pain or cramps possibly accompanied with nausea. Before he died, he vomited the contents of his stomach. Some of it, at least."

Monroe nodded. "I know he had allergies. He mentioned it on a hike Sunday. No details, but he carried an EpiPen."

Jim nodded, then looked toward Lois. "Well, if it was peanuts or nuts of some kind . . . we'll need to find out how or why he ingested them."

Monroe looked at his watch and remembered the lecture at 4:30. "Just thinking that maybe I ought to go to the President's Lecture Series after all to honour Eliot."

The constable perked up. "I saw the poster outside the door. I'd love to go. I once wrote an essay about Colonel Fawcett for a geography class at Queen's."

Jim frowned. "No kidding. Sorry, Ravi, it's not going to happen. I need you here. Well, unless we put up the yellow tape and get the forensic team here. I don't want to put a damper on your quest for enlightenment." Turning back to Monroe, he rubbed his chin. "This Spelt. Seems like an odd character to be a university president. Something about him. Know him well?"

Monroe shrugged. "Not *that* well. He's been OK—not great—as dean of arts. He's dealt with some tough family stuff," he added, filling Jim in on what he'd just learned. "Spelt put his name forward—or the chancellor did—for president last year. Eliot beat him out."

"Well, he's ready to run with it now," Jim said. "University politics. Dog-eat-dog, or polite and civil?"

Monroe thought for a moment. "I'm afraid mostly dog-eat-dog. Often disguised with high-sounding words. Turf wars and egotism all over the place. A lot of it petty."

Jim nodded. "Same as everywhere else. Was it common knowledge that Eliot had allergies?"

"Hard to say. He didn't hide it. In meetings in his office I've seen his EpiPen on his desk or on a shelf in the bookcase behind his desk. It seems to get moved around. And I've noticed that his muffin was packaged separately on the cart from Food Services.

Jim nodded. "Wait here a second, I want another look." Monroe sat in one of the padded chairs in the outer office and could hear Jim and Lois talking. When Jim came out again, he sat next to Monroe.

"OK, I think I've got a sense of this. The lab report and an autopsy should confirm what caused an allergic reaction. And things can then get back to normal."

Lois stepped out of the office, was removing her gloves. "About his leg, Jim."

"The scratches?"

"Yes, they seem odd. Why are they in the shin area? Everyone is instructed to jam those pens straight into a thigh. He would have known that. A clean hit in the thigh gives him maybe six or seven minutes. He may not have got his hands on the pen quickly enough. Possibly became disoriented. From the bruising on his cheek, I'd say he fell against one of the desk drawers."

Monroe frowned, his thoughts running ahead of the conversation. The drawers were all open, the top one on the left completely out and on the floor. Eliot had been searching for the EpiPen. It wasn't in plain sight. If he habitually doesn't keep it in the same place maybe he forgot where it was. Everyone does that.

Jim thanked Lois as she left and then phoned headquarters to ask the dispatcher why the photographer and forensic team hadn't come yet. When he hung up, he had instructions for Ravi. "I'm afraid we need you to stay put, no lecture today. And stretch some tape across the doorway, will you? I'm not done here. Oh, and when forensics gets here, tell them to be sure to bag the EpiPen as soon as they've got their photos."

Jim then took a closer look at Monroe. "You OK?

Monroe shook his head. "Not so much, actually."

Jim said nothing.

"He deserved better," Monroe said.

"You just get back to your students. We'll take care of it. I'll see what our lab people say."

"I wonder, though—"

"We'll take care of it, Bruce. You've got things to do. It's a police matter now. Later you may be able to help us with how this place operates."

"Of course." Monroe had confidence in Jim. But he still felt uneasy.

6

Monroe was up at 6:00. After porridge and a glance at the headlines, he bolted out the door. He retrieved his bike from the garden shed and headed down his back alley. He was still thinking about yesterday. *We'll take care of it*, Jim had said. To him, Eliot's death looked like some weird accident, nothing to get too worked up about compared to all the fentanyl-related deaths he deals with. A question of priorities. Yet Monroe had priorities too, and he wasn't so sure it was an accident. Of course there was plenty to do. Finish the book. Teach his classes. Prepare a grant application. But now a shadow hovered over everything. Eliot's big-picture ideas for the university—something hopeful, something Monroe had begun to be a part of—gone now.

As Monroe slipped into a higher gear and pushed hard on the pedals, he felt the familiar dull ache invading his lower left femur, a reminder of the stray javelin that had speared him all those years ago, killed his chances to take up a track scholarship at Cal Berkeley. Why hadn't he seen it coming? Actually, he knew why. He had been watching the Brazilian exchange student, María Cristina Ramos practising the high jump. She had set the bar higher than the school record and everyone, even Coach Jackson, had stopped to watch. Everyone, except Dawkins, the beast javelin thrower, who was oblivious to everything except flinging his Neolithic weapon. As soon as Monroe was hit, Coach Jackson sprang into action, pulled the javelin free, and ripped off Biggie Carlson's T-shirt to stop the bleeding. *Sorry, Biggie, we need it.* Coach taped it tightly to his leg and raced him to the hospital.

But, what the hell, it had healed. Mostly. And pushed him in a different direction. He became a reader and a serious student, which led to what he was now. Funny how good can come from misfortune. Or bad from good, come to think of it, in Grandpa Leonard's case. In the 1930s, he flipped out after he won the lottery and, in a drunken spree, gambled the money away along with his house, job, marriage, and self-respect. Yet Monroe figured he'd take his chances with a win in the lottery over a javelin in the leg.

His front tire flicked up a rock that hit his toe. Damn. The air was chilly, but his nylon jacket would hold the heat in. As soon as he generated some. He kept to a moderate pace for ten minutes or so and then swerved right at the turnoff to Beacon Hill. When he arrived at the campus, he unzipped his jacket and checked his watch. Twenty-four minutes. Not too bad.

After a few exercises, some stretches, and a shower, it was only a little after 8:00. Not many people in the gym this time of day. In a far corner, Hans Meyer from financial services flipped a towel over a well-muscled shoulder and closed his locker. Meyer would be about to hit the pool for his daily swim. *It must be twenty years that he's been doing this,* Monroe thought. Meyer was famous for his close scrutiny of faculty and staff receipts claimed against research grants and travel allowances.

"Morning, Meyer. Good to see you're not slacking off. How many laps today, fifty or so? Everything under control at Fort Knox?"

Meyer snorted. "You kidding? Your lot doesn't seem to realize that resources on this earth are finite. Whatever happened to frugality? The government may have to *impose* it. They've delayed this year's budget, which may mean cuts."

"Always the pessimist," Monroe laughed. "Part of your Teutonic background?"

Meyer paused as if to choose his words carefully. "Maybe. When an economy collapses, the crazies come out of the cracks like cockroaches. They're still there. Germany will never live it down. It can happen anywhere, even here. Losing Eliot may prove more costly than anyone thinks. He was a sensible man—balanced, ethical, cared about people, had the minister's ear. The deans already have their knives out."

Monroe wanted to hear more. "The deans? Are you sure?"

"Eliot was keeping them in line and now the zero-sum game is on again." Meyer slashed at his throat with a thick index finger. "My office is a front-row seat. When money's at stake, the beast comes out. And Spelt in the president's office? I don't like it."

"Well, I agree that losing Eliot is bad. We'll see about Spelt."

Meyer gritted his teeth. "Be alert."

Monroe sensed that Meyer knew something more. He stepped over a bench and started for the door and then turned back. "What do you mean by zero-sum game? In our context, I mean."

"Don't be naïve. You know. It's the art of playing groups off against each other. We see it in hard numbers, plus or minus columns. No fairy tales."

Monroe sighed. "Have a good swim."

◼

On the way to The Buzz, Monroe kept thinking about Meyer. He was a career-sergeant type. Grumpy exterior, but he cared about the place. He had a terrible job. It's bad enough to be an accountant, but having to uncover cheap little scams of faculty and staff had to get him down. Often enough it was probably petty stuff, thirty or forty bucks here or there.

Meyer couldn't stand cheaters. *Neither can I*, Monroe thought. *Why do they do it? They're not underpaid.* Monroe had once seen Ted Dickenson scrounge extra receipts in a restaurant after he had given a paper at the Ethics in Society conference in Seattle. The kind of thing that would make Meyer sick.

The Buzz greeted Monroe with the hum of high-voltage conversations. Just the way he liked it. People juiced with talk about books, ideas, travel, art, micro-biology, sports, movies, you name it. This was one of the reasons he'd become an academic. He sucked in the aroma of strong coffee. Relief from Meyer's pessimism, well earned though it was.

Monroe spotted Warren hunched over a newspaper at a window table. After getting his coffee, he scooted through the minefield of chairs, tables, knees, feet, and backpacks without, he noted with satisfaction, spilling a drop.

When Monroe bumped into his chair, Warren jumped but recovered quickly.

"I guess you got my message."

"Yeah, this morning." Warren paused. "Short-lived experiment. You're too attached to your bike."

"True, and a bit of a loner. Not a cheery type to chat with on morning commutes."

"You aren't too bad. I'm a bit slow myself in the mornings."

"Well, for grumpy, try Hans Meyer. Just saw him in the gym. Anyway, I owe you one. I'll drive sometime when your car's in the shop and it's raining. Or I'll have a go at that door on the passenger side."

"Yeah, if it comes to that. I may get some grease for it."

"Might work. But something might be bent. I'd like to take another look. Anyway, I'm trying a new schedule. Cycle in early and hit the gym before classes."

"Oh?" Warren raised his eyebrow.

"Was that skepticism?"

"Well, you've done it *once*. We'll see."

"Fair enough." Monroe sipped his coffee. "I keep thinking about Eliot."

"What about him?"

"Did you hear some of the details?"

Warren gestured toward the paper in front of him. "Just what's in today's paper. He was fifty-eight. Pretty *young* . . . and the death was sudden." Warren pushed a wooden stick into his coffee and stirred it cautiously as if it were part of a chemistry experiment. "I know you met up with him quite a lot. But nice things always get said when people die."

"The police seem to be viewing the death as routine, accidental."

"It probably was. We may have a nasty side, but we don't kill each other."

"But what if . . . ?" Monroe stopped as if struck by a new thought.

Warren poked at his stir stick lying next to his cup. "What if what?"

"Well, what if the police are missing something? I want to understand what happened."

There was a short silence and then Warren nodded his head.

7

Monroe glanced up at the clock tower as he and Warren walked out of The Buzz. "I've got a grad studies committee meeting in thirty minutes. But there's enough time to talk to Mildred Jones. She could be the last person who saw Eliot alive."

"Geez, he only died yesterday. The police will be checking it out."

Monroe paused. "Yes, but Martino's pretty busy . . . and treating it routinely. Come on, you don't have to say anything."

Warren raised both hands, palms out, in mock resignation. "OK."

"Besides, you're the psychologist, trained to observe people closely. You can pass on your thoughts later."

"Take it easy. I'm a cognitive psychologist who works with rats. They're simpler creatures than we are, and half the time I can barely figure out what they're up to."

"Rats—people, behaviours probably on a spectrum not different as such. They're smart, everything's related. How much time do you have? Fifteen or twenty minutes?"

Warren looked at his watch. "Yeah, meeting some graduate students at 9:30 and need to check my emails first. I'll tell them about your spectrum theory. You think Mildred will be in? Yesterday was traumatic."

As they got closer to the president's suite of offices, they could hear a high-pitched whine that almost sounded like a leaf blower. They entered and the sound got louder. Monroe put his hands over his ears and, looking at Mildred, scrunched his face into a grimace. She nodded and pushed a business card across the counter. It read Aziz Carpet Cleaning and included contact information. Monroe watched the reedy young man who had started to clean the carpet in the outer office. He looked to be in his late twenties, unshaven with plenty of black stubble, a Boston Red Sox cap on his head. The Northlake hoodie he wore, formerly navy blue, must have come from a thrift store although he could be a former student.

Monroe stepped over to the thick cord of the machine and yanked it from the wall socket. Silence invaded the room.

The young man turned to see what happened. "What are you doing?" Monroe asked. "Has this area been released by the police for cleaning up?"

"I didn't hear anything about police. I got an email work order last night from facilities management saying that my estimate for cleaning the carpets had been approved."

"Who signed the work order?"

"Uh, someone named Les, I think. Les Westrom."

Monroe knew a facilities guy named Wes Ahlstrom. He made a note in his notebook. "Well, it's a mistake. The area is off limits. The police tape should still be up. You'll have to leave. The police inspector may want to get in touch with you." Monroe looked into the presidential office, then turned back toward Mildred. "Mildred, who emptied this office? Inspector Martino said no one was supposed to touch anything in there. Where is Eliot's stuff?"

Mildred pointed toward a door across the room. "In boxes, in the Pearson conference room. Three men from central stores were packing his things when I arrived this morning." Monroe joined Warren, who was already standing by the door studying a black-and-white photograph.

"It is a great photo. You know, I've never really looked at it before."

Monroe took a closer look. Lester Pearson, frozen in time, one leg on a rock, smiling, cigarette in hand, looking slightly anxious, probably about a talk he was about to give.

"So young," Warren said. "Must have been my age or younger."

"Probably younger," Monroe said.

"Thanks."

"Look at him. Thinks he's ordinary. Unsure of the future, no idea that one day he will play a major role on the world stage."

"The Nobel Peace Prize is a pretty big deal. By the way, you sounded pretty official ordering that guy out. Maybe the police took down their tape."

"From the way Jim was talking yesterday, I don't think so." They entered the room and saw twelve or fifteen boxes stacked in one corner. Leaning against the boxes, askew as if placed there carelessly, sat Eliot's computer, its power cord dangling malevolently.

Mildred, leaning against the doorjamb, watched as Monroe and Warren surveyed the salvage. Monroe poked at a couple of the boxes, not really looking for anything in particular. "Is this everything? They even cleared the desk drawers?"

"I think so," Mildred said. "I arrived a little late, they were just finishing."

"What time was that?" Monroe asked.

With one hand, Mildred smoothed her dress. "About 8:40. I suppose the clean-up crew must have been here an hour or so to judge by all the work they'd done. I'm not sure. Buildings and grounds people start earlier than office staff. I normally get here at 8:30."

"I wonder what happened to the police tape. Wasn't it here when you left yesterday?" Monroe waited a few seconds and then caught himself. "Oh, I forgot you left early."

Monroe patted his pockets and looked at Warren. "Can I borrow your phone? Must have left mine on the kitchen table."

"Sorry. It's at home. I keep forgetting it. I only have it in case my car gives out on one of the bridges."

It figures. He gets a phone instead of upgrading the car, Monroe thought. He borrowed the phone on Mildred's desk and called Jim's private number. As he was dialing, Aziz returned, his tank emptied, and began to roll up the power cord. Monroe covered the mouthpiece and called to him. "I'm checking with the police. They may want to speak with you later."

"Jim, It's Bruce. . . . There may be a problem. I'm in Eliot's office. Did your forensic people finish up yesterday? The whole place has been cleared. . . . Yes, packed into boxes, and a carpet cleaner was in the outer office—"

Monroe pulled the phone away from his ear and thought even Warren and Mildred would be able to hear the expletives. It took more than a few seconds for the storm to subside. "At least you can still have another look at the inner office. The carpet cleaner didn't go in there yet. So what do you want to do? I've got a meeting in a few minutes."

Monroe looked straight ahead and nodded his head once or twice. "Right, well, maybe it can be stored in Warren Kingsley's lab in the psychology department. He has closets with locks." Monroe caught Warren's eye and cocked his head. Warren shrugged his shoulders—a reluctant assent.

"Yeah, he says it's OK. . . . Right, later then."

Monroe turned toward Warren and Mildred. "Well, you could hear Jim's not happy. The forensic crew finished, got their photos, and bagged some stuff. But he wanted to go over the office one more time before it was cleaned up."

"And now? Warren asked.

"Eventually, he'll be sending two constables to impound all the stuff in the conference room, but he can't spare anyone right now. In the meantime, it's going to your lab for safekeeping."

"For a few days, that's all—"

Monroe looked at Mildred. "Inspector Martino wants you to arrange for Central Stores to do the moving under the supervision of campus security. Please lock the door to the conference room and guard the key until they come."

"And Warren, will you be in your lab for the next hour or two to receive the stuff?"

Warren nodded. "Yeah, but I hope—" The phone on Mildred's desk rang. She scurried to answer it.

"Take this," Monroe said as he handed Warren a USB memory stick. "It's empty except for a book review I need to send off. Copy Eliot's files and correspondence. Just in case. Someone might find a way to get rid of something the police need. And don't erase my review, please." Warren looked reluctant, but Monroe gave him a little push toward the conference room.

Upon finishing her call, Mildred looked up and scanned the room. "Has Professor Kingsley left?"

"No, he's in the conference room. He thinks he dropped his keys. A little absent-minded." Monroe tapped the side of his head.

The door swung open and Evan Spelt marched in. "Hello. Thank you, Mildred, for coming in today. I know yesterday was hard."

It sounded genuine.

Spelt poked his head into his soon-to-be office. "I see there's been progress, but why did the cleaning stop?"

"I stopped it," Monroe said. "The police hadn't cleared the area yet."

"Oh? And you speak for them?"

"Hardly." Monroe smiled. "Yesterday, Martino said the office was a possible crime scene. After you left, I guess. I called him a few minutes ago and he was pissed off that it had been prematurely cleared out and a carpet cleaner was here."

"His name is Mr. Aziz," Mildred added. "A nice enough young man." Warren came out of the conference room. "Find your keys, professor?" she asked.

Warren paused, then patted his pocket and produced a passable grimace as if admitting absent-mindedness. Then with a flourish, he nodded at Spelt. "Greetings, señor presidente."

Spelt stared at him with a look of distaste. *Cheeky*, Monroe thought. "How much time does the inspector need?" Spelt asked. "Such a tragedy, losing Peter like this. But we do have work to do. He would have wanted us to carry on. Speaking of which, Mildred, can you come down to my office in, say, ten minutes? I'd like a complete picture of anything Eliot was working on. Bring that clumsy appointment book he used. Dreadful old-fashioned thing, could have been a remnant from Victorian times. I guess it was part of his charm that Peter was a little baffled by tech stuff, no idea of the advantages of our university system."

"Well . . . uh, I haven't had time to—"

"Inspector Martino has asked Mildred to keep watch until Central Stores and campus security arrive for the transfer of Eliot's belongings," Monroe said.

"A bit much." Spelt muttered to no one in particular. "Now the police are telling me I can't meet with my administrative assistant." Then he looked at Monroe. "Possibly you or, uh, Kingsley here could stay a while."

"Afraid not, I've got a committee meeting," Monroe said.

"I'm meeting grad students in my lab"—Warren studied his watch—"in seventeen minutes." Warren smiled. "But why don't you send someone from the dean's office?"

Spelt looked annoyed. Warren was pretty good at such digs. No one spoke for a moment until Mildred, looking at Spelt, broke the silence. "Could you give me thirty or forty minutes to get that list together? By then campus security should be here."

Spelt nodded. He turned quickly, and marched off at a time-is-of-the-essence pace.

Monroe looked at Mildred and shook his head. "Things are going to be different. With Spelt, you may need more staff. He seems . . . already so busy. You used to have a couple of assistants or secretaries."

"Yes, we still do. Sort of. Brenda Simpson is on maternity leave for another month and Leona Wong should be back from holiday next week. The truth is,

Mr. Eliot didn't want much staff. He did his own email correspondence and quite a lot of the phone calls." Monroe gave Warren a knowing look as if to say, *Good thing we copied his files.*

8

Monroe opened his notebook. "So, Mildred, can we just go over a couple of things? I'd like to get a clear picture of your day yesterday. It's important for me—for all of us—to understand how Mr. Eliot died. I have a meeting with Inspector Martino tomorrow."

Mildred nodded but looked away and fidgeted with some papers on her desk.

"Do you recall when you arrived at the office? Monroe asked.

"Yes, of course." Mildred sat a little straighter in her chair and pursed her lips as if to concentrate. "I parked in lot B at 8:15. The morning news had just finished and I waited in the car for the weather. It comes right after the traffic report. Then I walked to the office."

"So what took you so long to get to the office? You told us a few minutes ago that you arrived at 8:40."

"Well . . . yes. I ran into Janet Snider—she works in distance education—in the quad. She told me that her divorce had been finalized and she wanted to meet for a drink to celebrate. And she asked my advice about taking some courses in communications in order to move to the office of community outreach. I explained that it wouldn't be that easy. Communications, you must know, has problems these days. It went on and we agreed to meet for lunch later in the week."

Monroe jotted a few notes, torn between not wanting to interrupt Mildred and wishing to skip the details about Ms. Snider. "OK, you arrived in the office. Then what?"

"Nothing much. As usual, Mr. Eliot—he said to call him Mister or Peter because he didn't have a doctorate—was in his office. He arrives . . . between 6:00 and 7:00. But I didn't talk to him because somebody was with him and the door was closed. It sounded like an argument."

Warren leaned forward. "Couldn't you see who it was through the glass panels beside his door?"

"No, the shades were down. They're the type you can see out of but not in."

Monroe nodded. "Were you alarmed?"

"Not really. Mr. Eliot is sort of combative . . . *was* combative. Not a person to be bullied."

"And no one had made an appointment to meet the president?"

"No. That's why I was surprised. Early morning was Mr. Eliot's quiet hours to work without interruption. He avoided appointments before 9:00."

"OK, someone drops in on him. They have an argument. Only one other voice, I take it. A man's voice?"

"Yes, a man. I *think* only one. And I did hear Mr. Eliot say, uhh, sonofabitch in a loud voice. I don't think he would have said that to a woman."

Warren perked up. "Was that common?"

Mildred allowed herself a hint of a smile. "Fairly common, yes. But he never used language like that when speaking to me or the staff."

"A good person to have for a boss," Warren said.

Mildred took this as a question. "Oh, yes. Mr. Eliot trusted us, confided in us. Laughed a lot at . . ." Her voice broke and she stopped to compose herself. "Laughed at academics who patronized staff and people like him without PhDs." She glanced first at Warren and then Monroe. "*Some* academics, not all. He could imitate the way they walked into a room and looked down their noses at us as if we're all idiots."

"Can you think of anyone who might have been arguing with him yesterday morning?"

"Not really. Professor Halberg, the new chair of the sexual harassment oversight committee, yelled at him the other day about campus safety. But I would have recognized her voice, and I think he liked her. And you, too, Professor Monroe. He said you were a goldmine for getting him up to speed when he became president. And he liked Nicole Lavoisier, the French girl in charge of the foodservice cart. She gets here about 10:30 every morning for coffee break. Mr. Eliot was such an early riser that her arrival was almost like lunch for him. Even if someone was with him in the office, he would interrupt for the cart. Once he interrupted a meeting with Mrs. Kerr to attend to the cart's arrival. I sensed that she was annoyed at the way he passed the time for a while with Nicole and the rest of us in the outer office.

Nothing more important than the cart, he used to say, to create a convivial atmosphere. His word—'convivial.' Nicole was instructed to knock on the door if I wasn't here, but I usually am. That's when President Eliot liked to touch base. Sometimes, he'd share a joke or check on the schedule. Or just chat. I'm rarely out of the office from 10:15 to 10:45."

"Except for yesterday," Monroe said. Mildred remained silent although she slumped, perhaps taking this as a reprimand.

❖

Monroe flipped back a page in his notebook. "Can you remember anything else about yesterday morning?"

"The rest was normal. A few phone calls—nothing special." Mildred looked down at an appointments book on her desk. "Oh, yes, Professor Batalla called for an appointment and I made it for Friday morning. He keeps telling me that his name in Spanish means 'battle' and that's what he likes to do. He said he was ready to fight for a faculty position in Brazilian politics. Poor Mr. Eliot. He used to say that the infighting between programs and departments should stop."

Monroe and Warren remained silent as Mildred scanned the agenda. "Oh, here's one of my doodles: a tea pot and cup. Alicia Stuart from sociology—you know, the student advisor—invited me to sample her new blend of green teas. She said it's a great liver cleanser."

"A liver cleanse after talking to Professor Batalla sounds like a pretty good idea," Monroe said.

Warren said, "So you left the office for a tea break?"

"Yes."

"What time?" Monroe asked.

"I'm not sure. A little after 9:00, maybe. I was only gone a few minutes. Alicia's lonely, you know. Her husband took off with another woman. Someone named Judith who tends bar at the Cactus Club. She wanted me to go there with her to spy on her. But the talk about liver cleansings made me feel queasy and I didn't stay that long."

"When you came back from having tea with Ms. Stuart, was Eliot alone?"

"I think so. It was quiet. And then I left for my dentist appointment."

"But you didn't see Eliot before you left," Monroe said.

"No. The curtain was still down and his door closed."

"So you left around 9:30 or so." Warren suggested.

Mildred paused and scrunched her forehead in thought. "Closer to 9:45 or 9:50 because I couldn't find my keys right away. And the dentist appointment was at, uhh, 10:15? Yes, that's right. But the hygienist came in late and everyone was backed up at least half an hour. I had already gone to the drug store to drop off a prescription and then hurried back and had to sit there with all those old magazines. If I had known, I could have dropped by Home Hardware, my next errand, to buy some Drano. I finally finished at the dentist between 12:00 and 12:30, went to the hardware store, then had lunch at Olga's Organics. I got back to the office about 1:30. It could have been sooner, but I circled B lot a couple of times looking for a parking space."

Monroe said: "Right, so, you were away three-and-a-half hours and didn't actually see President Eliot at all that morning."

The phone rang. Before answering, Mildred excused herself. "Office of the president, Mildred Jones speaking."

Warren nudged Monroe and spoke in a low voice. "Looks like she turned an hour-long dentist appointment into a near holiday."

Monroe gave a little smile. "Ferris Bueller's day off."

"That was President Spelt," Mildred said. "He asked if the list is ready."

"Sorry, we've stayed too long. But just one more thing. Think carefully—details might be important. What happened when you got back to the office?"

Mildred paused, collecting her thoughts. "It was quiet. I knocked on Mr. Eliot's door several times and called his name. Finally, I opened it and he was lying on the floor next to his desk. I thought he must have had a stroke. I ran in and put my hand in front of his mouth to see if he was breathing. He wasn't. I don't think I screamed or anything. I closed the door, went to my phone, and called 911 and the campus clinic. Then I ran back into the office. I touched his neck to see if he had a pulse, but he didn't. Then I ran down to see Margo in the dean's office. Margo called the medical centre again. I felt sick and was short of breath and asked to go home, but I came back here first."

As Monroe left, he scanned the counter for Aziz's card, but didn't see it.

9

Monroe was in his office looking over some lecture notes when Rob Cunningham came by. "What's up, Rob? Is the essay going OK?"

"Not exactly. I'm having trouble narrowing it down."

"Let's see. . . . Your subject is violence and religion?"

"Yes, but it seems too vague."

"Right, getting it focused. Usually it's good to start with a question. Something that at first seems simple."

"So far, I had the idea that violence is often rationalized for some greater good. My essay would critique that idea."

Monroe gave a thumbs-up. "Excellent. That could lead you to look at torture, for instance."

Rob nodded. "Yeah and there's something about religion that can be part of it. If *God* wants it. And I've noticed that the process—if that's the right word—is often staged as a kind of performance or ceremony by church or state. As if it needs spectators."

"Yes, and spectators are needed, like a chorus in Greek drama, as part of the theatre that shames victims. Not just passive spectators but participants. And also experiencing punishments as exemplary."

"Exemplary?"

"The takeaway would be not to do whatever got these people in trouble. Two or three examples should do for the assignment."

Rob nodded as he wrote in his notebook: "Beliefs or acts? French Revolution, Stalinist show trials, inquisition, public executions, witches."

Rob stood up to leave. "This is more than I need. I think I'll concentrate on beliefs. Sorry to be so muddled. A lot of us have been thrown off by President

Eliot's death. I saw you in his office earlier today. It must be especially bad for Ms. Jones if she found him."

Monroe nodded. "She seems better today."

"Funny how life works. There she was yesterday morning exercising without a care in the world and with no idea what would be facing her later in the day."

"Exercising?"

"Well, sort of fast walking the jogging trail that circles the campus. She wore a coat with the hood on so at first we didn't recognize her."

"We?"

"Farshad and I. We were on the soccer pitch doing wind sprints."

Monroe had his notebook open. "What time was it?"

"9:15. The clock tower had just bonged the quarter hour and we congratulated ourselves on being already half through our workout."

"So Mildred at the far edge of lot E . . ."

"I don't think she saw us. She was near the corner of the parking lot where the trail drops away from the hill. Fairly close to where the German guy from finance parks his camper."

Monroe nodded. "Hans Meyer. He parks there to get a walk in before work. He's mainly a swimmer, but watch it, he may try to join you and Farshad for a few sprints one of these days."

Rob smirked. "Probably not. I think he's an early-morning type. We normally don't get out there until later, sometimes not till mid-afternoon. Coach Jenkins, out there a lot to get stuff from the equipment shed, even joked the other day that Mr. Meyer probably sleeps out there so he can work late and start early."

⚏

With Rob gone, Monroe began to pack up but paused to check his emails after hearing a ping that one had just arrived. From Jim, who wanted to meet him at the station tomorrow at 2:00. "OK," Monroe replied, "see you then." He hesitated over a pile of unread journals, shoved one into his bag along with several folders, and headed out the door. Only when he got to his bike did he remember that Warren had the flash drive with his book review on it. Damn, he had meant to read it over and send it today. Tonight would have to do.

Pedaling effortlessly now, Monroe took a few deep breaths. It felt like things were backing up. Small stuff like dirty dishes, a plate at a time filling the sink. After several days it becomes monumental. All normal stuff he usually did with zest—preparing lectures, meeting students, writing, editing, working on his book—had lost momentum after Eliot's death. He had to get back on track. But life on campus had become upended, mysterious in a way. Take Mildred Jones. What was she doing out on the walking trail?

Maybe things would change tomorrow after meeting Jim. Why did he want to meet? Maybe to team up a little more after the business with the carpet cleaner. Monroe reached the fork in the bike trail that circles the lake, and took the long route home toward the bridge over Eagle Creek and around Beaver Pond. After a quick stop at Gunderson's Grocery, Monroe picked up speed with dinner in his backpack. The bike felt good, the pedals solid under his feet, and the gravel of the bike path blurred into a single texture as he looked down.

Upon arriving home, he poured a glass of wine. Only then did he notice his forgotten cell phone. As he listened to his messages on speaker, he got the barbecue going, threaded chunks of chicken onto bamboo skewers and pulled out some rice, broccoli, and lettuce. *Hello, bad boy. This is the acting dean. Acting . . . I'm about to change offices and get my own associate dean. Weird here in the office with Spelt busy becoming president. He paces a lot. I think he's anxious to get into that corner office. Look, I'm rambling. I'm calling about tonight.*

Tonight, Monroe thought. What *about* tonight? *. . . production we agreed to attend starts at 8:00. Remember? I forget what they're calling it . . . people clumped in groups on stage to represent census statistics. So we're stuck. And there's a reception at 7:00. I'll swing by your place a little before then. See you then.*

Monroe groaned. Plans for the evening now up in smoke. So much for the simple life. The next message played, this one from Jim Martino:

Bruce: thanks for securing Eliot's office today. What the hell happened? Should have left a guard overnight. Actually, I'm calling about tomorrow. Let's move it back to 4:30 at the station, OK? I've got a meeting in Lynden in the morning. Politicians involved. Cross-border opioid trafficking. Most of it getting in on container ships, if you ask me. It's a crisis, man, as you know.

Monroe muttered as if in reply to Jim. *Crises everywhere. How many can one take on?* He gave his onions in the skillet a stir. Browning nicely, just about perfect now.

10

Monroe grumbled under his breath as he and Luce entered the cavernous room adjacent to the theatre where the Town and Gown production would be viewed. He was glad to feel anonymous, relatively unnoticed, as Luce's flatterers began to circle. The word had already gotten out that she was in effect now dean of arts. Monroe slipped to the table with wines and hors d'oeuves and spotted a *La Mancha Tempranillo* from Northern Spain. It had been quietly ignored in favour of some lower-level French vintages.

He poured a glass, swirled it, eyed the deep red rivulets flowing down the glass. Glancing around to see which members of the board of governors were there, he could see only Mrs. Kerr. She stood in one corner with Jean-Michel and they looked fairly animated. First, his turn to speak with plenty of gestures as she regarded him skeptically, then her turn as he looked on attentively. Serious talk? Kerr wasn't normally talkative, Jean-Michel had told Monroe, and rarely intervened in day-to-day affairs of the campus gallery, which carried her name.

Monroe considered joining them but Carlos Batalla, busy plucking morsels from the food table, caught his eye. Must be his dinner. As chair of Latin American studies, he was indeed combative. Monroe watched him bump into Ali Qasemi, head of Middle East studies, a smooth operator and elegantly dressed, as usual. Batalla's brittle smile magnified rather than concealed his contempt for Qasemi. But it was mutual and long running, probably stemming from the way Qasemi outflanked Batalla in building a small empire while Batalla spun his wheels making a nuisance of himself.

Luce was holding up. Smiles and eye contact for well-wishers laying the groundwork for future favours. More and more, the university seemed like a loose federation of special interests with programs, departments, and ideologies battling for resources. Vice-presidents of development fell all over themselves to solicit funds—ill gotten sometimes—for endowed chairs linked to a region, an economic activity, or a political outlook. Follow the money. The sectarian feel of the campus had been getting more cutthroat in the past few years and deans were often at the centre of it, either taking abuse or being courted incessantly.

Monroe felt protective and wanted to warn Luce. *As if she needed it.* They had dated for several years now and she was the rarest of principled academics, an excellent scholar and teacher. She also believed, tentatively perhaps, she could help make the university a better place from within the inner circle of upper administrators. He took another sip of his Tempranillo and, without moving the glass from his mouth, surveyed the room. He saw several people pretending to converse but their eyes darted side to side to spot someone higher up the food chain. One looked to be an investment banker or real estate developer from the cut of his expensive suit and designer silk tie. As Monroe shifted his gaze to Mrs. Kerr, they locked eyes and she flashed a little smile and lifted her wine glass ever so slightly. Jean-Michel had disappeared and she was alone, quietly presiding now rather than searching for company. Her expression conveyed how tiresome it all was.

Might as well, Monroe thought. He worked his way over to her. "Mrs. Kerr. How nice to see you." She opened her eyes wide in mock appreciation. "And you, too, Professor Monroe." She paused. "Of course neither of us means it. But we do our duty. Especially you, a real academic. I'm supposed to be one of *them*." At this point her eyes strayed briefly toward the crowd, then settled on Luce. "Now, Professor Drummond is something else, one of the rare ones unafraid to step away from the herd."

What's that supposed to mean? Monroe wondered. Academics prefer the safety of herd, living small lives encased in an academic specialty and unwilling to risk a turn as dean, vice president, or president? *That could be how she sees me.* She is a keen observer, she speaks her mind. He imagined her in a former life as a no-nonsense madam running a high-class brothel. She played the game but knew it to be *only* a game. A realist, she was suspicious of ideologues; smart, she distrusted academic obfuscations. Monroe remembered someone who'd said that family always had the key to your back door. It fit her, somehow. Kerr had come into the university through the back door. How'd she get the key? Certainly, she saw through storylines of selfless quests for truth and enlightenment. She saw coyotes with overde-veloped egos on the prowl. "So," Monroe said to change the subject, "we've got a new president. The board of governors has been busy."

"Not so much. We had to keep the seat warm." She paused, brushing an imaginary speck of dust off the sleeve of her silk blouse. "The chancellor wanted Spelt," she continued, "on the logic that he was runner-up in the last search. After some arm waving and fake sniffling into handkerchiefs, we agreed. It's temporary, after all."

"Arm waving or arm twisting?" Monroe paused in case she might respond. She didn't. "Well, Eliot was doing more than keeping the seat warm. I think he was up to bigger things. Losing him is a big loss, don't you think?"

Kerr barely nodded. "We understood each other."

"What do you mean?"

"Don't go there, dear boy." Mrs. Kerr idly reached into a small bowl and selected a single peanut, once again looking past Monroe and panning the room. *Well, this conversation seems to be over,* Monroe thought, just as a warm body gently pushed up against him and a hand draped over his arm. Luce had extricated herself from the chattering classes.

Mrs. Kerr met Luce's gaze. "Good evening, Professor Drummond. They have been keeping you busy." She said "they" in a dismissive tone that contrasted with her look of respect for Luce. Luce, smart, youthful, attractive, was now a go-between to broker projects, causes, and deals.

The crowd drifted to their seats to watch the production. It began with a kind of prelude. A director, three or four participants, and a local arts columnist marched to the stage and sat in chairs arranged in a half circle. They each took a turn to say what a fine production they had created. For a couple of participants, supposedly, it had been life changing.

How could that be true? Monroe wondered later. "Interminable," he said, as he and Luce inched toward the exit. When they were jostled near the door, he looked into the clear blue eyes of Howard Davis, chancellor of the university.

"Sorry," Davis said. "I was rear ended." He paused as if to give Monroe an opening to say something deferential. Then carried on. "Enthusiastic bunch tonight, but not sure why based on the little I saw. I'm Howard Davis. I've seen you at other university functions, but I'm afraid your name slipped through one of the crevices. They seem to be getting larger."

Monroe reached for Davis's hand. "Bruce Monroe from history, Chancellor Davis. A long time ago, we—"

"Pleeeze, it's Howard. Monroe, of course. Evan Spelt has mentioned your name on occasion. In fact, he did so recently in connection with our recent . . ."

"Yes, I was in the office with him on Tuesday waiting for Inspector Martino to arrive and—"

"Professor Drummond, our dean of arts pro tem, I didn't see you." Davis's gaze and interest had shifted sideways. "I must be spaced out," he continued. "A production like we just saw—dare I say it?—will do that. Good of you to come."

Luce smiled as she offered her hand. "Well, I didn't have much choice. I'm on Town and Gown duty for the Arts Liaison Committee. But I've seen worse. I didn't see you at the reception, Mr. Davis."

"I didn't make it. I'm currently playing in a squash tournament and had a match at 6:00."

"And may we ask how the match turned out?"

Davis beamed. He liked the question. "I won." He shrugged as if any other outcome would have been unthinkable. "A good competitor in better shape than me. But drop shots and lobs that die in the corners can wear down opponents like that."

The word on Davis, Monroe knew, was he liked to win. On the squash court or in high-stakes real estate. Even in his sixties with spiky grey hair, Davis stood his ground. Gossip circulated about his abrupt style in chairing BOG meetings. Monroe had himself just experienced it when Davis cut to Luce. It wasn't personal. A kind of ADD for grown-ups. No stomach for academics beating around bushes. But why was he so high on Spelt?

Monroe tuned back in.

"Then it was worth it to miss at least, uh, the first part of the evening," Luce said.

"In fact, I hadn't planned to come at all. I'm covering for Evan Spelt, whose daughter Chiara is playing in a concert with the Okanagan Symphony. In Kelowna," he added, with a token glance in Monroe's direction. "She's the featured soloist playing a piece by Bach. Amazing talent. No one will even notice Evan; he'll just be the guy carrying her cello." He laughed a little too loudly, quite pleased with the remark.

11

An hour later Monroe lay stretched out on his bed, one leg draped over Luce's. Occasionally, he pushed his face into her neck, inhaling deeply. The down comforter had become bunched up and disorganized, partly on and partly off the bed; the room, he now decided, sported a stylish look, the effect of some hasty disrobing. Actually, it had begun decorously enough, as they helped each other with buttons and fasteners, even folding Luce's blouse. But then everything sped up and clothing got dropped or flung onto whatever was nearby: a chair, a chest of drawers, a lamp, or the floor itself. Luce's underwear, it seemed, had just missed a branch of the *ficus benjamina* and his boxer shorts ended up covering the Christmas cactus. A kind of unstaged conceptual art: episodic, chaotic, modernist. Now neither Monroe nor Luce was sleepy, just relaxed and relieved to be out of the straitjacket of the evening.

"Do you ever wonder if you're on the right track?" Monroe asked. "Know what I mean? The politicking. Mean spiritedness. Tribalism. Eliot wanted to restore collegiality to Northgate. That's the word he used, but I didn't get a chance to discuss it with him. And now he's dead. And tonight. It was a time to stop, take stock. Instead, the show goes on. Full speed ahead in mediocre mode. Why no mention of Eliot? The chancellor shows up late looking smug and only thinking about his squash game. He should have stood up and said something about Eliot. Are we wasting our lives here, on the good ship Northlake, a ship of fools? Of course the evening ended well . . . here and now, I mean."

"Whoa, young man. If it's discussion time, have you got some of that Burrowing Owl Chardonnay in the house?"

"Geez, I forgot. I put a bottle in the fridge before we left."

She was half out of the bed. "I'll get it."

"The opener—"

"I know where it is. In the drawer by the dishwasher. Relax." Luce was almost at the door when she stopped. "Brr, it's kind of cold." She backtracked to the chest of drawers and pulled out a Harvard T-shirt, red, with basketball written across the front, and slipped it over her head with a smile and toss of her hair.

Monroe nodded. "I like the look. Maybe basketball's your sport . . . and red's a good colour, very dean like. Now, if you'll just step over here, I'll check to make sure the fit is right."

"Get *out* of here. So easily distracted . . ."

Luce was gone for what seemed like only a couple of minutes. "Your neighbour gave me a wave from her window," she announced as she glided back with glasses and the full bottle, beaded with condensation, sitting on a tray with a Toulouse-Lautrec reproduction.

"Mrs. Rigetti next door?"

"I got the big smile—and she might even have winked—but I sensed she might have been disappointed that it wasn't you."

"Oh no you don't. You just made her day . . . night. She loves it when she spots anything unusual. And what could be more unusual than a beautiful woman in a red T-shirt fooling around in my kitchen late at night?"

Luce settled the tray on a side table. "Easy, boy. Methinks it may not be that unusual."

"Well, she's seen you here before, and she doesn't miss much. But maybe she hasn't seen you in the basketball T."

Luce gave the T-shirt a tug. "Well, it took the chill off. Actually, not much of a cover-up, is it? Maybe the window sill's high enough for basic modesty."

Luce poured two glasses, handed one to Monroe, and then slipped under the comforter and draped her leg over Monroe's. She leaned back against the headboard and raised her glass. "Here's to you," she said, "scandal of the neighbourhood, professor, scholar, maven of the arts—and of . . . fine wines, and questionable t-shirts."

Monroe took a sip. "And to you: Madame scholar, dean of arts, star of an otherwise tedious reception."

Monroe reached for her hand as the two of them sipped the wine, both silent now, as if digesting the implications of their new roles. "The wine's a 2005. I think it won a silver medal in France . . . not that I could tell the difference between silver and a well-chilled *ordinaire*."

"This isn't an *ordinaire*. Wine is about occasion. But three cheers anyway for 2005. Now, where were we? You were musing about life and career at our glorious university. Case in point: tonight's Town and Gown production." Luce sighed. "Yes, it was bad. But not *that* bad. Everyone has to get through stuff like that. People try. Cut them some slack. You do it all the time with your students."

"I guess," Monroe said. "Actually, Davis manages it. I mean, he gets through things, minimizes the tedium. Comes late or leaves early. But is everything cut and dried for him? What about Eliot?"

Luce took a sip of her wine. "Yes, you might have expected a word. He's a minimalist. It's surprising that he didn't nail a seat by the door and slip out early. He could always fake another appointment, then head home for a cookie, a glass of milk, and a good book."

Monroe scrunched his face. "The art of having been seen. But I don't figure him as a book-at-bed person. More a double-scotch-on-the-La-Z-Boy-while-plotting-his-next-takeover type."

"He's not *that* hardboiled. He wasn't planning to come at all. Squeezed it in as a favour for Spelt."

"Yeah," Monroe said. "I wonder about that. Why?"

"He treats him almost like family. He knew all about Chiara's concert."

"Yeah, good of him to tell us the Okanogan Symphony is based in Kelowna. Who would have guessed?"

"Easy with the sarcasm." Luce picked up the bottle and topped up their glasses. "But I did notice his little joke about Spelt as Chiara's flunky. A little black humour. A male thing. Friendly . . . and a bit sadistic."

"You think? That's pretty strong." Monroe sighed. "When I went into teaching I thought I'd be joining a community of people wanting to understand things, explore ideas, share, learn from each other. I know it sounds naïve, but it sits in my gut like a lump of industrial pizza. Instead, tonight, we waste an evening with all that posturing and jockeying for position. Politics as usual."

"Two things," Luce said. "Nothing's wrong with wanting the university to live up to ideals. Good people—a few at a time, or one on one—can make that happen. You do it. Others, too. No one's perfect. People such as Jean-Michel, Warren Kingsley, Lynda Ellis, Sandra Halberg, and Catherine Weisskopf in my department. Me, too, if I may. And it seems that Eliot was beginning to envision the university as a place of sharing and cooperating. And just occasionally some of us have to take a leave from our first love—teaching and research—and do the dirty work of administration for reasons other than ego or power. That's the first point."

Monroe interrupted. "Kerr has already spotted you as one of those who step up. She said we tend to be too comfortable in the herd, just doing our thing. Indirectly, I think she was referring to me. Isolation is something I do to myself. And Eliot's death killed a sense of connectedness I was beginning to feel."

"Yes, but you can't let it defeat you. Which brings me to my second point. We both know that universities are never going to be utopias. They don't exist except in someone's imagination. People who try to create them are dangerous. In bad faith, they do terrible things to bring about their supposed utopia."

Monroe nodded. "I say this to my students. The means *is* the end."

Luce smiled. "Third point, don't lose your sense of humour. The human comedy is fun and funny. Enjoy the ride. Our time here may be shorter than we think. Losing Eliot so suddenly reminds us of that."

Monroe started to say something, but Luce beat him to it. "Let me finish. One last thing. If you feel strongly that there's something suspicious about Eliot's death, however unlikely that is, you should look into it. Our whole community has been wounded. But your main duty is to your students. Especially now. And my duty now as dean is to act with fairness, modesty, kindness, and integrity in an administrative position I never expected to hold. Goodness should trickle down from a dean's as well as a president's office."

Monroe was silent for a few seconds. "I thought you said only two points. There were four. No wonder you're a dean and I'm a professor."

Luce laughed. "Cut it out. I just said stuff you've said a hundred times. All of us keep forgetting the basics if we don't shut up and take a deep breath once in a while. As for the number of points: I had two when I started, then thought of a couple of others when I got rolling. Professional prerogative of us professors. Or our downfall, as our students might say."

Monroe reached for the wine bottle and tipped the last of the chardonnay into their glasses. *Take a deep breath. Why not?*

Luce put her glass down. "Now I'm getting too warm." She pulled off the T-shirt, dropped it on the floor, and snuggled up to Monroe.

A laser of sunlight sliced through an opening in the curtain and locked on Monroe's eyes, pulling him from a deep sleep. He turned his face into the pillow and reached over, expecting to encounter a warm thigh. Instead there was a cold sheet. Sitting up, he saw the comforter neatly pulled up, the red T-shirt folded near the pillow, and Luce's clothing gone.

The clock by the bedside showed 7:40, a little late for Monroe to bike early to campus. No real pressure, though. It was Thursday, the last day of September—and he had no classes, just a meeting with Jim in the afternoon. Luce would be in her office by now, or close to it. She had been right. Why wouldn't a university share the faults and foibles of ordinary society? Where did the idea of a university as a utopia come from? Why should it be different from drainage or commerce? Funny the way people can know things—or have grand opinions—and then not know how to live them.

What the hell *did* he know? Montaigne's famous question. Well, he knew he didn't like poseurs, fakes, and self-promoters, yet maybe he was one of them. He remembered something Luce had said about not being just a bystander—a typical professor shtick—and *do* something.

Still in his boxers, Monroe did some stretches and his pushups, an even fifty, with the last five or so coming pretty slow. For some reason, he envisioned Jack LaLanne, the guy could do pushups all day long, even into his old age.

Monroe cut that line of thought. *Get a coffee, put on a sweatshirt, and think about the day.* Bradley Reed from physics liked to joke that he had no idea who he was in the mornings until he checked his iPhone. He claimed that Aristotle said what you do is who you are. He *must* have said it, it sounds so right. It had evolved into a little routine: *Hey, Reed, got your phone with you?* Reed would pat his pocket, affect bewilderment, and shrug his shoulders. *Who's Reed? You talking to me?*

By the toaster, Monroe found a note from Luce: *Had to get to the office early. The wine was amazing. Is there more in the cellar? Save it for next time. Town and Gown wasn't so bad. Regards to Mrs. Rigetti. Xoxo, Luce. P.S.—feeling better this morning?*

At the kitchen table, he thought of phoning Luce but decided to check the headlines on his phone. One should know something about the wider world beyond the tantrums and thrashings of Northlake. He mentally ticked off what he'd find: the war in Syria, interest rates, unemployment, malfeasance in the financial sector, glib politicians, accelerating feedback loops from global warming. He hesitated, then turned off the phone.

Around mid-morning Monroe headed for campus. He had a few things to do before meeting Jim in the afternoon. The weather was good so he would take the lake-path route, which was flatter, longer, and more relaxing than Beacon Hill. Maybe he'd stop for a few minutes at the bench near Bueler's beach where a flock of flickers hangs out. He had even seen a Kingfisher there a week ago.

He was already down the driveway and partway along the alley when Mrs. Rigetti popped out of her flowerbed, garden gloves on and a three-pronged instrument in hand.

"Oh, Professor Monroe. Good morning. A relaxed start to the day, I see."

"Yes, no classes today. Meetings and *research*." As difficult and tedious as they could be, Monroe knew that neither counted as work for Mrs. Rigetti. In her mind, he was sort of mysterious, a man who seemed to live a leisurely existence and didn't do much. Real working people left the house at 7:30 every morning wearing overalls and carrying a lunch bucket and they returned at 5:30 or 6:00, covered in dust with a case of beer in hand.

"Well, I suppose you did have a late night," she continued. "I was up fairly late myself, with a touch of insomnia, and it looked like you had company."

"Yup, pretty late. Gotta go now, a lot to do."

At the university, Monroe felt free, with no appointments and no commitments. He stopped and looked at a cluster of hollyhocks, faded now by the cooler air of September but still tall and elegant in reds and pinks. Why hadn't he stopped to enjoy them more often in midsummer? At the inter-library loan desk, he requested a rare book that he knew was in the Benson Collection at the University of Texas, on the fifth floor, near the stairs, on a bottom shelf. He had consulted it there a couple of years ago. But the librarian, with a squint and pinched lips, didn't care that he remembered its location. Without fail she would search every library in North America before sending the request.

Back in his office, Monroe looked through some mail and wrote a reference letter for Bill Marston, a student he remembered vaguely from four or five years back, who had applied to work for Amazon. To run around a warehouse finding stuff? He hoped not but couldn't tell from the job title. What next? He started to look over his notes from talking to Mildred but instead decided to call Warren and get hold of the flash memory stick.

12

Monroe had been in The Buzz for several minutes by the time Warren got there. He had his notebook out, trying to get a few points down for the meeting with Jim. So far he didn't have much.

"Figuring things out?" Warren asked.

"Working on it," Monroe said. "Time and place of death and who could have been there. Or *not* there."

Warren looked unimpressed and Monroe carried on as if talking to himself. "Why and how. Words we use in all critical thought. Even if the death proves to be accidental."

Warren nodded. "It probably was. Anyway, the police are the ones who worry about all this."

"Yeah, waiting for lab reports and the like."

"They know how to work out who or how if it wasn't an accident."

Monroe twisted the top of his pen. "We might be just as good at it. It's problem-solving. What we as academics do all the time. Nothing fancy, just being observant and smart. T. S. Eliot said the method is to be intelligent."

"Did he? Probably talking about literature."

"It applies to everything. You think about something, figure out what you know and what you don't. Ask questions. In a crime, you check for alibis."

"And?"

"Eliminate those who could *not* have done it. See who's left."

"Right," Warren said. "From those, check for a motive."

"That's it. Your field . . . psychology. By the way, did you bring the flash drive? I've got to send my book review off."

Warren laughed as he fished the little black device out of his pocket and slid it across the table. "Your bloody review, the world is waiting. And the files from Eliot's computer. The same, probably, as on his computer stored in my lab, but these are the ones I got in the conference room. I copied them to my laptop in case we want to compare notes later. Bit of a rush job there in the conference room. I mainly got the emails. Thought I should come out when I heard Spelt's voice." Warren stood up and drained the last of his coffee. "I'd better get back to the lab. Good luck with Martino this afternoon."

Monroe walked toward his office. He smiled at T. S. Eliot's big idea. *Intelligence, it covers a lot of ground.* In his office, Monroe plugged the USB into the computer but resisted the impulse to dive straight into Eliot's stuff.

First, the damn book review. He looked it over one last time, tightened up a few sentences, and emailed it. Then Eliot's files: grouped under Budget, Board of Governors, Faculty, Renewal, Library, Correspondence. Some names caught his attention: Evan Spelt, Fred Turner, Hans Meyer, and Elizabeth Kerr. Also the higher education minister, Ryan Doyle in Victoria, and Chancellor Howard Davis.

In for a list of points Eliot had scribbled for a reply to Carlos Batalla wrote "deal with under new collegiality, cut infighting between programs and departments, more dialogue, university not an ant hill of specialized functions but a place of inquiry, curiosity, community. Brazilian appointment joint with political science or history?" Applied collegiality beginning to come on line, Monroe thought.

Eliot's correspondence with Fred Turner began on June 7, Eliot's first day on the job. Turner ingratiating himself with some clichés about challenges ahead and hopefulness about new leadership. The last of these was dated September 27, the day before Eliot died. The tone shifted. Turner, the insider orienting a newcomer, gradually became more aggressive to lobby for his Institute of War and Peace in the Age of Decentralized Globalization.

Eliot acknowledged Turner's big idea. Then pushed back pretty hard. The university had procedures to preserve it as a community. A centre cannot be a project to enhance individual's ego. It must meet larger tests for the common good through assessments by internal and external referees, with approval and input by departmental and university curriculum committees, and with appraisals by the library acquisitions staff of resources needed. All this before the proposal could go before the board of governors.

Monroe scratched his head. What was Turner thinking? His own department would view a proposal in this form as a red flag. Monroe himself knew that political science already had courses that dealt with a now decentralized world with any number of regional conflicts from the effects of climate-change refugees and the impact of failed states. With Eliot playing by the rules, Turner looked to be out of sync with Eliot's ideas about collegiality.

Turner's response? He lost patience. In a rant dated September 27, he charged Eliot with "protecting the fat asses of the old guard." Monroe laughed out loud. A bit rich given Turner's heroic rear end, which he normally draped in baggy corduroys.

Petty stuff, Monroe thought. *The kind of morass Luce would have to swim in?* Reluctantly, he moved to another file folder called "Turner Institute: outside assessments. All of them seemed to agree that the proposal had potential, but one from Douglas Snyder at Bowie State University in Maryland summed up the others. It was "half-baked in its present form," he wrote, "and lacks a convincing argument for why the centre should be separate from existing political science or international studies department."

Eliot used the assessments to draft a letter to Turner. Unfinished. Had he been working on it the Tuesday morning he died? Monroe checked the time stamps on the document: created 9/27/10, modified 9/28/10. Almost surprised he sat back in his chair. *Eliot started the letter on Monday and worked on it the morning he died.*

Eliot's letter was cautiously supportive but the institute needed "broader disciplinary reach to incorporate religion, culture, ecology, climatology, literature, and history to exist as a separate institute." He posed sample questions it might address. "How is political cohesion in democracies affected by immigration and multiculturalism with special attention to tensions in the EC and UK? How does climate change destabilize civil societies? How will states manage pandemics that close off trade, shut down economies, and require social isolation? How will failed states and authoritarian kleptocracies that destabilize other nations and regions be neutralized? How will social media fuel protest and rebellion as well as facilitate control and repression?"

This is rather good, Monroe thought, as he read further. Eliot asked Turner to develop the proposal further by proposing collaborators from other disciplines and universities. He should also check on anything that could be politically controversial. In particular, in an unfinished paragraph he worded—to himself it seemed—a question about immigrant communities on Canadian soil that supported political factions in their home countries. In WCSs—Monroe paused until he figured this was Eliot's abbreviation for worst-case scenarios—some of these groups were known to raise funds or find recruits for military operations against constituted governments.

Monroe sat back. What the hell? This, at least in part, must be what Eliot had wanted to run by him last Tuesday or on the weekend hiking to Whyte Lake. Eliot had thought it out and was improving the project. Why wouldn't Turner appreciate such thoughtful feedback? Ego, probably. Could he have been the angry voice in Eliot's office the morning Eliot died?

13

⚏

Monroe turned off the bike path at the back of the police station. No bike rack there, only an ugly patch of asphalt half filled with police vehicles. He suddenly felt disoriented. *Why am I even here?* he thought. He peered through a window near a steel door. It was some sort of basement. Gloomy, no one in sight with three doors labeled "Equipment," "Custody," and "Kennel." A kind of dungeon except the kennel appeared to have access to an outside run, where a German Shepherd lay with his head resting on a bandaged leg. Farther along he saw another door labeled "Breathalyzer" and "Finger Printing."

Behind him, a police car entered the parking area at speed and Monroe stepped away. The driver, a young guy in uniform with short hair and long side burns, lowered his window. "Hey, mister, what are you doing here? This area is off limits." Monroe said nothing but flapped his hand in something like a village-idiot wave. He figured he looked innocent enough—a guy wearing a Mountain Equipment fleece and wheeling a bike. If not, Jim would take care of it. He walked his bike to the front of the building and locked it on a railing by the entrance.

A female constable, tall and fit looking as if she had logged time in a weight room, was behind the counter. She sat at a desk equipped with a computer terminal and scattered with papers with more than a few coffee stains. On the phone and apparently in no hurry to ring off. Monroe didn't mind. It gave him a chance to look around. To his right he could see a glass-panelled office with the sign "By-Laws Officer." No one there now. *Likely out checking parking and noise violations.* Next to the entry, stacks of pamphlets lay in quasi-disarray with information on drug addiction, crime prevention, block watching, alcohol abuse, and distracted driving.

"Can I help you?"

Monroe read the nametag. Constable Hudson stood before him with a hint of a smile on her face. For a couple of seconds, Monroe hesitated. He couldn't believe it, but for a brief lapse he was tongue-tied, some sort of reversion to the intimidation he felt as a kid toward the police. The constable waited patiently, apparently used to this reaction.

"Yes, I'm Bruce Monroe. I'm here to see Inspector Martino."

She smiled. "Ah, yes, *Professor* Monroe. The inspector said you were coming. Follow me."

She covered the distance to Jim's door with an athlete's stride, knocked once, and opened the door without waiting.

"Jim, Professor Monroe."

"Thanks, Catherine." Jim rose.

"Geez, Jim, what kind of operation are you running? You show up at the university with Mendoza in tow and here at the station Ms Hudson is running the front desk."

Jim chuckled. "Steady, boy. No one gets hired here for their looks. Except yours truly, of course." Jim paused for Monroe's scowl, which came on cue. "But it's true," he continued, "it's not easy for women. A lot of sexual harassment in the culture. So many troglodytes . . . you've read about them in the papers."

"All the time. And not only in police and fire departments."

"I know." Settling back in his chair, he picked up a folder and flipped through several sheets of paper. "Let's see. I'm still trying to figure out how to use you. I can't, actually, not in any formal way. But I'm not too up on this case because of the opioid epidemic. Looks like we'll be headquartered at a farmhouse in Lynden. Even if it's mainly coming in containers. Ah . . . but you don't want to know that."

Monroe affected a puzzled look. "Know what? I didn't hear anything."

"For now, let's just to bounce some ideas around about Eliot's case." Jim pulled out a typed sheet. "Some basics. The medical examiner's report. Time of death: between 9:30 and 11:30. Cause of death: massive anaphylactic reaction. Confirms what Mendoza said. Plus there was a letter from Eliot's family doctor (dated August 30) reminding him to renew his EpiPen. Analysis of a piece of uneaten muffin from under the desk matches those from your campus Food Services."

"That's for sure then?"

"Yup, Ravi picked some up. The lab has confirmed the mix of flours they use—twenty percent durum, seventy percent all-purpose, and ten percent whole wheat. Sourced from Rogers from high-gluten winter wheat from Saskatchewan. The durum is a little unusual, supposedly makes the tops a little crustier."

Monroe shifted in his chair. "Right, I'll keep that in mind when I bake. But the killer was the peanuts.

"No doubt. In a muffin. Odd that Food Service does them if they can be lethal."

"We're confirming Eliot's allergy with his family doctor. Mendoza says it doesn't take much for people with allergies. One bite could do it. Could you double-check if the cart was on schedule and how they label the muffins? Eliot can't be the only person on campus with an allergy to peanuts."

"Sure, I'll talk to Nicole, the cart lady."

"Just keep it low-key. Some basic context for us." Jim looked down at his notes again. "The analysis of the stomach contents says that he ingested quite a bit, about a third of the damn thing. The coffee cup on his desk was about two thirds full. You can see it from the photo of his desk."

"On Cypress on Sunday I saw him tucking into some zucchini bread. Big bites. Maybe the coffee sped the reaction. So that's the story line for accidental death . . . yet I've heard that allergic types are pretty sensitive to smells or certainly a first taste."

"I don't know," Jim said. "Middle-aged men supposedly don't have a keen sense of smell. Mine's not that great and we're a little younger. Or maybe it doesn't matter. You're busy, not paying attention, not carefully sampling some delicacy."

Monroe wrote something in his notebook. "Something else. How did he get his hands on it in the first place? They keep them in a separate place on the cart."

Jim picked up a pencil. "Check it, OK? So we'll know exactly how they're wrapped, and how someone could switch one or mix them up."

Monroe shook his head. "I don't know. A few hundred people could have switched a muffin. Everyone loves the cart. It gets wheeled around the corridors and generates ad hoc socializing. A bell alerts office staff and seminar classes to break when it's coming. People crowd around and talk to each other. You serve yourself. In theory, someone could reach in and switch a muffin or pick one up, change their mind, and put it back in the wrong place."

Jim was doodling on one of the sheets of paper. "Your version of the office water cooler."

"I guess so. It follows a predictable schedule. The time limit for the switch would be the window between 8:45, when the cart leaves the kitchen, and 10:30, when it arrives at Eliot's office."

"Or *before* the cart leaves?" Jim asked.

Monroe twisted in his chair and crossed his legs. "I'll see what Nicole and the food manager say. But hard to narrow it down."

"Yeah," Jim said, looking discouraged. "It was probably some sort of accident. But if . . . *if* a muffin was switched with intent, we need a motive. Eliot can't have too many enemies after a couple of months on the job."

Monroe nodded. "By the way I've already done a couple of things that I can report on. Maybe jumped the gun."

Jim looked surprised. "Such as?"

"Well, you remember my call from Eliot's office yesterday?"

"Of course. I wish I knew who that sonuva—"

"While I was there, I asked Mildred Jones to give me the details of her movements that day," Monroe interrupted.

"Oh? That wasn't—"

"Wait, it was friendly. Here's what I figure. She arrived at the office Tuesday morning at 8:40—*about* 8:40, I think, because she's a little vague—and Eliot was already in his office, door closed and curtain drawn. Someone was there with him and she heard voices. *Angry* voices."

Jim leaned forward. "She doesn't know who?"

"Correcto. The main thing, though, Mildred's accounting of her time. She left the office about 9:50, she says, yet she was seen walking on the bark trail next to Lot E at 9:15. That's probably ten minutes away. Then she had errands: the dentist, hardware store, lunch, and back about 1:30, when she finds Eliot dead."

"Finding a way to stay away until you're sure that he is dead? Leaving earlier than she told you. That makes her a person of interest."

"I don't know what to think. Even if there was no foul play, her absence sealed the deal for Eliot. No one there to call to for help."

"True," Jim said. "And damn convenient for someone who knew she'd be gone."

"Look, I'm only a bystander providing some context. But one thing is bothering me."

"Yes?" Jim sounded curious.

"Before you arrived at the university, I went in and looked at Eliot lying on the floor. I didn't touch anything. Just looked. What bothers me is the condition of that EpiPen. I think it could have been sabotaged. If Eliot had damaged it by losing his coordination, it wouldn't have looked that way. He was an alpinist. Knew how to feel out the smallest cracks and outcroppings on rock faces. He could have jabbed an EpiPen into his leg in his sleep."

Jim didn't break eye contact. "Ah, Lois thought Eliot must have jabbed it into the floor as he lost coordination. You're saying the pen could have been wrecked beforehand and he never had a chance to use it."

Monroe nodded. "It's worth checking out. That would make it premeditation."

"Good observation. We'll check it again. You're pretty good at this stuff. By the way, how'd you find out Mildred wasn't straight about her schedule on the morning Eliot died?"

"By accident. One of my students, Rob Cunningham, was doing interval training on the practice soccer pitch above lot E Tuesday morning with his buddy Farshad. They saw Mildred."

"Was he sure about the time?"

"I asked. He remembered hearing the clock tower."

Jim made a note in the folder. "So with ten minutes or so to get there, she could have passed by the cart on her way to the trail."

"Yes, and switched the muffin."

"OK, that's opportunity. Ask this Nicole if she saw Mildred that morning. And we still have a little more than a half hour unaccounted for."

Monroe nodded. "Strange. Nothing out there but a trail and an empty parking lot. Well, almost empty. Hans Meyer parks his moth-eaten VW camper out there."

Jim picked up a pencil and tapped the eraser with one finger. "What else do we know about him?"

"Not that much. He's a German immigrant. From East Germany and somehow got to the West. Came to Canada in his twenties, I think, two or three years before the Berlin Wall came down."

Jim nodded. "1986 or '7 then."

"Still speaks with an accent," Monroe continued. "Works in financial services, as chief auditor, I think. Gruff but decent, principled, eccentric. Fitness buff but doesn't look it. Kind of thick around the middle but strong. Parks as far as possible from his office to get extra walking in and he swims every morning in the pool. Never takes an elevator."

"How old?"

"About fifty. Some grey hair, salt and pepper."

Jim made a couple of notes, then looked up. "What if Mildred was meeting up with Meyer? A little bed and breakfast before getting her molars looked at. Let's check the time of her appointment." Jim stepped to the door, looking back at Monroe as he opened it. "Let's see, Tuesday the twenty-eighth. Last name Jones, right?"

Monroe nodded.

"Be right back."

Jim returned in less than a minute. "Constable Hudson's checking local dentists. Meanwhile, you said you knew who was in Eliot's office that morning."

"I'm not *sure*. But I think it was Fred Turner from political science. I should say *we* think, Warren Kingsley and I. We copied Eliot's email files to a flash drive yesterday and I looked at some of them earlier today and—"

There was a whack on the door and Hudson poked her head in. "Jim, code 30 from Ravi in Surrey. Dispatch sent two cars, a local at the scene, fire crew on the way, probably there in a minute or two. Ambulance on the way."

"What is it?" Monroe asked.

"Ravi's been shot."

14

Jim was on his feet in a second and heading for the door. "Is he OK?"

"He said it's just a scratch, but you know Ravi."

"What the hell. He was only doing surveillance," Jim muttered. Coat in hand, he looked toward Monroe. "Wanna come? We can talk after I see him." He didn't wait for Monroe's answer but called back to Hudson. "I'm taking the black Ford."

He drove quickly, silent except for a single comment. "He'll be in good hands if fire and ambulance are there." Monroe could tell he was worried.

At the hospital Jim pulled into a zone reserved for emergency vehicles. A bulked-up parking attendant waddled up, arms stuffed into a red nylon jacket, lips frozen in a fake smile, eyes cold. "Hey there, pal. Can't you fuckin' read? Let me help you: Emergency Vehicles only. Now get your asses out of here or my boys at Busters will drag you away."

An annoyed expression crossed Jim's face as he reached into his inner pocket and pulled out his ID. "Look, buddy, since you're such a reader, have a look at this. Then see if your pea brain can register the number on the license plate. This is a police vehicle and we're on police business. Get it?"

Jim managed the exchange without breaking stride. The attendant turned red in the face but remained silent and gave just a hint of a nod.

"Gosh," Monroe said, "you were kind of harsh with that guy."

Jim smiled grimly. "Those types piss me off. Too much time in the weight room. A little power and they think it's a license to push people around. Show a little politeness, you get some back."

At the emergency desk, Jim flashed his ID again to the triage nurse and asked if Constable Ravinder had arrived yet. "Yes, inspector, probably five minutes ago. Took him straight to the trauma centre. Just go down—"

"Thanks, Ms. Johnson. We know the way."

"How'd you know her name? Do you come here that often?"

"No, just read her nametag."

At the trauma centre, two doctors were looking at Ravi's arm as he sat on an examining bench. They had removed his Kevlar vest, cut away his shirtsleeve at the shoulder, and were cleaning what looked like a gash on his deltoid. "Uh oh, here comes the boss," said one doctor.

Jim smiled as he walked straight up to the doctor and grabbed one shoulder in a meaty grip. "How's my man doing here, doc?" Then he made eye contact with Ravi. "You OK? This wasn't part of the plan."

Ravi shook his head. "Sorry, got careless. It's nothing, just grazed me"

"What were you doing? Taking a nap? That old Hyundai is supposed to blend in."

Ravi winced as the doctor swabbed out the gash on his shoulder. "That was the plan. Yeah, I was half asleep. A guy pulled up next to me in one of those delivery trucks—United Parcel, big brown thing—and slid open his door with a big smile. When I rolled down the window, he asked where 2015 Elm St is. I was thinking that I didn't know any Elm street in Surrey when he pulled out a Glock."

Monroe looked puzzled. "And you had time to start the engine and take off?

"Actually the engine was already running because I had the heater on. I dropped to the floor, shoved it into drive, and floored the damn thing."

"You're a big guy. You squeezed under the steering wheel?" Jim asked.

"Don't know how I did it. Didn't have time to think. The seat was back, sort of lounging position. Of course I had no idea where I was going but I knew that it was clear for at least 100 metres. I went by feel, just keeping wheels on the passenger side against the curb. Probably ruined the tires."

"Clever," Monroe said.

"More like dumb luck. The whole thing was pretty stupid. The engine running was a giveaway. Should have known delivery guys don't act like out-of-town yokels needing directions." Ravi looked embarrassed. "I wasn't thinking."

Jim nodded. "It happens. But in this case, I'm *glad* your engine was running. Otherwise I doubt that we'd be talking here right now."

Jim looked at Monroe. "By now I'm sure there's a report of a stolen delivery truck at the crime data centre. A gang took Ravi for a rival maybe setting up a hit. They wouldn't knowingly take down one of us, not at their front door. We'll get our hands on that truck and see if we can get some prints. Hansen can do a sketch of the shooter with you." Ravi nodded.

Monroe stood a few steps away. "Those guys must be crazy to shoot somebody like that, even if he was from a rival gang."

"A guy from a rival gang wouldn't talk to us. So not a factor. But they've made a big mistake. We're close to raiding that house. Trying to cut their supply of fentanyl—a big stash there we think, which is a death sentence for a lot of people. I'd like to catch the guy in the truck and link an attempted murder to that house. Our computer guys will listen for any info coming over their wi-fi network. I doubt if they know they've shot a cop."

Ravi scrunched up his face. "They'll be using burners."

"Well, sometimes they get careless. For now, go home and rest." Jim turned to the doctor. "That about right, doc? Even a flesh wound is trauma. And keep this confidential, OK? I don't want the drug guys to know they shot a police officer. Say the victim was unidentified in your paperwork."

"No problem," the doctor said. "Rest and desk duty for at least a week. And I'd like to have another look at that arm tomorrow." Ravi nodded. Jim grabbed him by both shoulders and looked him in the eyes. "You scared the hell out of me. Take time off. As much as you need. Then we'll ease you back. Got me? Glad you're OK, man. Having that engine running saved the day but not without some fast thinking. Impressive response under fire, Ravi. One for the books. But next time, bring a bloody coat."

15

Jim practically ran out of the building. "Hospitals give me the creeps," he said to Monroe. "Too many mistakes, misery, doctors overworked and jaded doctors, people dying."

"Yeah, and we're both on the way. What happened to the old dying with dignity as the family gathered round and sang 'Abide With Me'?"

"That wasn't so great either," Jim said. "What I remember is the priest finishing grandpa off with a blast of his garlic breath while slathering on the unctuousness." Slowing down, he squinted toward the horizon. "Sun's going down and you've got to bike home. Got time to finish our conversation?"

"Sure. After that trauma room, I could use a coffee."

"Mario's is up the street. Brews only beans from Central America."

Monroe puffed his cheeks and blew the air out slowly as if doubtful. "I thought your idea of a good cup looked like something dredged from the Alberta oil sands."

"Very funny." The two men entered Mario's and Jim headed toward the counter. "I'm buying. You're getting the bitumen double espresso, light on sand, no sugar. Grab a table."

Monroe settled in the corner next to a window. When Jim arrived with the coffees, he said: "Nice view. Inconvenient for potential assassins on the sidewalk."

Monroe kept a straight face. "Unless they're on the roof of Home Hardware with a rifle or something." Monroe dropped his spoon into the cup and stirred. "Where were we?"

"Well, you had made copies of some files from Eliot's hard drive. That, by the way, is a little aggressive. Your job is context. Leave the actual evidence gathering to us. What's up with you anyway?"

Monroe shrugged. "It's my patch. I'm not going to just sit by and—"

"Easy. It's about finding a balance. I don't want someone coming after you with a gun. But, go on, you think Turner is the mystery man who was in Eliot's office, right? Based on something you found on Eliot's computer?"

"Right, a bunch of emails about an institute Turner wanted to set up."

"And?"

"A political science thing about political instability in the contemporary world."

Jim looked interested. "Syria?"

"All over the place: North Korea, Somalia, Iraq, Sudan, Afghanistan. Even the UK and the US, in a way."

"Curriculum stuff? How does Eliot fit in?"

Monroe sipped a bit of coffee. "Turner wanted Eliot to fast-track an institute. He was impatient, probably still is. Eliot had told him the proposal needs more work and more vetting in the university. If Turner was in the office that morning, he had opportunity and motive, for he's hot to get this thing off the ground and he wants to head it."

"Are you serious? Someone might kill for something like this?"

"I know. Sounds crazy. But could fit with white-collar crime, about ambition, careers, greed. You know, the office psycho—"

"Hold it, I've got a text." Jim read his phone for a few seconds. "Hudson confirmed Mildred Jones's appointment was at Johnson's Dental Clinic at 11:15. She arrived late. They phoned her work number, but no answer. The time stamp on her Visa bill was 12:22. Oh, and Eliot's doctor has also confirmed the peanut allergy."

"The allergy's no surprise," Monroe said. "No answer when they phoned must mean Eliot was dead by then."

Jim nodded. "Probably. Or he may not have picked up."

"Timing's right, though: Eliot eats the muffin around 10:30 and is dead within a few minutes. As for Mildred, she's at the dentist's office for just under an hour."

There was a soft ping and Jim looked down at his phone. "Wait. Hudson again: The dental receptionist, Janet Yu, on her way for a swim at the Y on her lunch break, saw Mildred in the window table at Olga's. Time about 12:30."

Monroe rubbed his ear. "So Mildred is having lunch. Alone or with Meyer?"

"We can ask Janet if she saw his camper." Jim tapped the screen of the phone.

"I could also ask Meyer or Mildred directly, you know."

"Yeah, we can do that, too," Jim said. "So far, though, it looks like Mildred uses her visit to the dentist to make a day of it. Leaves the office early, walks to the far parking lot to meet Meyer. They have a couple of hours. Close to it, because you can drive to town in fifteen minutes."

"After lunch, they return to the university and she finds Eliot. That's Mildred, not necessarily Meyer. Not yet."

Jim had scribbled the times on a scrap of paper. "True, but in the parking lot and in town he has little opportunity to switch a muffin on the cart."

"Right, his morning swim is too early for the cart. But I keep wondering about Mildred. Why would she lie?"

Jim shrugged his shoulders. "Most people don't publicize their affairs. Or she could be trying to protect Meyer. Is he married?"

"Yes, but not sure how happily. I've only seen him with his wife once. A concert on campus and both looking glum."

"Maybe the woodwinds were out of tune." Jim paused but Monroe didn't bother to react. "Look," he added, "Mildred was playing hooky from work. She wouldn't want that known."

Monroe nodded.

"All of this seems innocent enough. A bit seamy, village gossip stuff. I still think this whole thing will end up as a case of misadventure. But go ahead and talk to Mildred again."

"Anybody else?"

"Well, it won't hurt to talk to Turner and Meyer, perhaps. Turner's the only one with a possible motive."

"Mildred lied and cheated. Should I ask her a few pointed questions?"

Jim shrugged. "Not yet. First, see what Meyer and Nicole have to say."

Jim's phone rang once again. He looked down: "Hudson again, she's busy. Says Ms. Yu saw a man park a VW camper in front of Olga's. Middle-aged, rotund, receding hairline and big forehead, strong looking. Had briefcase."

"That's Meyer," Monroe said.

Jim sat up straighter. "Briefcase. Hmm, is this a tryst or a business lunch?"

Monroe shrugged his shoulders. "OK, I've got a few people I *could* talk to. I can probably get Warren to help when he's not out bird watching."

"I'll be there as much as I can. You're doing some sharp work. You caught us out on that EpiPen. Just don't overdo it."

"Yeah, I know. Stick to context. I'll start with another look at the stuff from Eliot's computer. Speaking of which, when they retrieve the computer from Warren's lab, could your tech people check Eliot's hard drive to see if anything was erased recently?"

Jim opened his notebook again. "OK, looking for something deleted about the time he died, September 28."

Monroe nodded as he massaged his leg near the old injury. "If some files were deleted, Mildred herself had the best opportunity to do it. She was all alone after finding the body. I don't suppose her fingerprints were on the keys?

Jim nodded. "You have a bit of a fixation on her." He flipped through the pages in the folder and looked at the forensic report. "Here it is. Her fingerprints were on, uh . . . on some folders, his door handle, the desk, the stapler, and there's a partial print on his EpiPen. Geez, I didn't notice that. No motive, but I guess we have to keep her in mind."

"She's got that timid exterior," Monroe said, "but psychos can be innocuous. By the way, how'd you get her fingerprints for comparison?"

"Easy, from the cup on her desk." Jim smiled. "You're not the only one doing detective work around here, you know."

16

The campus was eerily quiet on Fridays. *True, it's early,* Monroe thought. *But 7:40's not that early. Certainly, there's time for a coffee. Go to The Buzz or wait for the cart? Wait, and deal with emails.* A little after 8:00, there were two raps on the door. Rob Cunningham poked his head in. "Good morning, Professor Monroe. Do you have a minute?"

"Sure, looks like you're going for a workout."

Rob glanced down at his frayed sweats. "Yeah, and still on the new program. Already done some reading for a lit class. All first-year students should get the tip to start early."

"I'm sure it's recommended at new-student orientation. Before you're ready for it."

Rob nodded. "Anyway, I have a quick question."

Rob had been reading Robespierre's speeches and wanted to check a translation. *Few students are so conscientious,* Monroe thought. *He's got the instincts of a scholar.* Monroe clarified a few points and reminded him that the assignment was an essay. "Your argument, Rob. Keep it moving forward. Stick some of the detail in footnotes."

"It's interesting, though. Thanks. I'd better run now so the porridge has time to settle."

Rob was halfway out the door when Monroe called him back. "Oh, one more thing, Rob. On the way to the workout last Tuesday, did you and Farshad notice anybody else in the quad?"

"Well, some guys with a van near the library. Unloading boxes. And a few students. I wasn't paying much attention."

"Any faculty?"

"Oh yeah, Professor Turner. Walking toward the admin building or possibly

The Buzz. He was wearing a raincoat and his hair was messed up. Farshad said he must have burned an all-nighter with all that high living."

"High living?"

"No disrespect. Just that racy new Tesla he's got. Bright red. Farshad's brother Ali—you remember him?—he's in law school now. He got to park it. Works as a valet at the Four Seasons on weekends. Turner showed up, dropped off his car, and met four or five rich-looking guys in suits at the main entrance."

"A Tesla, huh? A bit rich for most faculty. Do you remember what time you and Farshad saw him that Tuesday?"

"Just before 8:00, because the clock tower bonged just as we sat down to eat."

"Thanks, Rob. Have a good workout."

❖

Monroe decided to try to catch Nicole at Food Services before she left on her rounds with the cart. First, though, he ran into Harvey Iverson, the manager. "You've probably heard that Eliot died from eating a peanut muffin. Any idea how that that happened?"

Harvey's smile disappeared. "What do you mean?"

"Just wanted to clarify your procedures for people with allergies."

"Right, well the police took a couple of our peanut muffins last Tuesday. Nothing out of the ordinary that day on our end. We always provide a warning. *Only* for peanuts, not every other crazy problem people imagine they have. Well . . . except for gluten. Everyone now is worried about gluten so we have to do gluten-free. But gluten doesn't kill anyone, does it? I personally—"

"I'm not sure, maybe people with celiac disease."

Harvey seemed impatient as he shrugged his shoulders. "Anyway, I package Eliot's muffin every morning. The peanut-free muffins go into plastic boxes on the bottom shelf. Peanut muffins stay in a separate basket on the second shelf. We put quite a few of them on the cart—they're popular, although I don't much care for them."

Monroe nodded. "You're *sure* you put the right muffin into the box?

"Yes, yes. It's a fail-safe system. Peanut-free has no contact with peanuts. Ever. They're prepared on the other side of the kitchen and baked in a separate oven. We go to a lot of trouble."

Seems pretty damn sure of himself—has he heard of Murphy's Law? "How many allergen-free muffins go onto the cart on any given morning?"

"Only Eliot's and one or two extra, also wrapped separately. Most people with a serious allergy avoid our baked goods because we warn them that even plain flour can have trace elements of nuts. Look, I don't blame anyone for having allergy problems, but I'm not going to lie, it's a pain in the ass for us."

"What about the plastic boxes and labels? Anything special about them?"

"Nope. Standard food-grade clear plastic containers number 1. You see them at deli counters in supermarkets. We use different sizes for take-away salads or servings of beans or beef stew with rice, that sort of thing."

"Sealed?"

"Not with tape or anything. They're closed."

"So one can pop the lid off quite easily. What about labels?"

"Avery file folder type. Maybe they look a little amateurish for food packaging, but they're cheap and do the job. There should be some right here." Harvey picked up a small box from a shelf above a desk covered with papers and handed it to Monroe. "I would normally write Eliot's name on one of these and stick it to the top of the box."

Same ones we all use, Monroe thought.

"OK, Harvey. Thanks for your time. I'd like to have a few words with Nicole if she's still around."

"Make it a *few*. She's running late."

Nicole pulled off a food-safety bonnet and let down her hair, which was loosely tied in a ponytail. She smiled, seeming unaware that she was Harvey's secret strategy to sell stuff.

"I've been trying to work out how Mr. Eliot died. Do you remember anything special about your round with the cart last Tuesday?" Monroe asked.

"Oh, wow. But I thought it was an accident."

"It could have been. But the police are checking. President Eliot died from anaphylactic shock after eating a muffin with peanuts in it."

"But how? I gave him his special muffin in the box with his name on it, same as always. . . . Did I do something wrong?"

"No, I'm not saying that. It looks like Harvey packed it in the normal way. Do you remember where on the cart it was?

"Well, the usual place on the bottom shelf. We, uhh . . . he always puts two or three of those muffins in boxes, although Mr. Eliot is the only . . . ahh, was the only standing order with his name on it."

Monroe nodded. "So Mr. Eliot's muffin was doubly protected: separated from the peanut butter muffins."

"Yes, they're in a basket on the second shelf."

"That's what Harvey said. It looks like someone switched a peanut muffin into the box meant for Eliot somewhere between here and his office."

"And switched the other muffin out?" Nicole's voice was barely audible as if she were replaying it.

"Do you think such a switch possible?"

"I *guess* so. . . . It's easy enough to open those boxes. People reach in and help themselves."

"Do you think someone could have had a box ready with Eliot's name on it with a peanut butter muffin in it?"

Nicole looked doubtful. "It's possible. Easy to get a peanut muffin and a box and one of the labels."

"Right," Monroe said. "Two more questions. First, at certain points on your route do you leave the cart unattended? Secondly, are there places where it's more crowded so it could be easier to switch a muffin without being noticed?"

Nicole took a few seconds before answering. "Yes and yes. For a few weeks now, I take a coffee and muffin into the student-aid office for Jan Dillon and we chat. She's on crutches from a ski accident and can't carry her standing order, a low-fat blueberry-oat and medium coffee. She's the only one in that office. But that part of the corridor is fairly busy because it's close to the English department."

Good memory, Monroe thought. "Three or four people could have walked by while you were talking to Jan."

"Sure, I don't guard the cart or anything. The honour system, you know."

Monroe rubbed his chin. "Of course. I wonder . . . student aid is sandwiched between Economics and Political Science and English—"

"Yes, English, by Student Aid, is one of the busiest stops. Professor Kennedy always has three or four students in his office and they usually buy Danish pastries."

"Anywhere else?"

"You mean where there's a crowd?"

"Yes."

"Those are the main spots, history too, in the arts building" Nicole said. "And fairly busy in Communications, after English. But even at less busy stops I talk to people and don't pay much attention to the cart. Everyone's friendly and people do their thing. Oh, guess I already said that."

Monroe smiled. "That's OK. So you rounded the corner and passed along the north side of the Academic Quadrangle. I suppose you saw the dean and his staff?"

Nicole paused in thought. "I saw Professor Drummond . . . uh, your friend. I recall that she was wearing a linen blazer, ivory coloured, and a beautiful scarf. But Dr. Spelt didn't poke his head out that day." *That memory again*, Monroe thought. "I noticed because usually everyone lets him go first. Wait, now I remember. That day he was down toward the English department. Standing next to the department chair and wearing a raincoat, kind of baggy on him. They were having words."

Monroe made a note in his notebook.

Nicole frowned in concentration. "Wait . . . I also saw him earlier at Food Services, then—"

"Food Services? That same morning?"

"Yes, he was looking for Chiara. I told him he'd just missed her."

"Wait, so Chiara was there too? What was she doing?"

Nicole laughed. "She was all dressed up—a classy black dress—and about to go to the Conservatory for a recital. She was starving to death—that's what she said—and had to eat something because she couldn't play on an empty stomach. She bought two muffins and a we made her a cappuccino. She's a nice girl, spoke a few words of French with me. But she took off in a hurry."

"I don't suppose you remember what kind of muffins."

"I do. She took a blueberry oat and an orange pecan. Then I think she went back to her father's office because he was going to drive her to the concert."

Monroe jotted something in his notebook. "Can you remember what time this was?"

"Sure, the clock tower had just struck 9:00. A lot of our staff hadn't arrived yet. Mr. Iverson isn't too strict unless we're more than five minutes late. They were cutting it close."

Tight ship, Monroe thought. "So Chiara was here for four or five minutes, got her breakfast, and left. And then Dr. Spelt arrived maybe a couple of minutes later?"

"That sounds right. He asked about Chiara and I told him she just left. He then asked me to go find Mr. Iverson, that he wanted to speak to him."

"So you left him here while you searched for Iverson?"

"Yes, but I couldn't find him. I was falling behind schedule so I gave up and told him that he must be in a meeting."

"Then what?"

"I told Dr. Spelt I had to start my rounds. He apologized for delaying me and said he would see Mr. Iverson later. He told me he had bought a muffin and had put something in the tip jar."

How generous of him, Monroe thought. But if he was in such a hurry to find Chiara in the first place, why ask for Iverson and hang around while Nicole looks for him? "OK," Monroe said. "So, just to review. After this meeting with Spelt in Food Services that morning, you saw him again in the corridor talking to the chair of the English department. That would have been your last stop before his own office. At the dean's office, did Margo Johnson and some of Spelt's other staff come into the corridor for their coffee?"

"Yes, but I don't recall all of their names. Several tea drinkers in that office. Margo was there. She reminded me that she owed some money from Monday and she borrowed some change from Professor Drummond to pay the extra."

Monroe thought for a minute. It was pretty typical for a dean to have a quick word with a department chair as he moves around the campus. Probably had the raincoat on because he was about to take Chiara to the concert. "I'm keeping you from your work. One last thing. After the dean's office, you took the bridge connector to the administration building."

"That's right," Nicole said. "And, as usual, I arrived at Mr. Eliot's office at 10:30. Maybe just a bit later because of the crowd at English. At first I was surprised that Mildred wasn't there. I wanted to tell her that I was admitted to the MA program in communications. She helped me with the application."

"Congratulations," Monroe said.

"And you didn't see Mildred anywhere in the corridors? Maybe she got a coffee or muffin from the cart at another point on your route?"

"No, didn't see her at all."

"So the outer office was empty, but Eliot was there. Was he alone?"

"Yes," Nicole said. "It was a little unusual because I knocked on his door twice before he answered. Usually, he expected his morning break and sometimes even opened his door in advance. That day he was working at his computer. He said he was typing an important memo."

"Is that all he said?" Monroe asked. "Any little detail might help."

Nicole looked away as she thought. "Well, he looked serious . . . something about disappointing people and the buck stopping. I'm not sure what that meant."

17

Monroe ran into Warren emerging from Greenwood Hall. "You look worried."

"Someone's been in my storage closet and Eliot's computer is gone."

Monroe thought for a second. "Do you know when it was taken?"

"It was there yesterday afternoon but not an hour ago."

Jim was going to have his tech people check the hard drive for erased files. Monroe pulled out his phone and spoke briefly while pacing several steps away. "It's all good. Jim sent someone to pick it up yesterday around 6:00."

"Well, what the hell. I'd like to be informed when they're going to come into my space and rummage around."

"You're right. They should have left a note. I'll tell Jim you were miffed."

Warren looked only slightly appeased. "I shouldn't have given them a key."

"Yeah, but you did. Let it go. The rest of that stuff will probably be moved out soon. Meanwhile, their tech people are working on the hard drive right now."

"Cops, they have too much—"

"Here's the deal, Warren." Monroe slipped into a more soothing tone. "Eliot's files could be worth checking carefully. I had a quick look yesterday and he was nixing Turner's institute the morning he died. Likely Turner's was the angry voice in the office."

"Interesting."

"It is. When you copied Eliot's files, do you remember seeing any files labeled with Turner's name or with War and Peace Institute? It could be in a folder of Word documents."

Warren shrugged his shoulders. "It's a blur now. Why, by the way, did you shove me into the conference room like that?"

Monroe paused. "Not sure. I thought she might be hiding something.

Anyway, I'll be looking at those files this weekend. Anything to do with Turner. Want to coordinate?"

"Sure. But I have to go to a brunch on Sunday with people from the department. And Saturday I'm going to a home DIY show at the convention centre. I need to get my place winterized."

"Good luck. That cottage of yours is like a wind tunnel."

"It's not so bad compared to my cabin. The rent's cheap and the place is great in summer. Five acres and I'm at the edge of the wooded section where I've put up a lot of nesting boxes. Think Walden Pond."

"Small detail: no pond. For the cottage a few basics would help: some double panes, something to fill in the cracks. Your landlord can afford it."

Warren nodded. "That's the plan. He's loaded but cheap. I'll pick up some brochures for quick fixes. My talking point to seal the deal—get it?—is to offer to sign a three-year lease. And remind him that I take care of the dog when they travel."

"Hardly a chore to look after Boswell. I'd take him for nothing."

"I know. It's only a talking point."

"I'll phone you," Monroe said as he headed toward the dean's office.

Monroe knocked on Luce's door and almost immediately it opened. She had been putting things into boxes.

"Full speed ahead on the transition?"

"Half speed. It's too rushed and feels too permanent. Spelt is only acting president—why don't I stay in this office until things settle down? Why move me out to the big office?" Luce paused. "What are you thinking? You were someplace else just now."

"I was agreeing with you. Why *not* just stay put? Your term as associate is about up. You've wanted to get back to teaching and your students. Would you consider a full term as dean if they asked you?"

"The old ego trap. Otherwise, someone less competent will do it, right? I might, actually. It's OK to take a turn. We all should. Administrative work shouldn't be monopolized by bean counters trained in business schools. Students don't belong in a for-profit nexus."

"Or abstracted into full-time equivalents," Monroe added. "The FTE is an F word—it poisons the way universities think about students." Monroe paused, almost surprised at his vehemence. "Still, why are things moving so fast?"

"I'm not sure who's driving it," Luce said. "Spelt, I guess. He seems keen to be settled in the corner office. A symbol of success. He's just about out of here. Only a few odds and ends left, which he told the movers he'd take care of himself."

Monroe looked through Luce's doorway toward Spelt's mostly empty shelves and desk piled with books in random-sized stacks. On the shelves several photos remained. "Mostly of Chiara or her sister, and one or two of his father. One with his mother, I'm guessing."

"Yes, the father. Emeritus in physics at Minnesota, with dementia or something."

Monroe walked a little closer. "Good-looking dude. Must have been quite a force in his time. Looks like a hockey stick on the wall behind him. Must have been an athlete. Nice picture on the left with Chiara and her sister."

"Spelt doesn't talk much about her but looks at the pictures a lot," Luce said. "And he's definitely attached to the father. Phones a lot. And he always sounds patient, not the way we usually see him in the office."

Monroe stepped over to the bookcase. "Look at this picture of Chiara from a few years ago. Cello's about as tall as she is. She already knows she can play. What, maybe about twelve then?"

"Sounds about right," Luce said. "She's still on the small side but maturing fast. Recognize the man standing next to her?"

"Yo-Yo Ma," Monroe said. "Look at him, that big smile. So casual in corduroys, hand in his pocket, ignoring the camera, looking at Chiara."

"I can't imagine a better mentor. Maybe just finished a master class with her and still giving her his full attention."

"Here's a question for you," Monroe said. "What's the deal with kids like this? Why so talented at such a young age? Don't you think it's sort of freakish?"

Luce smiled. "In fifty words or less? Who knows? That's *my* answer." She paused for a few seconds. "Apparently, the older sister had talent as well. But not so much Spelt himself. I've heard him try to whistle a song."

"Maybe it comes from his wife," Monroe said. "I can't remember her name.

It's clear, though, that he's ambitious for Chiara. And for himself, I guess. And he cares for his father. Or maybe trying to live up to his standards."

"Well, he wouldn't be easy to live with. It hasn't been much fun sharing this office with him the past few years. Or much fun for Chiara. He dotes on her but drives her as well. Quite a few master classes, some far away. The other day I heard him on the phone checking on flights to Vienna."

"Ex-pen-sive." Monroe drew out the syllables.

"Maybe they've found an angel. There are foundations that help young musicians."

"Some make high-quality instruments available on loan to them."

"True," Luce said. "I've seen Spelt scouring catalogues from dealers. I think the sky's the limit, especially if you want the equivalent of a Stradivarius. Crazy expensive."

"Mostly you hear about violins," Monroe said. "Not so much cellos."

Luce gave a shrug, then stepped back into her alcove, retrieved a clipping from her desk, and passed it to Monroe. "Something to show you."

Monroe began reading aloud: *Three-day getaway to San Francisco: Friday night to Sunday night, stay at the Four Seasons, all-inclusive, $600 per person based on double occupancy.*

"What do you think?"

"Not bad, but—"

"I could squeeze in a visit to the Bancroft Library. You know, I've wanted to see the Mark Twain papers there. Even a half-day with the indexes. Enough to get started on a grant application. But that would be just a sidebar. Let's just go. We'll rent a car, a convertible, put the top down, drive to Napa. Taste some wines, catch some sun, get away from here for a while."

Monroe hesitated. Who in his right mind could say no to this? Yet going on a getaway now seemed like abandoning something he had to finish. "It sounds wonderful. Really. But I can't let go of the Eliot thing. Not right now. Not knowing what happened to him and why. It keeps eating at me."

Luce nodded, her lips tight, as she pushed the clipping aside dismissively. "Yes. Well, it is what it is. Maybe later, then, when this mess is cleared up."

There was coolness in her tone. She was pissed off. Monroe tried again, picking up a pencil and staring at it as if he had never seen one before. "Look, here's a thought. If you're worried about losing momentum on your research, you should be able to tap into some travel money to get to Berkeley for a few days. Deans have access to funds, don't they?"

"What? Go there alone?" Luce asked. "You don't get it. This isn't about research, it's about us."

Monroe felt cornered. "I didn't mean it that way. I meant in a week or so, you could go down a day or two early to work in the Bancroft and I could fly down and meet you. Hasn't Spelt been doing quite a bit of that? Linking his university travel to Chiara's travels?"

Luce looked doubtful, as if suspicious about Monroe changing the subject, but she answered anyway. "Possibly. . . . And possibly his trips are more about Chiara than university business."

"Oh?"

"Something our office staff has been doing," Luce said. "When Spelt books a trip for university business or to attend a conference, they look for news that Chiara is going away. The local paper sometimes had stories about it or Bernadette knows because her son, Tom, has the same math tutor as Chiara. I don't pay too much attention—people have to gossip a little."

Monroe nodded. "It's harmless, I guess. Although it would be a way to defray some of the costs for Chiara's travel. Padding expense claims isn't unheard of around here, as Meyer would say."

"I think he exaggerates," Luce said. "If true, it borders on fraud, but to get it by Meyer would take some clever bookkeeping."

"I'm not accusing him. But he has expenses."

Luce paused. "He makes a lot more than faculty. All administrators do. Even I do, a lowly associate dean. And as acting dean, my salary will jump up. It's the business model. Administrators are upper management, faculty mere employees—pesky ones, all too often—who deliver the product, education, to clients. People we used to call students."

"Don't get me started," Monroe said. "I was bending Eliot's ear about this." As if talking to himself, he murmured, "So Spelt just got a big raise."

Luce thought for a moment. "OK, here's my take on Spelt. He's not the best person to head this university. Or any university. He is self-centred, mean-spirited, lacks vision, and tends toward cronyism. I think appointing him acting president is a mistake. You would be a better choice; I would be. But I don't think Spelt would be stupid enough to defraud the university."

Monroe nodded. "You *must* be right. Although—"

Luce looked impatient. "Yes, yes, anything is *possible*. Except getting you out of here for a weekend."

Ouch. Monroe felt Luce's annoyance like a slap in the face. Her phone rang, but she got one more point in before picking up. "We all have a tipping point, you know." She raised a hand to cut off further conversation. "Dean of arts, Luce Drummond speaking."

Monroe signalled that he had something more to say.

"Oh, yes," Luce said. "I was just reviewing your memo. Can you hold for a second?" Luce had put her hand over the phone. "Make it fast. It's Charles Hamilton from anthropology and I've already put him off a couple of times."

Distracted by the term "tipping point"—was Luce reaching hers?—Monroe, had trouble getting back to his question. "Do you remember seeing Spelt here in the office on Tuesday morning?" he managed. "Chiara might have been here."

"Gosh, I don't know. . . . Another detective question? Tuesday? Chiara *was* here, but she disappeared and Spelt went to look for her. Ask Margo."

Monroe waved goodbye and mouthed *call me.* Luce pointed toward Margo's desk in the outer office as if dismissing Monroe. He walked straight to it.

"Margo, do you remember anything about Chiara being in this office on Tuesday?"

Margo thought for a minute. "Well, she had her cello and was going to play in a recital at the Music Academy. I think the plan was for her dad to drive her there and catch her performance."

Monroe nodded. "Luce said she went missing for a while."

"Oh, that. She'd slept in and hadn't had breakfast. Ran down to Food Services to grab something."

"And?"

"Well, Spelt came out of his office ready to take her and was all hot and bothered when she wasn't here. I told him where she'd gone. He did a little rant. Not serious enough about her music and all that. Imagine getting so worked up over such a small thing! Then he went to find her. Funny thing, she was back before he was, waiting quietly with her muffins and cappuccino."

"And so he got back and drove her to the concert and all was fine?"

"Not quite. He charged in and told her she'd have to take a taxi because she had screwed up his schedule and now he wasn't going to her concert. It didn't make sense. He was ready to go, even had on that Burberry raincoat he got from his father. Too big for him and not even raining."

"How did she take it?"

"Not well. She was in tears. Then I think she was ashamed and embarrassed when Spelt ordered me to call the taxi. *Ordered* me. He then pulled a twenty out of his wallet, announced it was for the taxi, and flipped it onto my desk. Abusive behaviour to both of us, if you ask me. I almost told him to bugger off."

Monroe shook his head and sighed. "Then Chiara left?"

"Didn't say a word. Just put on her coat, grabbed her instrument, and started to go. Spelt tried to talk it back a little. But too little and too late. The girl kept her poise, but she was hurt. I don't think it was the first time he'd acted this way. She had eaten only one muffin and was no longer hungry. I tried to get her to take the other muffin to eat on the way to the conservatory, but she told me she felt queasy and left it on Spelt's desk. Anyway, I called the taxi, made sure Chiara took the money, and walked her to the bus loop, where she was picked up."

"And Spelt, was he in the office when you got back?"

"No."

18

That Friday night, Monroe opened a bottle of Chilean cabernet and sat at the kitchen table scribbling a list of tasks he could do . . . or *should* do. He wasn't thrilled. Odd to be working on a research grant application on a Friday night. Shouldn't he be socializing or something? Maybe something grooved into his brain at adolescence.

He thought about the conversation with Luce, how he'd poured cold water on the San Francisco getaway. She was pissed. Could he repair things in a week or two? You never know. Life is now, you make decisions. She might go alone, might meet somebody. People researching in archives and libraries become comrades in a hurry, fast friends sharing ideas and stories. Then just as quickly they return to their real lives.

He took a sip of wine. It was no use. He had one thing on his mind. He'd have to try to get some slack from Luce until the mystery of Eliot's death was solved.

The doorbell rang. Monroe jerked the door open, ready to say no thanks to solicitors, but he relaxed when he saw Mrs. Rigetti, who held out a plate covered with plastic wrap.

"Carrot cake for you, professor. So you'll be ready for the race tomorrow."

Monroe eyed the cake. It looked good. "Race?"

"Don't you remember? When you donated to the Parkinson's campaign last summer you were automatically entered in the 10K race around Stanley Park."

Monroe tried to think. "Something about 'Around the Park against Parkinson's'?"

"Exactly. I'll be at Second Beach at 10:00 to give you your number—or one of the other volunteers will. And remember the race starts exactly at 11:00."

Monroe's first thought was to back out, quickly and cleanly. *Why not,* he thought. *It'll only take an hour or two. Fresh air. The best ideas come when you're moving. Maybe how to repair relations with Luce. And a damn good cause.* Parkinson's had taken Hugh, his mentor and thesis advisor in grad school, way too soon. Monroe reached for the cake. "Thank you, and thanks for reminding me."

Later, back at the house, Monroe threw some clothes into the washing machine, iced his leg, put a couple slices of carrot cake on a plate, and turned on the TV. He found a baseball game in progress but turned it off after a couple of innings. He was fidgeting, wondering what Jim's tech people had come up with on Eliot's computer. He dialed Jim.

"Jim. Monroe here."

"What d'ya want?"

"You sound grumpy. In the middle of something?"

"If you must know, I *was* watching the Yankee game on TV."

"I had it on myself. Still two to one?"

"Yeah, no change since the third inning. The pitching's good. But you didn't call to talk about Severino's curve ball."

"No, actually, was wondering about his fastball command." Monroe paused for a comeback but didn't get one. "OK, I called to see what your tech guys found on Eliot's computer. Any erased files from last Tuesday or Wednesday?"

"As a matter of fact, yes. I was going to call, but it's Saturday. Thought you'd be out with Luce or working in the garden. Hold on. . . . I'm getting my notebook. Bob Seaker, our lead tech guy, found something called 'Notes on Institute' and 'Turner re: Institute.'"

"Can you send them?"

"Hudson already did, yesterday. Check your inbox. They're encrypted but the program to decipher them and the password are in separate emails. Hudson usually puts something generic in the subject head.'"

"OK, they could be in the spam folder. Oh, could I get my hands on Eliot's computer now that you're done with it? Maybe you could drop it off at my house. Tomorrow or Monday should do."

"What for?" Jim asked. "You think we missed something?"

"Probably not. I'm not even sure what I'd be looking for, but maybe there's something."

"We can't release the computer," Jim said. "But I'll drop off a copy of the hard drive. I'll be out your way this evening or tomorrow to visit my mum."

"She doing OK?"

"Well enough. The hip healed, more or less, but she needs a walker for the street and a cane in her bungalow. Assisted-living vultures hover, but she'll have none of it. Treats them like real estate solicitors."

"Oh my. They'd better be careful. That cane can be a lethal weapon. Could be a scene out of a Clint Eastwood movie."

"Yeah. She's feisty. And still strong. Makes bread for the neighbours every weekend. Maybe see you later."

"You know where the key is. Just bring it in and lock up after."

Jim laughed. "Oh my god. . . . Still under the pot with the geranium on life support. First place any self-respecting B&E artist would look. I need to get the property crime boys to stop by and clue you in."

Monroe realized he was a little lax, but Jim didn't know about Ms. Neighbourhood Watch next door.

■■

It was Sunday morning and Warren was sitting at Monroe's kitchen table cradling a mug of coffee. "It was either brunch with colleagues," he said, "or taking Jensen to Ambleside to observe a couple of nesting Kingfishers. He asked and it's a good idea to keep him off the roads. I've wanted to observe them for a while anyway. What exactly are we looking for?"

"I'm not too sure," Monroe said. "Almost a week since we lost Eliot and Jim's coming to campus Tuesday. Not exactly full-blown suspects, but to talk to Turner, I suppose, about being in Eliot's office that morning. If—"

Warren finished the sentence. "If he was. If only Mildred had been more curious, thought of an excuse to open his door, we'd know."

"Yes but that's not her. By the way, my student, Rob Cunningham, saw Turner early Tuesday morning heading toward the administration building. And a couple of hours later, Eliot was writing up his decision on Turner's proposal. That's when Nicole arrived with the cart and told her he was writing a memo that would disappoint someone. And, get this, we now know that memo was erased on the day Eliot died."

"That means—"

"Try this. It means Turner has words with Eliot, leaves to go teach his class, and Eliot is alive around 10:30 when Nicole arrives. Turner sees the cart on the way to his class, switches the muffin, teaches his class, and returns to erase Eliot's memo."

We would need to establish where he makes the switch," Warren said. "Good luck."

"I should have asked Nicole if she saw him at the cart before she got to Eliot's office."

Warren slapped his mug down. "Even if she saw him, it's unlikely she saw him switch a muffin. There are too many ifs. *If* he switched the muffin. *If* he was even in Eliot's office early. It's not enough that your student saw him early and heading in that direction."

"You're right, but it's a start," Monroe said. "A reason to ask him. And I'm curious about why he is now driving a new Tesla."

"*That* surprises me." Warren stared out the kitchen window. "Well, what else don't we know? What about Hans Meyer?"

"Meyer goes to the gym early every day and he may stop by his office on the way." Monroe paused and squinted toward the window. "We should also talk to him. But I have trouble with motive. He respected Eliot, was working with him to uncover something suspicious."

"Maybe it's far-fetched but what about the possibility that Meyer was in on the take for whatever he was investigating," Warren said.

"Devious. *Pretending* to investigate and when Eliot seemed to be getting too close he wrecks the EpiPen and switches the muffin. He certainly had access to Eliot's office."

"A muffin is a weird murder weapon," Warren said. If someone switched it, for example, it could have been unplanned, something done on the spur of the moment—almost a prank."

"I don't think so," Monroe said. "There's planning here. Someone knew how lethal peanuts would be to Eliot. Knew the route and timing of the food cart. Knew how to get access to Eliot's office in advance, maybe several days or even more, to sabotage the EpiPen. Maybe even knew that Mildred would be out of the office that day."

Warren didn't seem convinced. He stood up to reach the coffee, refilled his cup halfway, and held the pot in Monroe's direction.

Monroe waved him off. "Same thought. How many people would have known Eliot's regular times to be out of the office? To disarm the EpiPen, for example?"

"Mildred, of course. And she lied to us. She could have erased the files, although why would she?"

Monroe didn't answer. He felt that he and Warren were circling the proverbial dead horse now. "We need other days," he said.

"Here's what I think," Warren said. "We're not looking for sociopaths, cold-blooded types. We should imagine someone high-minded."

"What do you mean?"

"I should say a distorted high-mindedness. Possibly with a twisted idea to eliminate a perceived threat to the university or some idealistic cause."

Monroe played with his coffee spoon. "So in Turner's case, his pet project gets turned down, dismissed and even ridiculed he imagines, and he thinks it is such an injustice that he must push back."

"Yes, something like that," Warren said.

"It's a kind of insanity," Monroe said, thinking out loud. "Conflate personal advantage with an imagined greater good. Or pretend to. Yet killing someone is extreme."

"Of course," Warren said.

"Think more about Eliot's early going," Monroe continued. "Thoughts about collegiality could be perceived as dangerous if it meant cutting or combining programs, shifting priorities, dismantling mini-empires, or regrouping thematic and area studies programs differently. Change might be viewed as a threat. You could look for that sort of thing and I'll try to focus on individuals."

"Turner, Meyer, and Mildred?"

"Yes, and Spelt. He has big expenses and resented Eliot's appointment as a kind of injustice."

"Spelt, huh?" Warren had dutifully written down Spelt's name and then doodled jagged lines around it.

Monroe nodded. "Let's meet early Tuesday at The Buzz. Jim will be around to check out Turner. Join us if you want."

19

✥

After Warren left, Monroe turned to his computer to have a look at the files Hudson had emailed. She had pressed the forward button on what the tech guys sent to her: *Hudson: attached deleted files from Eliot's hard drive for Professor Monroe. And copies for our files. Not necessarily in that order (ha, ha). We're still looking for other deleted files, but this may be it. Cheers, Bob.*

A Word document labeled "Notes on Institute for the October BOG Meeting" had been created on Thursday, September 23, and modified on Tuesday, September 28. So these notes in progress for nearly a week and worked on the day Eliot died.

Monroe wondered if there was an email that linked to this document. In a few minutes, he found an exchange between Eliot and the higher education minister, Ryan Doyle, dated September 23, at 7:31. Doyle's note originated from his Gmail address rather than his official government one. Off the record then.

Peter: the premier likes that proposal for an institute. He got word that it might mean a big pot of money for our party—I mean big—as well as a trust fund to support the institute. Win-win, no? There is a small quid pro quo. They have been in touch with Professor Turner directly and asked for a few revisions to the proposal to emphasize the central role of China in the new world order. We'd like you to support this version, when it comes together, to the BOG. In case Davis and Spelt oppose it, we've still got the votes if it comes to a showdown. Monroe took a deep breath. *You've probably seen the opinion piece by Vaughn Palmer in the* Vancouver Sun*—we don't know his source—where he calls it a Trojan horse, a so-called Confucius Institute set up to spread Chinese Communist Party mis- and dis-information. Apparently, they've approached Kerr and she told them to take a running jump. She would rather abstain at the level of the BOG, but the premier will buy her off with a package of funding for the gallery. See if you can bring her along.*

Your assessment and presentation of the institute will be crucial. For now, play along but postpone action. The usual bullshit should do: needs more focus, more time for execution, a plan for long-term budgeting, possible outside funding, how gifts from donors do not compromise freedom of speech, academic integrity. Yada yada yada. Cheers, Ryan.

Eliot's reply was dated September 23, at 7:31 a.m.:

Ryan: I didn't expect such a cynical take. I won't be a party to it. The art gallery deserves budgetary support on its merits, not in exchange for Kerr's vote in the BOG. And Turner's institute, should it find a home at Northlake, should be placed in the political science department, where academic freedom is in place. All of this is our decision. So stop interfering. A university's not a glorified propaganda machine for special interests with deep pockets. Let's be honest, the premier has no idea what higher education is about. Critical thinking will always be in short supply and it comes from across the spectrum: the arts, humanities, sciences, as well as engineering and computer programming.

Let's fight this out in person with a decent bottle of single malt. Have a backbone and tell the Chinese no thanks. For now, postponement is our best bet because Turner is a bit of a dick and his proposal does need work. But it's not for sale. So we've got a standoff. But I've got a six-year term and you're standing for re-election in two years. Cheers, Peter.

Monroe sat back in his chair and took a long breath. What the hell? Eliot under siege. Trying to fight back with university politics scaling up with the Chinese bribe to the provincial government along with their project to own Turner's institute. That explains Turner's Tesla. They're tossing him a bone.

Monroe glanced through the rest of Eliot's emails, which mainly consisted of routine matters, luncheon dates, and invitations to attend meetings. Finally, though, he saw one he hadn't seen before that had been deleted and recovered by Bob, the police tech. It was Eliot's note to Turner dated September 27, at 4:07 p.m.: *I've reviewed your proposal for an institute along with peer assessments. It's a good proposal. Yes, it needs legitimate outside funding, but it must be with no strings attached. I like the idea to run a journal out of such an institute, but where are the details? A new journal or an established one? We need details about an editor, an editorial board, and a budget.*

I've been in touch with Minister Doyle, who has told me that he is freezing university budgets next year except for increases linked to increased enrollments.

Proposal will not go before the board of governors with my recommendation until you strengthen it in areas the assessors identified. As for the released time from teaching you requested, you must negotiate this in the normal way through your chair. You must also do more to convince your department colleagues to support your proposal. Best, Peter.

Turner fired back a reply at 4:17. *This is bullshit! I'm not taking it lying down! I've worked my ass off and you put me off by passing the buck to Doyle. I myself am aware of donors interested in supporting the institute. The proposal deserves more respect than some warmed-over crap about budget constraints. I'm breaking this to the* Gazette *for what it is, the opening salvo of a fight to preserve the university. You, Doyle, and the political hacks in Victoria can go to hell.*

20

❖

As Monroe locked his bike near Sterling Hall on Monday morning, he spotted Jean-Michel about to enter the building. He walked slowly, his head drooped. *Hung over?* Concerned, Monroe followed him. "Yo, JM. C'est moi. Where are you?"

Jean-Michel peered around the corner of his work area, hanger in hand, still hanging up his coat. "Ahh, didn't hear you come in."

"What's up? You look out of it. Rough night?"

"Didn't sleep so well, actually. Trying to figure out how I can survive around here."

"What do you mean?" Monroe moved closer.

Jean-Michel looked away for a few seconds. "At the Town and Gown Kerr said our whole operation here is under fire. Eliot told her that funding for the gallery could be cut unless we can attract more private funds. The premier is behind it all, so I don't know where we are now with Eliot gone."

"I don't either . . . but I do know Eliot supported the gallery and the arts generally." Monroe thought of Eliot's memo to Doyle. *This seems like part of the premier's plan to get her vote for the Chinese version of Turner's institute. And Eliot's counter was to push for her donation, enough and soon enough to put the gallery out of danger.* "Even if the gallery is under fire, I don't see *you* getting the chop."

"Collateral damage," Jean-Michel said. "At best I'll be parachuted into another department. History or humanities. I suppose I could develop some art history courses."

"We should be so lucky. You've been doing courses in art history anyway. Students flock to them."

"Does history take asylum seekers?"

Monroe poked his shoe at a paper clip at the edge of the desk. "Stop talking that way. The gallery's not dead yet. Don't underestimate Kerr."

"We both know that cutting a program is the university's easiest way to terminate tenured professors. I'd hate to be displaced from the gallery. I've built a program here over eight years. You can only move around so many times."

"Don't panic. Mrs. Kerr won't let the ship go down without a fight. And I'm sure there was no Eliot-Doyle coalition. I think Eliot was playing Minister Doyle in order to keep the arts programs intact."

Jean-Michel moved an easel to one side. "Too complicated for me. I've got to run."

Monroe left the gallery feeling more confused than ever. What a mess. Kerr pressed for money by Eliot, not understanding that it was a tactic to put the gallery out of reach as a blackmail target of Doyle and the premier to get her vote on the BOG for the Chinese takeover of Turner's institute. Is it possible Doyle organized a poisoned muffin for Eliot to get him out of the way? Possible that Kerr herself was now in danger? And who knows now how Spelt will fit into this dismal picture."

With a class in twenty minutes, Monroe normally would have sat quietly in his office reviewing notes. But on impulse he ducked into the basement of the administration building to see if he could get hold of Eliot's ID and password for university webmail. What if there were emails of interest still on the server that Eliot had not downloaded or seen? Something from Kerr perhaps or about the gallery that might throw more light on Jean-Michel's situation.

The secretary of IT sat perched on her chair like a resident flicker surveying a patch of sod. Except she was chewing gum. She ignored Monroe long enough to annoy him, avoiding eye contact as she adjusted some papers in precisely the right order and then carefully stapled them. Finally, she looked up. Glancing at his watch, Monroe said he needed to speak to the administrator in charge of webmail. "That would be Kevin Renwick," she said, "but I think he's busy with a client. Could you come later?

Monroe took this as *let him wait while I take my own sweet time,* a small gesture of power sometimes enacted by bored bureaucrats. She has no idea whether Kevin is busy or not. "Just tell me where Kevin is and I'll take it from there."

She blinked, gave her gum a crunch, then said to try number 106 at the end of the corridor. Monroe found Kevin leaning in his doorway chatting with someone mirroring the same pose in the doorway across the hall. Kevin was a middle-aged guy in baggy pants with keys clipped to one side of his waist and a cell phone holster to the other. He wore a tired-looking golfing shirt that must have begun life as red but had faded to blotchy orange. Monroe interrupted the chat by saying that he had urgent business connected with a police investigation. "Can we do this in your office?" he asked.

Kevin smiled at his colleague as if this was just another joke and gestured toward his door. "Let's do it."

Monroe heard, "Watch your step, Kev," as they entered the office. He explained that he needed access to Eliot's account on the server as part of the investigation into his death. "The log-in name and password should do."

"No can do. Breach of privacy. Right at the top of the seven deadly sins around here. Sorry." Kevin clearly was not sorry and he pushed several packs of business cards to one side of his desk and reached for some papers as if the conversation were over.

"What do you mean 'breach of privacy'?" Monroe asked. "The president is dead and this is part of a police investigation."

Kevin shrugged his shoulders as he raised his arms with palms up. "Sorry. I don't see a search warrant. They tell us that the police will be after us if we give out private information."

Monroe stood to leave and nodded toward the business cards. "Mind if I take one of your cards?"

"Actually, those aren't mine. I run some off for a few colleagues and am currently redesigning a new one for myself."

Monroe left Kevin's office without another word and cut across the lawn on a fast track to retrieve his notes and get to his class. It would have helped if Jim had been with him, he thought, but he brushed off his frustration once he was in a groove lecturing his class. After class, though, the problem bounced back into his head. Should he call Jim and get a warrant? Or call Eliot's widow? *Wait, what about good old-fashioned rank pulling? What if old Kevin got a phone call from the top?* Monroe grabbed his notebook and headed for the administration building and Evan Spelt's office. He waved at Mildred, who was tapping away on her keyboard and looked up but didn't slow down. Spelt's door stood half open and Monroe took that as the equivalent of a welcome mat.

"Hello, Evan. Got a quick minute? I need your help."

"Of course. How's it going, by the way? Have you been able to help the police find their way around? They must be about done."

"I hope I've helped a little. Jim Martino will be on campus tomorrow."

"Think of it." Spelt stood up and paced a few steps toward the window and then turned back. "Not quite a week ago Peter died. Seems longer. Peter's wife doesn't want a memorial service on campus, you know."

Monroe said nothing but wondered at Spelt's familiar reference to Peter. As if they had been buddies. It reminded him, though, to write a note of condolence.

"They cremated his body on Friday. Just the family. And next Saturday will be a private celebration of his life with a larger group. His two sons came back for the cremation."

Monroe frowned. "Nobody from the university invited?"

"No," Spelt said. "They seem to be blaming us for his death. That's the impression I got from talking to her on the phone. But you didn't come here to talk about that."

"No. I'm afraid I unleashed a little bad temper at an employee in IT in trying to see if there are any of Eliot's computer records still on the server."

Spelt chuckled. "Ill temper can sometimes be a sign of character, not suffering fools gladly. I'm guilty of it myself on occasion."

That's no secret, Monroe thought. "I don't really know if I'll find anything. Probably not. More of a fishing expedition to help the police close this thing out. He gave me the privacy runaround."

"Ah, yes—" Spelt paused. "Everyone does it because the middle ground is muddied, fear of making a judgment call. Cases of depressive students have been kept from parents. I'm against that."

Spelt's voice broke and his face had grown red. His eyes darted briefly toward photos on his shelf. *He's taking this personally*, Monroe thought. "So you're think I might help?"

"I thought I'd try."

Spelt stood and paced as he thought. "The truth is, I don't exactly have a free hand. I'm already getting unwanted advice from the minister's office and members of the board of governors."

"Well, this is low-level stuff. I'm thinking a direct call from you to this Kevin person might advance the cause."

Spelt turned abruptly. "OK, I'll do it. It can't do any harm and you won't be publicizing anything you find, uh, of a sensitive nature."

"No, of course not." Monroe had tried—unsuccessfully, he knew—to keep his voice free of irritation.

Spelt picked up the phone, pressed the intercom button, and asked Mildred to get Renwick from IT on the line. Only a few seconds later Evan's phone buzzed and he began to speak, calmly, convincingly, with a surprisingly detailed exposition of the true intent of the privacy policy and the need to be smart, flexible, and not bloody minded. The last came like a knife thrust after luring someone into dropping their guard. "Get the information that Professor Monroe requested right away. Email it or leave as a phone message within the next ten minutes, please."

As he was closing the deal, Evan caught Monroe's eye and flashed a thumbs-up, clearly enjoying his little performance. *Completely different style than Eliot's,* Monroe thought as he made his way back to his office. No profanity, no bluster, no gesture toward dialogue. Spelt sounded, well, presidential.

■■

21

Renwick had already sent Eliot's log-in name and password by the time Monroe got back to his office. No greeting, no sign off. *He's annoyed,* Monroe thought as he signed into Eliot's account. A pop-up notice appeared announcing that the account would be terminated on October 28, because the owner was deceased. *Closing the account one month after the death or an extra dig from Kevin?*

Only three emails came up. The first from Professor Johnson at the University of North Carolina. Monroe skimmed it: *sorry the assessment is late . . . proposal quite good. If possible, get it moving right away to stake out the territory because someone at Cornell is thinking along the same lines. Turner is adequate as interim head, but you might want someone more senior (and less prickly) for the long run. All this in more detail in a report I'll send next week.* Well, not quite in sync with Eliot's decision, but Northlake isn't going to compete with Cornell anyway.

Another email from Mrs. Kerr was dated September 28, at 1:05 p.m. *Peter: Stop rushing me. I need more time. I'm not Warren Buffett. Yes, I have one or two assets, but will need six months or so to cash them in. It will make a big splash, big enough to secure the gallery and without any expectation of a quid pro quo as with other so-called donors hovering about. Let's meet later in the week or next Monday.* Eliot was dead by the time Kerr wrote it. *How interesting,* Monroe thought. Kerr indeed knew that the point of her donation was to give Eliot space to say no to the Chinese.

Then there were a couple of notes from Eliot's sons, Mark in Rome and Julian in Paris, replete with observations about life, love, art, and the high cost of cafes, bar tabs, and fast trains. Hint, perhaps an infusion into the bank account? Monroe smiled grimly, too sad to think about families torn apart. Young men finding their way, sharing their adventures, then, wham, Dad is no more. But a poignant PS from Mark caught Monroe's eye: "Thanks again for Mumford. Perfect for the e-reader. Ancient Rome as predatory, passive, parasitic, and addicted to spectacles of torture and death. Straight talk for a change."

A single tap on the door coincided with the chair secretary's town-crier voice calling out "department meeting in five minutes." Monroe reached for the agenda, a single page stapled to a thick sheaf of supporting materials. He hadn't read them.

After the meeting, Monroe collected his bike and was about to head home when he saw Jean-Michel emerge from the library. He called out and they converged at the centre of the quad near the Lloyd Kerr bench. "Nice time of year for the bench," Monroe said. "One sometimes sees Mrs. Kerr stopping by for a chat with Lloyd."

Jean-Michel nodded. "So to speak. The reds and yellows of the leaves are about as bright as they'll get thanks to a couple of cold nights."

Monroe had one hand on the trunk of a coral bark maple whose leaves were a softer yellow than the other maples. "This one looks interesting all winter."

"It's a Sango-Kaku," said Jean-Michel. "Maxes out around twenty-five feet."

"How do you know *that*? You should be on the committee to design a memorial for Eliot."

"I doubt he'll get one. . . . Well, maybe a bench. But who knows if I'll be around? Don't forget the gallery may go down."

"Well, I've got something on that." Monroe mentioned Kerr's email to Eliot.

"One or two assets? I wonder—"

"Any idea what she meant? Seems to be something big."

"Nope. There's something secretive about her."

"You must know something. You run the gallery."

Jean-Michel paused. "Well, don't quote me. But it's pretty well known Lloyd used to pick up promising paintings in out-of-the-way places, bargain prices often with gaps in provenance. Some unsigned, yet potentially quite valuable. Don't forget Velázquez himself didn't sign most of his paintings. So unsigned not necessarily fakes because fakers *always* sign. Lloyd judged them by the art itself and he had a good eye."

Monroe took a little time to think about this. He plucked a single yellow leaf and held it by the stem toward the sun. "This yellow . . . amazing when you backlight it. I should take up photography." Jean-Michel flashed his here-he-goes-again smile. "Of course, photography will be your next big thing. Big in the art world these days."

Monroe slipped the leaf into his pocket. "How about this? Kerr still has an inventory of Lloyd's treasures but they're only suitable for private buyers."

"That's what I meant," Jean-Michel said. "But how does this relate to me?"

"It probably doesn't. We both know it's not criminal to sell a painting with weak provenance. It only lowers the price. Such sales would only be unethical if they were fakes. Or stolen. I think we agree the Kerrs didn't cross that line."

❖

Seated at a corner table in The Buzz the next morning, Monroe had his notebook open and his pen out. Jim would be along in ten or fifteen. At the top of the page he had written "Tues. Oct. 5," and he'd started to make a few notes when a hand came down on his clavicle, gentle but firm, and Jim slid into an adjacent chair.

"Today's big ideas? Always organized. You'd be a good role model at the station where the crew'll be working on a second donut about now. What've you got?"

"You're early, I just started. Eliot's been gone a week now and I don't feel like we've got very far."

"Patience, man. A week is nothing in a case like this."

Monroe nodded. "So far, I've got a few ideas, but no clear direction. More going around in circles."

"That's normal. At this stage, we're poking around, sorting, putting things in piles. I haven't been much help, but work on some of my other cases may be easing off."

"I hope so, for your sake," Monroe said, noting that Jim looked tired. "So today we're talking to Turner."

"Did you set up an appointment?"

"No, I read somewhere that you get more out of someone if you drop in cold."

Jim pursed his lips as if he wasn't sure he agreed. Monroe carried on with what he had on Turner and Jim made a few notes. "OK, I'll take the lead," he said when Monroe finished. "I don't want him to think that a colleague is grilling him about police stuff. Jump in, though, if you feel like it."

At Turner's door, the sound of music seeped under the door and Jim, poised to knock, stopped to listen.

"Sounds Russian," Monroe said. "Not Tchaikovsky, maybe Shostakovich. But what do I know? I'm a Mozart man—like Einstein."

Jim nodded. "Right. You and Einstein, two of a kind." He rapped twice. Not a student's excuse-me-sir knock but one that said open the damn door. Turner seemed to recognize the difference. Instead of his trademark shout to come in, dripping with annoyance, he cracked open the door.

"Police," Jim said, holding out his ID. "I'm Inspector Martino and you, of course, already know your colleague Bruce Monroe. He has been designated as liaison in our investigation of President Eliot's death."

Monroe repressed a smile upon hearing his new title. Turner did a double take. "Liaison? What the hell for? Last time I checked, Monroe here was a mere professor like the rest of us."

Jim ignored the comment and glanced toward the speakers. "Sounds Russian. Sort of wild. Shostakovich?"

Turner perked up. "Yes, actually. His life interests me, more than his music. Lived under Stalin, got denounced a few times, and later got some prizes. He didn't know which end was up, was half out of his gourd most of the time, lots of tics and stress. Of course I've lived under Eliot rather than Stalin, but not for so long."

Monroe came half out of his chair. "Are you crazy? Comparing three months with Peter Eliot to a lifetime under a murderous sociopath?"

Turner started to say something but then squeezed his lips together in a smirk as he reached over and turned the music down almost to zero. "Just an analogy." Jim waved Monroe toward a chair as if to change the subject and pulled up a second one for himself. "If you don't mind, Professor Turner. Thanks for your hospitality, by the way. We won't take much of your time. Since we're on the topic of Eliot . . . where were you last Tuesday morning, between 9:00 and 11:00?"

Turner scratched awkwardly under one eye with his little finger. "Simple. I teach at 9:30, a seminar: Machiavelli in the age of the United Nations. I would have been in my office, say, around 8:30, no later than 8:45, to get ready to teach.

Oh, and that morning I had essays to hand back so I needed to write the marks in my grade book." He gave a pat to a small blue book on his desk.

"Is that all?"

"That's about it. Want to know if I sliced a banana into my cornflakes? Or stopped for a piss before going to the class?"

"Did you buy a coffee of the Food Service cart that morning?" Monroe asked. "It seems like you might have passed it on your way to class."

Turner looked toward the far wall as he paused to think. "As a matter of fact, not that morning. I usually do. Normally when the cart's by the dean of arts office. For some reason, the cart must have been a little late."

"Hmm," Jim said as he pretended to jot something in his notebook. "It seems that you're quite easily annoyed, Professor Turner. Did you, by the way?"

"Did I what?"

"Slice a banana into your cornflakes or stop to pee?"

"What is this, harassment or something? You can't be serious."

"Oh, I'm serious alright. Let's try to sharpen the picture a little. A witness saw you early that morning looking hung over and walking toward the administration building in your raincoat . We think you were on your way to Eliot's office. Was it to threaten him? To attack him?"

Monroe, without thinking, tossed something into the pot. "Your voice was heard in his office."

Jim leaned back in his chair and studied the ceiling. "Not the kind of civilized exchange one expects in the ivory tower. But, of course, the stakes were high, emotions run high, the institute means a lot to you."

Monroe noticed what he thought of as Shostakovich-like tics playing across Turner's face: the hint of a smirk at Jim's invocation of ivory-tower cool followed by the jaw clamping shut at his mention of the institute. He lifted his gaze from the desk and started to speak, but nothing came out. He clenched his hands into a fist and then studied them as he stretched them open as if to release words that had been in his grasp. "It means everything," Turner said finally in a soft voice. "I've worked toward it my whole career and this newbie, a man without an academic background or advanced degrees, had the nerve to say it wasn't good enough."

Jim nodded. "What happened then? Did you kill Eliot?"

Turner took a deep breath and blew it out slowly as if gathering his patience to respond to a befuddled student. "What a question. I was pissed off, I admit it. But I'm not stupid, not a killer. Yes, I did go to his office that morning. Eliot was working on his report for the board of governors meeting, something he told me he would be doing in an email the day before. He was forthright, I give him that."

"And?"

"Well, I hardly slept that night. I decided to try to change his mind, reduced to begging, goddamn it. All I wanted was a couple of weeks to address some points the assessors made. Nothing serious. The proposal was sound, but you give them what they want. This is standard practice; he should have supported it. I had even begun to attract some outside funding that could become a trust to support the proposal in exchange for a few tweaks."

"A few tweaks?" Monroe said.

"We believe those Chinese businessmen were asking for more than that when they came forward as donors," Jim said. "And what's in it for you person-ally? What will we find when we examine your financial records? It's interesting that you're going around in a flashy new car these days."

"Ah, the car. I only get to use it for a couple of months. They leased it. I didn't receive anything else now except . . . they offered a deal. I re-jig the proposal to put China as the centre of the new world order and once it goes through, with gifts to the university and a trust to fund the institute, the car is mine. Oh, and they want two people to sit on a board of three directors that would oversee appointments and curriculum."

Jim glanced at Monroe then back at Turner. "So you would sell it out like this? Is this what you call academic integrity? Born of bribery and sheltered by the university as a virtually independent propaganda machine."

"I can't believe this," Monroe said. "Eliot wouldn't have gone for this; he smelled a rat."

"Possibly," Turner said. "But the provincial government was interested. Eliot, though, was a stubborn man; he was stonewalling me."

"Stonewalling?" Monroe asked.

"The worst kind of stonewalling: bureaucratic, passive aggressive. He seemed tired. He kept repeating that the proposal had merit and should be put forward again next year. But the support for it should have had no strings attached. Big money was waiting in the wings. Meanwhile, he claimed that the budget was frozen and it would be a better fit in a year because something more urgent needed attention now. He said something about fixing a cancer in the institution."

Monroe leaned forward. "Cancer? What did he mean?"

"He didn't say. That's when I lost it, must have yelled at him. I thought he was making it up. But that's all I did. I didn't hit him or anything. I don't even know how he died. Wasn't it a stroke or a heart attack? When I left him, he was alive and well and working again at his computer."

Jim stood up and leaned against a bookcase. "I need to ask you some questions now and I'd like you to think carefully before you answer. One, when did you leave Eliot's office? Two, did you return to the office? After teaching your class, maybe?"

Turner paused, rubbed under his eye again. "I was watching the time. It's only a ten-minute walk to get to my class. But I forgot some notes and needed to swing by my office and pick them up. Since the class begins at 9:30, it must have been 9:10. Give or take a minute or two."

"And the second question?" Monroe asked.

Turner scowled in Monroe's direction but remained silent for a few seconds and then reached over and turned the music off. "The answer is yes. I couldn't concentrate on my teaching and dismissed the class early. The seminar is supposed to run for two hours and I packed it in a little before 11:30. Somehow discussing Machiavelli's ideas with my class cooled me off and I began to accept a certain logic to the way Eliot assessed the institute. His phrase 'no strings attached' kept running through my mind, for it showed more respect for my proposal than I myself had when I flirted with guys sent by the Chinese government. I guess some part of me wanted to find a way to team up with Eliot, strengthen the proposal , and push for it next year. Curiously, I think he would have liked that. But another part also wanted to try one more time to get the proposal approved right away."

"How did you find him?" Jim asked.

"I think you know. I took a roundabout route back to the office. Mildred was gone, the office quiet. I knocked on his door and then opened it and saw him crumpled on the floor. I couldn't believe it."

"So you deleted files from his computer instead of calling for help," Jim said, with a nod of his head as if agreeing in advance that one might reasonably do this.

"Well . . . yes. I'm not proud of it. I became delusional, telling myself he would have given me a couple of weeks to rework the proposal. So I deleted the memo he was writing to me and also a document he called 'Notes on Institute' or something like that for the BOG meeting. It was a stupid thing to do."

"Then you walked away," Monroe said, "leaving him for someone else to find."

"That's about it." Turner paused and seemed to collect his thoughts. "I didn't leave him to die or anything. He was beyond help. Gone. I've had first aid training and I felt for his pulse. Did I mention that? Well, maybe not the best just to leave him. But I didn't want to explain our disagreement. I thought I now had a second chance to edit and resubmit my proposal to the acting president. I wiped off anything I had touched with a tissue from a box on his desk and walked out."

"So that's why I saw you standing outside the administration building when the fire and ambulance people came," Monroe said.

"Yes. I knew what they were finding. I couldn't concentrate on anything at that point and just wanted to be there."

"We may want to talk to you again," Jim said.

<hr/>

Later, Monroe and Jim were sitting at a table in Ten Days, a pub named after *Ten Days that Shook the World*, John Reed's eyewitness account of the Bolshevik Revolution. The owner, a great nephew of Reed, set it up in the sixties as a hangout for leftist students and faculty and it became a place to plan demonstrations of one sort or another. Students now viewed Bolshevism as a kind of gangster interlude of mass murder and the lust for power. Posters urging the revolution on and photos of liberated workers acted as the cover story for the projects of madmen who in turn were eaten up by their nightmare utopia. For a time, students seemed to view these images as ironic kitsch. But not so much anymore. Vladimir Putin's kleptocracy with assassinations of opponents and journalists had come to mirror the authoritarianism of Stalin. But, what the hell, the clientele came here now for ten draft beers at the best prices in town and the two-for-one happy hour on Friday afternoons.

Monroe and Jim settled in with a local pale ale and Monroe allowed his eyes to roam over the oversized black-and-white photos and posters. One of John Reed himself, scribbling at a makeshift desk, always caught his eye. A blown-up photo of Putin, shirtless, next to a motorcycle in a James Dean pose, gave the update. A kind of little-buddy Gilligan imitating his heroes.

Monroe broke the silence. "What did you think of Turner?"

Jim paused to put his thoughts together. "Troubled. I don't trust him. Ambitious, obsessed, paranoid, opportunistic. Otherwise, a real sweetheart."

Monroe glanced over at a giant poster screaming *Peace, Bread, Land.* "Without going Freudian on you, that comment about Eliot being the equivalent of Stalin—"

"Deranged, over the top. Shameful to call it an analogy. I'm no psychologist but he seems to have issues, sort of unstable. Those tics and his music? Lucky you clued me in on the Shostakovich."

"Still pretty fast on your feet. I think it disarmed him."

Jim rubbed his chin. "A fluke. Anyway, what do *you* think? Is he a credible suspect?"

"Hard to say. He's erratic. Not sure about his story about changing his mind. After Machiavelli he's suddenly ready to call a truce with Eliot, finds him dead, and yet goes ahead and erases files on his computer. Did he really have second thoughts about taking money from the Chinese?"

"Just a new car." Jim said with a smile. "Tried to make it sound as if he was playing them rather than falling for a bribe. I don't buy it; potentially a high-risk situation."

"What do you make of the cancer thing?"

"It may be important. Check his computer again, will you? And let's talk to Meyer. Maybe on Friday."

"Wait, you lost me. Why Meyer?"

Jim shrugged "Well, just that word. 'Cancer' makes me think of something deadly but hard to find. Why not some sort of financial malfeasance, which by definition is clandestine. Something one has to be *uncover.*

22

◼

At home, Monroe cooked up his version of a bolognese sauce loaded with chopped red and green peppers, mushrooms, and grass-fed ground beef and had it with spaghetti and a green salad. He poured a glass of Montepulciano d'Abruzzo: *soft on the tannins, dry, unassuming,* the label read. Not to mention cheap. He was nursing a second glass when he phoned Warren. Turned out he slept in after a late night watching *Enigma* on the TV. "Good film," Monroe said, "although Polinski once cornered me in The Buzz to complain, in great detail, that it ignores the role of the Polish cryptologists."

"He would know," Warren said. "Sociology has several who ride shotgun on their ethnic heritage." After catching Warren up on the meeting with Turner, Monroe asked him to look through Eliot's computer files again that night.

At 11:30, as Charlie Byrd's Jobim album pulsed softly from speakers in his study, Monroe was about to call it a night when the phone rang.

"I think I found something," Warren said. "An email to Hans Meyer dated September 9, and in the trash file. I'm reading it: 'Got your notes about hocme that you left with M. Keep looking, and don't send anything by email.'"

"About what? Spell it."

"H-O-C-M-E. It's a code, a simple one."

"Go on."

"At first I thought it must be an acronym. No luck. Then I thought anagram and, bingo, there it is: chemo."

Monroe remained silent for a few seconds. "Chemo to fight cancer. Great work. We're getting somewhere."

After ringing off, Monroe poured another glass of wine and searched for "hocme" in his copy of Eliot's files. Nothing. As a final idea though, he opened the Word program that had been on Eliot's hard disk to see what might come up under "recent documents." And there it was, the last in a list limited to nine. But when he tried to open the file, the computer said it couldn't be found. Where was it? He emailed it to Bob, the police tech, with a copy to Jim, and went to bed.

The next morning, Monroe checked his emails at 9:00 but there was nothing yet from Bob. He took a scenic route to campus and went straight to Warren's lab to see if he wanted to accompany him to talk to Mildred. Warren, still engaged by his discovery of last night, agreed right away even though Wednesday was his busiest day. At the president's office they found Mildred talking to Leona Wong.

Mildred smiled but looked tired. "Leona's just back from her Cancún vacation. She hadn't heard about . . . Mr. Eliot." She lowered her voice. "She met someone named Jesús and has already called him twice this morning."

"Sounds pretty generic," Warren said.

Mildred smiled. "It happens every year. Last year it was Felipe something or other. I don't know how she—"

Monroe interrupted. "Look, we don't need to take up too much time. Can we go over a couple of points?" Mildred nodded and turned to Leona, telling her she'd be with her in a few minutes.

"Did you ever hear President Eliot speak about some deep concern he had about the university?" Monroe asked. "Perhaps he called it a 'cancer' or something along those lines?"

Mildred paused. "No, I don't think so. He didn't exactly treat me as a confidante, you know."

"I think you know more than you're saying. We should be clear." Monroe paused to look at Warren, who nodded on cue. "We know you weren't entirely truthful the last time we talked." Mildred turned white and seemed to have trouble swallowing. "Can we just agree," Monroe continued, "that you're going to tell us everything we need to know and stop making stuff up? Stop wasting our time and yours, out of respect for Peter Eliot. This is about how and why he died. It may be homicide and you could be in the thick of it."

Mildred crossed her arms as if to protect herself. "Fine."

"So, start with what you were doing out by lot E last Tuesday morning."

"Taking a walk."

"To meet Hans Meyer in his camper, right?"

Mildred glanced across the room at Leona and lowered her voice. "Yes, if you must know, we've been meeting on Friday mornings. Last Tuesday was extra. We meet on Friday because that's when President Eliot has weekly meetings with the deans and vice presidents. There, satisfied?"

"Geez, couldn't you meet in the evenings or something?" Warren asked. "I mean, you're taking time out of your workday."

Mildred twisted her hands. "I wish . . . no, his wife expects him after work and, well, Hans said it was like taking a coffee break and should be OK if we stayed a little later in the day to make up for it."

"Some coffee break," Monroe said in a low voice as if to himself. "Look, Mildred, we don't have to know all the details. We're not accusing you of anything criminal. But we need to be clear about what was really happening, even if it didn't directly contribute to Eliot's death."

"Something small could be important," Warren added, "such as your time away from the office that day."

Mildred took a quick intake of breath and looked down at her hands. "That's completely . . . I would never have. . . ." She stopped for a breath. "Except I feel ashamed, ashamed that I cheated the university, ashamed that I wasn't here to call for help."

Just then a buzzer sounded. "Excuse me," Mildred said as she quickly got up and walked to Spelt's private office. Monroe picked up Mildred's appointment book and started glancing through it, moving backward from September 28. After a few minutes, he pulled out his notebook and began to write. "What have you got?" Warren asked.

"Tell you in a minute." Monroe kept flipping pages back and forth. Mildred eyed Monroe when she returned. "Dr. Spelt was also looking through it just yesterday," she said.

Monroe looked up. "Oh? Did he say why?"

"Not exactly. He said he wants everything on the university online system, that Eliot wasn't up to date with this old-fashioned book. He was checking to see if he had missed anything."

"But last Wednesday you were already making a list," Warren said. "He interrupted our meeting with you to get it."

"I *did* do it." Mildred paused as if looking for the right words. "He didn't trust the list I gave him.

Monroe nodded. "Hard not to take something like that personally. But I noticed something just now. Meyer was booked for appointments on July 19, July 26, and August 2. Regular weekly meetings. And then they stop. What were they about?"

"I don't know. After the third one, Mr. Eliot told me not to write his name in the book anymore."

"He didn't say why." Monroe was thinking out loud. "What's this 'Budget Committee Preparation' for a week later in the same time slot? Was that code for another meeting with Meyer?"

"Yes. That's what Eliot . . . uh, Mr. Eliot, said to put down."

"Any other codes you're aware of?" Monroe asked.

Mildred's eyes darted from side to side. "I can't think of anything. . . . I didn't know this was important."

"What about a project or file named 'hocme,' h-o-c-m-e?" Warren spelled it slowly. "A file with that name was erased from Eliot's computer."

Mildred's eyes darted from Warren to Monroe, but she remained silent.

"Did Meyer ask you to erase it?" Monroe asked. "Maybe when you phoned him after finding Eliot dead."

Mildred nodded. "I didn't know what to do. I phoned Hans and he said to phone 911 and the campus medical centre. I told you that before. But what I left out is that he said it was urgent that I find that file and trash it because it was life-and-death confidential what he and Mr. Eliot were working on."

Monroe banged his hand down on Mildred's desk. "Finally. You need to get it straight that your loyalty isn't to Meyer or to your reputation or to anything but the truth. You tampered with evidence by erasing that file. I know you cared about Mr. Eliot. So I'm going to ask you for the last time to think about things and tell us anything—I mean *anything*—that might help explain why he died. It's quite possible that Inspector Martino could charge you with obstruction of justice, which is a felony."

Mildred collapsed forward in her chair, head in hands, and started to cry. "Honestly, that is all."

Warren flicked a stray paperclip in his direction as if to signal that they weren't going to get any more out of her now. "Just keep thinking," Monroe said, "and call me when you're ready to talk."

As soon as they left the office, Monroe realized that he had only a vague idea of what obstruction of justice means and he called Jim.

"What you said is about right," Jim said. "She lied and tampered with evidence. Damn it, I didn't expect this from university people. A judge might treat it as a misdemeanor, but the way judges and lawyers work out those things is a mystery. All I know right now is that your place up there could give some of those con artists from Lehman Brothers a run."

"Although we do it for petty cash. They pushed the world to the brink and then gave themselves bonuses with bail-out money."

"Petty cash or not," Jim said. "I didn't expect this from university types."

∷

Monroe needed to get back to his office to meet with a grad student working on a master's thesis. Crossing the quad, he ran into Hans Meyer, eyes down, walking quickly toward him, jaw clenched.

"Meyer, are you in a race or something?"

"What?" Meyer looked around as if to get his bearings. "Ah, Monroe. I was miles away. Trying to catch the five o'clock ferry and avoid the bottleneck at the tunnel."

"Lucky you. Going to Victoria or the cottage on Salt Spring Island?"

"There's *no* cottage," Meyer said impatiently. "Victoria, for a meeting."

Monroe glanced up at a shaft of sunlight striking the corner of the administration building where Spelt had his office. He couldn't tell who was there, just saw some movement and a flash of light. Monroe imagined Spelt standing at his window with a glass of single-malt scotch surveying his kingdom.

"I won't hold you up. We all know the tunnel can become a bottleneck after 3:00. But let's talk when you're back. Friday? Eleven o'clock in your office?"

Meyer paused and stroked his chin. "Let's see, I usually . . . yes, I can do it." *So much for the regular meeting with Mildred*, Monroe thought. They both turned to go and Monroe glanced again toward Spelt's office. The window looked normal.

The ride home cleared his head, as the sound of his tires tracked over gravel and pavement and birds exchanged pleasantries and insults. The thought of Meyer stuck in traffic somewhere near the Deas tunnel made him shudder. About halfway home, his stomach disrupted his blithe feelings. He had forgotten to eat lunch and hunger had attacked. Pasta tonight, he decided, and at home he found something to bring it off in style: a bag of yellow morel mushrooms left at the front door by Mrs. Rigetti.

He went straight to the kitchen and sliced them. While they sautéed in butter and olive oil, he chopped fresh parsley from the garden, grated a generous portion of Parmesan cheese, and boiled some linguini. The cheese was firm but broke off in crumbly bits. And there it was with only Carlo's olive oil and some black pepper to finish it off. He poured an Argentine Malbec that Luce had brought a few weeks ago and finished with a green salad and a perfect pear with more chunks of cheese.

Afterward, sipping a fresh glass of wine, he thought of Meyer going to Victoria. Did it have something to do with his meetings with Eliot? Monroe put on some Boccherini, the cello sonatas, and began to pace the floor. Plato had the idea that musical compositions, their development and resolution of ideas, helped the brain work out other problems. Something Kennedy once said in The Buzz. It could be true.

If Meyer was meeting Doyle, why now? Could it be something to do with getting Turner's institute back on track, packaged with support from the Chinese donors? With Eliot gone, the premier and the minister might imagine that Meyer could lobby Spelt for the deal.

Monroe set his wine glass down and opened Eliot's drive. He re-read the note he had found earlier in which Eliot declared his independence from Doyle. And from the premier, too, which could have been serious if they had only backed him because they thought he was a yes man. What if they decided to deep-six Eliot? Eliot had been increasingly isolated but had teamed up with Kerr to keep the gallery safe.

Monroe did searches for "Doyle," "hocme," and "Meyer" with no results. On a whim he tried Doyle's first name and found an email to Eliot.

Look, Peter, let's not fight over the big question. That's a war that won't be fought, much less won or lost, in either of our tenures. So for now we agree, sort of, on the proposed institute. Fine. As for your phone message. I'm with you. Indeed, proceed with Operation Meyer. If he's onto something as serious as you think, we need to stop it fast. It would be a tremendous credit to you to do this and it would reflect well on this government and, if I may say so, my ministry. So full speed ahead. Your idea to have Meyer work on it full time has my support, whatever face you want to put on it. Keep me posted. Ryan.

Monroe read it again. So a peace treaty over the institute and an agreement to support Meyer's secret investigation. That's got to be the reason for Meyer's trip to Victoria. Monroe forwarded the message to Warren and Jim, and then called it a night.

❖

In the gym the next morning Monroe had a session with Brad Smart, who had been giving him a few tips on self defense. Brad had been an amateur boxer and was a karate expert with a few barroom brawls to his credit. Once the kids in elementary school started calling him Brad Dumb, he learned to fight back. Now he was showing Monroe how to throw and parry punches and also some basic karate moves.

In the change room after showering, Monroe automatically glanced toward the corner Meyer normally occupies. *Creatures of habit,* he thought. *Thursday morning, he would be wishing he were here in his routine instead of messing around in Victoria.* With forty minutes or so before his class, Monroe decided to swing by the gallery and see what Jean-Michel thought about Kerr's email to Eliot sent the day he died. Madame Kerr keeps popping up, what else can he learn about her?

23

Monroe stretched out his legs from the chair he had settled into. "This thing is comfortable even if it looks like hell."

"What are you talking about?" Jean-Michel said. "B.C. Binning himself designed and built it, sat on it out on his deck. It's a work of art, beautiful cane work, has a history, probably should be on display with a plaque on it."

"Sorreee. Actually, you're probably right." Monroe shifted cautiously and studied one of the chair's weathered arms for a few seconds. "Hey, I'm trying to figure out Kerr. What's the deal with her?"

"What do you mean?"

"Well, more generally. There's the gallery connection . . . but how does a woman like her get appointed to a university board of governors?"

"And reappointed," Jean-Michel added. "Who knows? She's capable, has a strong personality, is sharp, knows art. She isn't an academic type. She keeps an eye on the gallery but isn't chummy with faculty. Doesn't want us jumping on the furniture."

"I agree. Academic types don't often get appointed. One or two as tokens but not enough to shape discussion."

"She also has connections. There's some gossip out there that Kerr and the premier were an item back in the day, in the seventies, when he was mayor of Vancouver. I didn't pay much attention. Besides, why does it matter one way or another?"

"Probably doesn't."

"They're still friends, I think."

"You must be right." Monroe scratched the back of his head. "I remember when the premier was here to dedicate the bench after Lloyd Kerr died. He and

Kerr were chatting like it was old home week."

"He also spoke when the gallery was renamed the Lloyd and Elizabeth Kerr Gallery."

"Lloyd had a pretty decent run," Monroe said. "He was quite a bit older than Madame. They got on famously—a lot of good cheer when they were hosting dinners or receptions. Some pretty substantial fundraising."

"They were a power couple. She was more jolly when Lloyd was alive. Now more reserved. He had a reputation as a charmer and maybe a bit of a rascal."

Monroe nodded. "Yeah, I recall rumours that he worked the edges. But everyone liked him. As for Kerr's long-running seat on the BOG, I think you answered it: the special friendship with the premier. Board appointments come as orders-in-council, a cabinet decision without any oversight and hardly any publicity. There's a tradition to limit appointees to two terms, but more than two can be spun all kinds of ways: pro tem, ad hoc, ad interim, whatever."

"Or not spun, if no one pays attention," Jean-Michel said. "A timely gift would smooth the way. Lloyd would have handled that part. Kerr's been serving a long time, I think on her fourth term now."

Monroe crossed his leg and rubbed his knee. "Cash infusions, donations for the next election. All legal. Opens the inside track. The bigger gift would have come when the campus gallery was renamed. But what if Lloyd organized it all as a kind of money-laundering arrangement?"

"Something illegal?" Jean-Michel asked.

"Not exactly. Try robber-baron light. Good for the university, good for a donor who pads his reputation as a benefactor. You make a pile of money, add in a few shady deals, set up a foundation, give some away, and get a tax credit. You're now a benefactor but have kept most of it for your mansions, hobby-horses, some works of art, with plenty in the vault for the next generation. They get sent to Ivy League universities, acquire polish, marry well, inherit, and, voilà! You have a kind of aristocracy. The narrative stresses merit, hard work, thrift, focus, taste, maybe a little luck, and generosity, rather than strike breaking, price fixing, tax evasion, and sweet deals with politicians."

"Let's not get carried away," Jean-Michel said. "Sounds pretty cut-throat. This isn't New York." Jean-Michel paused, glancing at a Penhall landscape on the far wall hanging near the university's only Emily Carr. "So tell me how this might have worked."

"Well, Lloyd might have arranged it when the premier was making the jump from mayor of Vancouver to premier of the province. What if he mentions that he has some old photos of the candidate cavorting with the beautiful Elizabeth Kerr? Nothing too risqué, but enough to tarnish the image and swing a few votes to the opposition. At the same time, he dangles some funds for the cause and makes the case that the university needs to polish its image as a cultural centre by beefing up the art gallery. Kerr's appointment to the BOG would accomplish that. The stick *and* the carrot."

"That sounds like Lloyd," Jean-Michel said. "A knack for presenting things as win-win. Funds flow to the university from the sale of dodgy artwork or paintings donated to the collection while payments flow back to the Kerrs in expense accounts, travel vouchers, entertainment rebates, honoraria, and consultation fees."

"Not so nice," Monroe said. "Of course this is only speculating. For now, I'd like to keep the focus on Eliot's murder. Kerr may or may not be relevant for that. I don't have much, only that email on Eliot's hard disk that I mentioned to you."

Jean-Michel picked up a small canvas on stretchers and began to fidget with it, turning it and poking it gently at the back to test its elasticity. "The one about liquidating a couple of assets?"

"That part sounds like something left over from Lloyd's assets. It was Eliot's strategy to counter the premier and Doyle who blackmailed Kerr to support the Chinese takeover of Turner's institute in the BOG or else. It amounted to her being in a crossfire. And she let slip when you were talking to her. "

Jean-Michel leaned forward. "That makes sense. Kerr was rattled because Eliot was rushing her. Lloyd always handled the marketing and, without him, she needed time to figure out how and to whom to sell. With a large enough payout to protect the gallery."

"As for the politics, she wouldn't have talked openly about this. Not to Doyle or Eliot. So in the email it's business as usual while working out making a sale. If the BOG meeting came up before she had got the money together she may have been ready to get Eliot to announce up front that a large donation was in the works."

"Speaking of assets," Jean-Michel said, "whatever she has stashed away, I'm pretty sure she and Lloyd donated a picture that has or will have serious value."

"That beach painting?" Monroe cocked his head toward a small canvas on the easel next to the desk. "Something about it . . . unfinished but compelling."

Jean-Michel smiled. "Well, I think it's a Gerald Murphy. Unknown before now."

Monroe stood up quickly, barking his shin on a frame leaning against the desk. "Really? That would be huge. A link to American ex-pats in the twenties: Fitzgerald, Hemingway, Dos Passos, MacLeish, Dorothy Parker, Cole Porter."

"They clustered around the Murphys," Jean-Michel said. "Generous, attractive, stylish, rich. They got the Americans together with Picasso, Léger, Stravinski, Diaghilev . . . I don't know who else."

"What about Murphy as an artist?"

"Pretty good. Arguably the first American to tap into the modernist style. Picasso liked his stuff. But only a small output, maybe fourteen canvases. Seven survived."

"Now eight then." Monroe added.

"I hope. This would be a kind of postscript. His heyday was the twenties, and then came the thirties and the death of his two boys. It crushed him; he stopped painting; he never recovered. He and his wife Sara carried on into old age but they were hollowed out, shells of their former selves. The memory of that exuberant time on the Cote d'Azur—life itself as a work of art—mocked them for its hubris. The only consolation: Honoria, their daughter, survived."

Monroe felt the word "hubris" as a kind of blow, a perfect fit for the fate of the Murphys. "Did you tell Kerr," he asked with a catch in his throat, "about the attribution?"

"Not yet. We still need an expert to confirm it. A curator at Yale is our best bet. For now, I'm keeping it quiet. Security here is almost non-existent."

"But what about Kerr herself? Knowing this could be a big help if she has financial pressures."

Jean-Michel thought about it for a few seconds. "Possibly, but only indirectly. The picture already belongs to the university. That email makes it seem like they expect new money. But, yes, the picture could be our Mona Lisa, the killer draw that brings people into the gallery, justifies modernized security, proper lighting, and, eventually, I hope, an endowment to build the collection. You need something visionary to attract donors. A single painting with this resonance would be a start. I'd like to collect at the edge of modernism—less expensive sketches, drawings, and etchings—that link to Murphy and his circle. Maybe spiced up with a few more expensive pieces. A Léger, for example."

"Big money for a Léger," Monroe said. "A few drawings by Picasso could help—there are thousands out there, no? What about that famous sketch he did of Murphy's wife on the beach at Antibes?"

"Anything by Picasso, even a napkin he scribbled on, is probably out of reach. That particular sketch could be in the family . . . or in the Musée Picasso in Antibes. We'd need a Bill Gates or Craig McCaw to dream about it."

"If it's really a Murphy," Monroe said, "wouldn't it put the gallery out of reach as a bargaining chip for Kerr's vote on the BOG?

24

Monroe ran into Warren in the quad after teaching his class. Warren was leaning back and looking at an old acacia tree. "A Brown Creeper working this tree—never seen one on an Acacia before. Cute little guys."

"Did you read the email from the minister to Eliot yet?" Monroe asked.

"Yes, this morning. So, 'Operation Meyer.' Odd to put Meyer in charge. He's a weird character."

"He's an ace accountant."

"Really? How hard can it be to keep track of a couple columns of numbers?"

"Gotta be more to it. Like where the numbers come from and whether they're padded or faked? He's been sniffing out that kind of thing for years. Sounds dismal, actually."

Warren looked unimpressed. "At least Eliot trusted him for the chemo investigation."

"And the minister. Approved his release time so it was a big deal."

"Nice for him. Leisure time to meet up with Mildred in the parking lot."

"You're a cynic, Warren. As we speak, Meyer's returning from Victoria. Maybe he conferred with the minister about whatever Eliot was so worried about."

Warren rubbed his chin. "You're right, it must be serious if the minister's involved. Especially given Eliot's strained relations with him. Otherwise, why not pass it on to a dean or department chair?"

"Why indeed." Monroe said.

At 10:55, Monroe walked into the outer offices of Financial Services. The receptionist, a former student, greeted him, but he couldn't remember her name. Odd, he could remember other things about her. Her boyfriend played on the rugby team. She always sat four rows back in the middle. "I'm sorry I forgot your name."

"Laura Kelly," she said. "I'm not surprised. After all, it's been eight years and I was one of the shy ones."

"Of course. Laura. Eight years? No, you spoke well and wrote well. Your boyfriend used to wait for you after class."

"That was Ben," she said as she marched with Monroe toward Meyer's door. "We're still friends. He's married now and has two kids. And so am I—married, that is. No kids."

Laura punctuated "kids" with a push on Meyer's half-open door, gave Monroe a little wave, and backtracked toward her desk. Meyer waved him toward three chairs, only one of which wasn't covered with papers and file folders. "You probably want to ask me about Victoria," he said, not bothering with small talk.

"Yes. What was it about?"

"Well . . ." Meyer took off his glasses and carefully began to clean them. "Coffee? I need one." He went to the door, and asked Laura if she could bring two cups when the fresh pot was ready.

As the coffee was getting organized and before Meyer was fully settled back at his desk, Monroe heard Jim's voice in the outer office. "I'll show myself in," he said. And in he came, all purpose and energy, one hand on Monroe's shoulder, the other thrust out toward Meyer. "Inspector Jim Martino, major crimes, fourth detachment."

Meyer extended his hand, fleshy with short, thick fingers that looked as if they'd been designed for propulsion in water. Jim seized it, then cleared one of the chairs and sat down. His presence changed the atmosphere. Meyer switched his demeanour toward deference in some indefinable way.

"Let's get right to it, Mr. Meyer. You may know that we're investigating Peter Eliot's death. We learned from Mildred Jones that you advised her to erase a file from Peter Eliot's computer. She also mentioned your regular meetings with Eliot. We need for you to fill us in on this."

Monroe leaned forward. "We also know about your meetings with Mildred in the parking lot. In fact"—Monroe looked at his watch—"just about now would be the time for one."

Meyer sat back and, with an unsteady hand, reached for his cup. "I had nothing to do with Eliot's death. I deeply respected him. He was a good man, way better than most people around here knew. What can I do to help with the investigation?"

Jim leaned forward. "For starters tell us about h-o-c-m-e, or maybe it's easier to refer to it as 'chemo.'"

"Right, our code word . . . Eliot's idea. He decided to be secretive, not sure who he could trust. Peter was concerned about irregularities in the Dean's Research Fund. They dated back to President Bancroft's time, touched on inconsistencies in how funds were awarded and how well documented the expenses. He asked me to check it."

"With the minister's approval," Monroe said.

"Yes. That's what my trip to Victoria last week was about. The minister asked me to come. Basically just told me to carry on. But if he knew I was talking to you about it, I'd be in big—"

Jim held up his hand. "I know, I've heard it before. Politicians always try to control information. But an investigation into a suspicious death trumps everything. I'll deal with him if necessary. Go on."

"Well, it all started when Peter asked me to review some complaints by faculty that President Bancroft put in a file. I found some questionable transfers of funds taken from the Arts Faculty Research Grants budget. It's not clear who tapped into them. Not too noticeable, not a lot at a time, but they added up. When I mentioned this to Peter, he went ballistic, going on about it being a betrayal of public trust, showing a lack of integrity, short-changing students. Dishonesty was a sore spot for him."

"So you began to meet regularly." Monroe checked his notebook. "Here it is, from Mildred's agenda. On July 19, 26, August 2, and from August 9, entries called 'Budget Committee Preparation.'"

"Right. We met on Mondays and Eliot decided it should be noted generically. He knew I use the scheduler on the university platform but didn't want me to mention it there. Old-school privacy thing."

"Was the dean himself under suspicion?" Monroe asked.

"Well, it was hard to—" Before Meyer could finish his sentence, a whoosh and an explosion rattled the window and shook the room.

25

All three men jumped up and looked out but nothing was visible. Monroe rushed to a bank of windows of the reception area where he saw a ball of fire and a billow of black smoke. "What the? There aren't any buildings out there."

"Wait," Meyer said. "My camper." He ran for the door, hesitating briefly to call back to Laura to phone the fire department. Monroe and Jim followed. The three of them were only a quarter of the way there when they heard sirens. A couple of hundred metres from the fire, Monroe could see that the camper was twisted and charred with flames pushing out shattered windows.

They watched silently as the trucks arrived, rolled out their hoses, and shot water onto the van. The captain, as soon as he could get close enough, hooked something to the shattered propane tank and dragged it away. "Nothing in it now," he said, looking at Jim. "We'll examine it later." He paused. "A battery-powered timer, blasting cap, and detonating cord—cordtex, I think—were wrapped around the tank. Once the propane blew, the gasoline did the rest."

Jim gestured toward the pile. "They knew what they were doing."

The captain nodded. "Do you know who the owner of this vehicle is?" Meyer gave a little wave of the hand.

"Well, mister, looks like you've got some serious enemies. Time to think about who might have done this. Maybe it was just a warning since it was timed mid-day."

He walked away to talk to one of his crew. Jim looked at Meyer. "It wasn't *just* a warning. Someone knows your routine, expected you to be here."

Meyer seemed sick. "Please, I'd rather think—".

"Did anyone know you had changed your meeting today?" Monroe asked.

Meyer glanced back toward the clock tower. "I'm trying to think . . . uh, no. I didn't even tell Mildred until mid-morning, around 10:00, didn't even arrive on campus till after 8:00."

Monroe said, "Someone could have watched you arrive and set the device to explode when you and Mildred would be here."

Jim nodded. "Why? To stop the investigation? Why now just after you're back from Victoria? We need to talk some more. What do you say, Meyer? Your place tomorrow morning? Can you get a ride home?"

Meyer nodded. "Why don't you come with us?" Monroe asked. "There's not much you can do around here. Or do you want to watch them mop up?"

"A few more minutes," Meyer croaked. Jim gave him a pat on the shoulder and waved at the fire captain. "Call you tomorrow, OK?" The captain nodded and Jim and Monroe moved away through the remnants of onlookers.

"Can you make it to Meyer's tomorrow? I should have checked first. I some-times forget you have your work. Not to mention a life."

"Ah, yes. My so-called life. This *is* my life now. First, Eliot's death and now a bomb in the parking lot. I'm coming. Meyer looks rattled."

"Well, a bomb tends to do that. This thing"—he cocked his head in the direc-tion of the still-smoldering van—"has 'insider' written all over it. Knowledge of Meyer's routine if not the bomb making as such."

Monroe groaned. "Well, Meyer's schedule is predictable. Except for arriving late today and missing his swim. The nooners with Mildred may not be so well known. Parking in such an isolated spot makes the van an easy target."

"Right," Jim said. "Plant the explosive and off you go on the jogging trail."

"Possibly, a jogger could have seen someone unusual on the trail. Runners notice each other. We notice non-joggers, especially way out here."

Jim sucked in his breath and then blew it out again. "We'd have to get lucky. Doesn't seem that busy."

"No, especially on Fridays. But I'll check around."

"What about your forensics people?" Monroe continued. "Will it be possible to trace the timer or figure out where the explosive came from?"

"We'll be giving it a try."

26

Saturday morning Monroe awoke to an eerie quiet. No cars, no sounds from Mrs. Rigetti's house. He waited a bit, then walked to the window and opened the curtain. "No way," he blurted out. A blanket of snow covered the garden.

Snow on October 9th? The garden barely knows it's fall. Monroe turned on the radio as if to demand an explanation and, sure enough, a meteorologist, dripping with self-importance: " . . . [H]ighly unusual, although with weather anything . . . true, no one saw this storm coming but skiers are pleased to see an early start to snow accumulations in local mountains." The "rest of us," he said, "can look forward to a return to Indian summer, with clearing skies and mild temperatures beginning late Monday or Tuesday. Meanwhile, watch those slippery roads for the next few hours and bundle up for cold temperatures tonight."

Monroe turned off the radio, made a coffee, pulled out some rarely used rubber boots from the furnace room, and ventured outside on the off chance that the paper-delivery person had come. Then he phoned Jim for a pickup. Best to keep his car parked with the tires getting a little bald. Jim said he'd be by a little before 10:00 so Monroe settled in with the morning paper. Nothing much caught his interest until he got to page six, where there was a large photo of Chiara Spelt. She had been invited for a second year to study at Colluvio, a prestigious international music class in Vienna. For once, simple good news.

A smaller headline on the next page, "A Musician's Gift," piqued his interest. Aiko Tanaka—a concert violinist, teacher, and founder of the Yokohama String Quartet—had come to Vancouver to donate her Carlo Bergonzi violin. The instrument, valued conservatively at $900,000, was a rare treasure made in 1737. It had been secured in a vault at the Vancouver Recital Society and Alex Morton, president of the society, was helping Ms. Tanaka find a recipient for the violin. She wished to present it in memory of her daughter Haruko, a promising young violinist, killed in Hiroshima in 1945. "The instrument wanted to come to Canada," Ms. Tanaka explained through a translator, "because her distant relative, Kazuyoshi Akiyama, former conductor of the Vancouver Symphony Orchestra, believed that it could serve as a symbol of peace, goodwill, and rec-onciliation for Japanese Canadians who were interned during World War II."

※

Jim's horn interrupted Monroe's reading. He ran out to the street. "What's the plan with Meyer?" he asked as Jim avoided a clump of snow. Jim said nothing at first but nodded his head slightly as if to indicate he was thinking. "Try to get a clear picture if fraud is involved. And it'd be good to get some names to follow up on."

At Meyer's front door Monroe had a look at the mailbox. *Good spot for another go at him. Stuff some plastic explosive into it with another timer and take out the whole front of the house.* Actually, he had no idea how explosives worked. He felt a little debased that such a scenario had come to mind.

Meyer opened the door and wordlessly motioned them to a table in the dining room. "The wife's gone to the store," he said. "We're out of coffee and what my wife calls tea tastes like clippings from the back lot. So I can't offer you anything. I don't feel much like eating or drinking anyway."

Jim nodded. "About yesterday . . . do you have any idea why someone would blow up your van?"

"No, none." There was urgency in his voice. "I've thought about it. I have no enemies that I know of. I'm not exactly Mr. Popular, but I get along. Mostly. A lot of smart asses on campus treat me like a nobody doing busy work."

"Plenty of one-upmanship games," Monroe said. He looked over at Jim, who said nothing, and carried on. "But this is a bomb, for god's sake. And you nor-mally would have been in the van when it went off. Don't you think it had to be about the investigation you were doing with Eliot? To stop it?"

"Possibly the same motive for Eliot's demise." Jim said softly as if thinking out loud. "Although a completely different style, something to look like misad-venture, the second, straight-up terror."

Meyer looked panicky. "For god's sake, I'm just an accountant. This *is* a university, after all. People have opinions, they express them, they disagree—"

"What about Mildred's husband?" Monroe asked.

"What about him?" Hans glanced toward the door. "He's long gone. In California somewhere. Split last winter."

"We had to ask," Jim said, "just to eliminate the jealous husband skulking about. And your wife? Does she know about you and Mildred? Is she capable of organizing something like this?

Meyer laughed. "No way. She's boring but kind. Wouldn't harm a living thing, much less set a bomb."

"So it again comes back to this chemo thing," Jim said. "Tell us more about it."

"Well, in a nutshell——" Meyer stopped and peered out the kitchen window as if looking for a better way to say it. "A nutshell is what I have right now because Peter's idea of security was to work only with hard copies. Eventually, I'll be able to retrieve most of what I had because I was backing it up with my sister in Germany who is a computer whiz with expertise and resources for keeping data secure. So my working files were in the van, where I had a laptop with a wi-fi connection and a printer."

"Right, your base for the special assignment," Jim said.

"Yes. Time in the office was for being seen, looking normal, checking correspondence, making a few phone calls. Then I'd slip away as if for a meeting or something. Weird, I know. That's what Eliot wanted after he began to worry that someone was watching us. And that's how my affair with Mildred began. Eliot sent her out to help me set up the office and her drop-ins became routine."

"OK," Monroe said. "So you were hiding out in your van while doing at least some of the work, and temporarily, at least, that work is gone."

"Exactly. I watched the van until the fire crew had finished. The files were destroyed, the laptop a lump of burned plastic. I felt badly enough losing momentum and having to bother my sister about it. But then the president's call to cheer me up seemed creepy."

"Spelt called you?" Monroe asked.

"Yes, last night. Commiserations for the accident. He said he was glad that no one—"

"He called it an accident?" Jim asked. "I phoned him in the afternoon and told him it was arson, that explosives had been involved."

"That's odd," Meyer said. "He had a theory that it must have been a leaky propane tank and asked if Mildred's husband threatened me."

"Check," Jim said. "He knows about your meetings with Mildred, knows your van has a dodgy propane tank strapped to it, and therefore he might have known the van was a secret office. How?"

"Well, we were discreet. At least, I was," Meyer said. "I found out just the other day that Mildred was making little drawings of a VW camper in the president's agenda. But how could anyone have known what that meant?"

"How indeed," Jim said. "But let's get back to what you were working on. Investigating some sort of fraud."

"Yes, money was disappearing. Mainly from the faculty small grants budget. It is supposed to fund expenses to give papers at conferences and the research to prepare applications for large grants from outside funding agencies."

"Research grants to do research grants," Jim said softly.

"All together, how much money are we talking about?" Monroe asked.

"Well, it looked to be in the neighbourhood of $150,000." Meyer pushed his hand back up and over his forehead through the thinned-out hair. "A surprising amount had been awarded to faculty who were not publishing much or who were not known to be active researchers. Possibly the money was meant to encourage them? They were fairly small grants in the $5,000-to-$10,000 range."

"Any names come to mind?" Monroe asked.

Meyer said. "Let's see . . . Lou Fraser in archaeology is one. I mentioned something to him in the gym. You know, how's the new research project going. That type of thing. He got mad, thought I was mocking him."

"Maybe later today you can make a list of names you can remember and email it." Jim pulled out a card and set it in front of Meyer.

"If the supposed recipient doesn't know what you're talking about, they might be a bunch of ghost grants," Monroe said. "Some sort of system to cut cheques for researchers who didn't apply for funding and won't ask where the money went when it doesn't arrive. But I still don't see how someone cashes a cheque made to someone else."

"Not difficult," Meyer said. "A cheque can easily be deposited into anybody's account and then transferred to other accounts."

Jim considered this and then asked, "How would you fake the receipts?"

"Easily enough," Meyer said. "Change the name on a receipt or plane ticket or use summary claims: max out x number of days at the per-diem allowance."

"Clever," Monroe muttered. "Target the faculty who publish less."

"Exactly," Meyer said. "There's a fairly big pool of people to choose from."

"Did you find out how cheques issued to such people were sent out in the first place?" Jim asked.

"Didn't have time. I'm guessing through internal mail or maybe posting the cheque to a fake address off-campus."

Monroe rubbed his chin and frowned. "But don't the banks . . . the banks must take note when a cheque made out to Joe Smith gets deposited into the account of Al Jones."

"Apparently not," Meyer said. "Not for sums under $10,000 or so. As well, it's possible to make ATM deposits. These aren't checked at all, too many to process. Endorsements aren't even required."

"Sounds impossible to nail it down," Monroe said. "What if we started looking at the other end? Identify someone with more money than usual?"

"Could be a good bet," Meyer said. "Some of it would look ordinary: some extra travel, extra payments on a mortgage or on credit card debt . . . or possibly something flashy: a new car, jewelry, or a painting."

27

On Monday morning Monroe was settled in The Buzz with a large cappuccino when Warren arrived. After talking about the freak snowstorm, Warren asked about Meyer's camper getting blown up.

"Nothing new," Monroe said. "Haven't heard from Jim since Saturday when we went to his house. But it was clearly arson. Something called Cordtex wrapped around the propane tank and set off with a blasting cap."

"Someone trying to kill him?"

"Looks like it. Timing's right."

Warren tapped the table with his fingers. "Mildred, too?"

"I don't know. Mainly Meyer, if it's about his investigation. Yet the timing indicates a willingness to take Mildred out, too. His records in the camper wiped out but most of them backed up with his sister in Germany. She's a tech person." Monroe glanced toward the entrance and saw Rob and Farshad coming in. They looked to be in a serious conversation. When Rob spotted Monroe, he shook his head as if something were wrong. Upon reaching the table, Rob pulled the student newspaper, *The Norwester*, out of his backpack. He laid it in front of Monroe. "I thought you should see it right away."

A large photo of Monroe covered most of the front page. He was talking to Meyer in the quad and wearing an Inspector Clouseau trench coat with the collar turned up, briefcase in hand. The headline read: *Conflict of Interest or Interest in Conflict?* Monroe skimmed the text.

Popular professor of history at Northlake, Bruce Monroe, has been dividing his time since the death of President Eliot on September 28. On campus and off he shifts identities at a moment's notice, from mild-mannered professor to amateur detective investigating Mr. Eliot's death. Why? Isn't this police business? Professors are paid to teach students, share departmental and university governance, and conduct research. Who asked Professor Monroe to scurry about questioning the good citizens of Gotham ... er, Northlake? Who gave him clearance to collect information and access files normally off limits due to privacy regulations? Perhaps someone should ask the board of governors what this is all about.

"Is this copy for me?" Monroe asked.

"Yes," Rob said. "But I'm afraid it has gone viral." Rob pulled out his cell phone and showed him the links being shared on Twitter and Facebook. There was the same doctored photo with a slightly different article. Its headline was *Prof Says President Was Murdered* and it went on to say that Monroe was "running amok, investigating without the police, and compiling his own list of suspects."

Warren looked at the paper and Rob's phone. "What is this? Where'd they get this information?"

Monroe bit his lower lip. "I didn't tell anybody that Eliot was murdered. . . . Maybe I thought it."

"They're making it up. To get you off the case. First Meyer, now you."

"At least they didn't bomb my office." Monroe paused but Warren didn't smile so he continued. "Actually, I don't see a connection between Meyer working on fraud and me looking into Eliot's death. Maybe the joke's on me: a bungler, out of my depth and looking foolish. Whoever did this I think I know where and when the photo was taken. In or near the president's office on Wednesday morning, right after we talked to Mildred."

On the way to his office Monroe felt self-conscious as if everyone had seen the story and was wondering if he'd gone off the rails. A couple of Post-it Notes were stuck to his door. One said that Marsha Fleming from *Citytv* had requested that he phone her. Another, from the department chair, Jake Miller, asked Monroe to come to his office as soon as he got in. Monroe pulled both notes from the door and sat at his desk trying to get his bearings.

A soft knock interrupted his thoughts, a gentle two-rap tap that conveyed *sorry to bother you, but it's necessary.* Through the opaque glass he saw the departmental receptionist.

Monroe pulled the door open. "Hi, Diane. Got your notes. I was just settling in." He saw her eyes drift toward his desk with the newspaper on it.

"Not very nice, that picture," she said. "And the nasty story. Ms. Fleming called again and asked what time you get to your office. I think she was implying that you should be here by now."

Great, Monroe thought. *She'll make that part of the story.* "Would you mind phoning her back and telling her I'm in a meeting. I think I know what Jake wants."

Jake greeted Monroe with a grim look. He was pacing the floor. From long experience Monroe knew that his main concern was not rocking the boat.

"You've done it this time," he said.

"Done what? Got sucker punched when minding my own business?"

"Well, you've been going around asking a lot of questions."

"And that's supposed to be a crime? I want to know why Eliot died. You more than anyone should be saying that I have not compromised my normal responsibilities. Surely, you don't believe this scurrilous bullshit."

Jake put his palms down. "Take it easy. It's out of my hands now. Spelt wants to see you. And don't worry about your 10:30 class. I'm supposed to arrange for it and your other classes to be covered until further notice."

"The bastard," Monroe said. "So it's a done deal. This is the kind of support I get from my chair? What did you say in my defense, Jake?"

"Well, you know that I spoke for, uh—"

"Stop, I don't want to hear it. You said nothing."

Minutes later, Monroe gave a little a wave to Mildred and went straight into Spelt's office.

"What the hell's going on? Jake says I'm suspended from teaching. Is this your doing?"

Spelt leaned back in his chair, pushed his hands together palm to palm, then pointed toward a chair. *Mr. Reasonable now.* "Well, not exactly. You see—"

"Don't tell me this is the result of that idiotic story and doctored photo."

Monroe paced the floor. "Is this how professors are treated on this campus with some half-assed fake news?"

"Relax. No one said you're guilty of anything. It just looks bad. Bad publicity. Especially that claim that you've been broadcasting that Eliot was murdered. I hope you didn't actually say that. Anyway, Davis and the BOG want you off stage for a bit. As of now, you are relieved of all duties on campus until we run this through the committee on charges. It's pro forma to let things cool down. They'll review the claims, interview you, and reinstate you. You get a week or so off with pay. The public will see that we've done due diligence. We've got enough problems with Eliot's death without the extra publicity of a professor claiming there's a killer on the loose. That's what it looks like from out—"

A rap on the door interrupted Spelt and a nervous-looking Mildred entered and began to speak rapidly as he glared at her with his what-*now* look. "Sorry to interrupt. Mr. Banyon called from Chicago and said it's urgent. He has obtained the instrument and will meet you Tuesday at his offices at 3:00 p.m. He hopes you will join him for dinner and asks you to contact his assistant at this number"—she waved a piece of paper—"in case of any changes on your end." She held out the paper to Spelt, who shoved it to one side on his desk and nodded curtly in her direction, which she took as a dismissal. Before she closed the door, Spelt stood and took a step to one side. "Mildred, no more interruptions, please."

"But you said—"

"For *any* reason."

As Spelt was distracted, Monroe, feigning interest in a small photo of Chiara, looked at the paper Mildred brought in. Only the bottom left edge with the beginning of a telephone number, 312, was visible. Monroe changed the subject. "Nice picture of Chiara. I saw the article in the paper on the weekend."

Spelt seemed thrown off balance at Monroe's change of tone. "It's actually not from that article. Similar, though."

"She's looking grown up. Getting lots of attention."

"Yeah, we're proud of her. This was taken in the same shoot as the one in the paper, same dress. Just before her appearance with the Okanagan Symphony. It will be the last time she uses that cello—the consortium keeps their instruments on a short leash—and we need to get her comfortable with her new instrument before Vienna next summer."

Monroe grimaced. "Must be hard to keep up with expenses like that."

"Tell me about it." Spelt's shoulders drooped. Then he gathered himself and his expression hardened. "But we're off topic. I need to get back to work."

"Of course," Monroe said. "Speaking of photography . . . do you do any yourself? Some nice views of the quad from your big window."

"What kind of a question is that?" Spelt frowned and stood up. "Unfortunately, I'll need you to leave the campus now. Use your time away as productively as you can. I could probably find the funds for a flight to an archive or research library if you need it. Don't bother with a formal application; just fire off a letter outlining the purpose of the trip and a projected budget. I should be able to fast-track it, one way or another."

I'll bet you can, Monroe said to himself. "Well, I'm editing the final draft of my book now so I'll be doing that."

"As for your suspension . . ." Spelt now slid into bureaucratic vagueness, "the committee on charges will report back to Chancellor Davis and me. The board of governors will ratify your return in a week or two. Meanwhile, please stay away from the media."

As he was leaving the office, Mildred intercepted Monroe. "I wanted to say that I'm sorry about that scurrilous article in the paper," she said. "I want to help any way I can."

"Thanks, Mildred. You can help. Can you think back to last Wednesday and let me know who came to see Mr. Spelt after Professor Kingsley and I left?"

Mildred glanced toward Spelt's office door and nodded. "I will call you in your office."

Monroe moved down the corridor as if now a stranger on his own turf. He wondered if his clumsy question about photography had signalled his suspicion that the *Norwester* photo had been taken from Spelt's office. Or damn near it. Spelt's offer of a research grant had been a surprise. Was it a gesture of kindness or a ploy to get him out of town?

The entrance to financial services was just up ahead and he decided to check if Meyer had thought of something new. Laura Kelly waved toward a copy of the *Norwester* at him as soon as he entered. "This is mean. And the one in Facebook is worse."

Monroe smiled grimly.

"It's just me, but I think somebody is spooked," Laura continued. "Panic mode. But if someone had done this to a prof in my time, just because he was asking some questions about a suspicious death, the students would have been marching. They're way more docile now. What will happen to them?"

"The department chair's looking for a stand-in. I hope only for a week or so. How's Meyer doing? Is he in?"

"Yeah, the bear retreated to his den. He was out here a while ago growling at his mail, barely managed a hello."

"I'll go on in. Meyer had his back to the door and was hunched over the bottom drawer of his file cabinet. "Reorganizing the files?" Monroe asked.

Meyer looked up and wiped his palm across his brow. "Packing up. Stress leave."

"That was fast. When did you apply?"

"I didn't. I was notified by Spelt in the campus mail—all official and signed by the chancellor. I'm on medical leave effective today at full pay. I'm to vacate my office and am eligible to return in two months with a doctor's certification that I'm free of symptoms of PTSD."

Monroe patted Meyer on the shoulder. "That's good, isn't it? Give you time to recover from the shock and get back to normal."

"What the hell is normal? I feel normal. Sure I wasn't happy to see the old camper blown up, but I'm not losing sleep over it. What I'll miss is the work and—this is going to sound a little strange—my morning swim. I'm going to keep it up unless they post a guard."

"And the meetings with Mildred?" Monroe asked.

"That's none of your business."

"No one will notice you at the pool," Monroe said. "You get there before anybody's up . . . well, most people. Come to think of it, I wonder if I'll still have access to the weight room. I've just been suspended from teaching."

"What? Because of that moronic hatchet job in the student paper? Laura showed it to me. Who would take that seriously?"

"The chancellor, supposedly. I think it was set up in advance. The picture is of us talking in the quad on Wednesday. Your camper is blown up on Friday, and here we are on Monday, both removed from campus."

Back at his office, Monroe checked the internet and found that area code 312 was downtown Chicago including the Loop. Could be near the Art Institute, he thought. Then he outlined lecture topics for the coming week and left a set of essays to return, thinking he wouldn't be suspended for long. He delivered these materials to Jake and told him to get his suspension lifted as soon as possible, even if it meant that he sign an agreement to stop investigating Eliot's death. He knew he wouldn't, not now, but he could be less obvious about it. He also insisted that all student assignments be delivered to his house—or made available for him to pick up on campus. "Don't be such a wimp, Jake," he said. "Stand up for us, your colleagues, and our students." Jake nodded.

Monroe was about to send out a notice to his students that he would be on temporary leave for a week or two when his phone rang. "Hello, Professor, this is Mildred. I've checked President Spelt's appointments from last Wednesday and Professor Turner came shortly after you left. He had a sheaf of papers under his arm and I saw part of the title was 'Institute.' They were interrupted briefly when Mrs. Kerr came by and President Spelt stepped out to speak to her."

"Thank you, Mildred. That's helpful."

Monroe stared at the wall for a moment, then phoned Jim to propose lunch or a coffee at The Ten.

28

Jim was seated beneath a poster-size black-and-white photo of Stalin. The cold, pitiless eyes together with the smirk of a psychopath made Monroe uneasy. "Did you have to choose this table? He gives me the creeps. The whole place does. Irony is fine but we're talking here about mass murderers."

"You're right," Jim said. "Cheap beer doesn't override the vibes. I guess people felt differently about these people in the sixties. An age of innocence. Radical chic or something. I'd be up for an ordinary Joe's diner with formica tables and linoleum floors. Any ideas?"

"Nope, they hardly exist anymore, overrun by an invasive species called fast food."

"Let's tough it out; I'm only here for a minute," Jim said. "Coffee?" Monroe nodded and Jim caught the eye of the young barman in a leather vest with a ring poking through one nostril.

"You're in a hurry," Monroe said. "What's up?"

"A new case. An elderly woman found dead on Grouse mountain yesterday."

Monroe pulled his attention back from the barman who had plunked a mug of coffee in front of him. "A hiker? I didn't hear about a search. When did it happen?"

"Probably Friday night. But they just found her an hour ago. A famous violinist caught in the snowstorm."

"The one who came to donate a valuable violin? I just read about her."

"Yeah, she went to the Grouse Mountain Bistro, and a few flakes at 4:30 or so turned into a blizzard along with a sudden drop in temperature, down to minus four or five. Weather on the mountain gets underestimated all the time."

"But it's only a short walk to the Sky ride from the bistro."

"Well, she didn't get there. A busboy saw someone matching her description walk with a man toward the Centennial ski run after the storm became intense. She had on light clothing and carried a small handbag. That's all I know."

"Walking *away* from the Skyride?" Monroe asked. "Mind if I tag along? I've been suspended from teaching."

"What?"

"There was a story in the student paper that claimed I was neglecting my teaching while playing detective, and had announced to everyone that Eliot had been murdered. And it went out on social media."

"You wouldn't say that."

"Of course not, someone made it up. For now, I'm out and it goes to a faculty committee."

"Maybe someone doesn't want you nosing around. Could be we're getting somewhere."

"Take it easy, I wasn't planning to lose my job. They also put Meyer on PTSD leave without even consulting him."

"Interesting," Jim said. "Both of you. Is he OK?"

"Feisty as ever. Pissed off about it."

"Some guys can be in denial. We've seen it in the force."

"I'm not sure what it accomplished if someone wants him silenced. I guess he'll get his files backed up with his sister in Germany sometime soon."

"Anyway, I've gotta go. You're welcome to come with me."

Riding the gondola, Monroe watched Jim review his notes while taking occasional glimpses back toward Vancouver, the Georgia Strait, and the lake behind Cleveland Dam. "Never get tired of that view," Jim said. "Should get up here more often." At one point, Monroe remembered, Jim had been an excellent skier, competing in downhill and slalom races. At the top, Constable Hudson was waiting. She walked quickly toward them.

"Hello, Professor," she said, looking surprised. Then she turned to Jim. "We've searched the ground between here and where the body was found."

Jim squinted out toward the Expo run, where Ms. Tanaka had ended up. "Where exactly was she?"

Hudson pointed. "In a hollow under that second tower. Stuck. We found her bag tossed into the bush near the body. No cash, but credit cards and driver's license. Possibly a robbery."

"How do you know it was tossed?"

"It was in a thick growth of salal a good twenty feet from the tower. "

Jim nodded. "Did you get the name and contact information of the busboy who saw her leave with a man?"

She flashed her notebook and nodded.

"Spoken to all the restaurant workers?"

"Only briefly with the busboy and dishwasher. We left them for you."

"Right. Thanks, Hudson."

Jim led the way to the bistro with its large deck overlooking the city. He identified himself to the manager and held out his photo ID. "We're looking for the person who served Ms. Aiko Tanaka on Friday afternoon before she went missing."

The manager was short. His skin looked greasy as if he had been standing at the deep-fat fryer for a few hours. "Yes," he said, screwing up his face in an attempt to convey bereavement. "Terrible mishap. We can't understand how she got onto the Expo run or why. Wrong direction . . . away from the gondola."

"Well, someone may have taken her that way," Jim said. "Did you see anyone with Ms. Tanaka or anyone who might have had any direct contact with her? Who waited on her?"

"Mary Barnhill." He called over to a young guy setting a table. "Dean, where's Mary? These gentlemen want to talk to her."

"Outside, looking after her addiction. Want me to call her?"

"Yeah, tell her it's important."

Dean went out the side door and returned a couple of minutes later with a slender, shorthaired blond girl with large brown eyes. As she approached, the manager took a call on his cell and walked away.

"You wanted to see me?" Mary asked.

"Yes," Jim said. "We're checking on Ms. Tanaka's movements before she got lost on the mountain Friday night. The manager said that you served her."

"I did." Mary looked toward a window table halfway across the room. "She sat by the pillar over there. Good view of the mountain. She ordered a large pot of tea and a plate of sushi and just sat quietly."

Jim said. "When did she arrive and when did she leave? Did you speak to her at all?"

"She arrived about 4:00 and left a little after 6:30, about a half hour after the snow began to come down really hard. She paid with her Visa well before she left. About 6:00, I'd say. She complimented us on the sushi. Nice lady. Peaceful."

"Did you notice anything else?" Monroe asked. "Cell phone? Notebook?"

"No, only that it seemed unusual to see someone sit quietly without being glued to a phone. She did look at her watch quite a few times. When she pulled out her Visa, a Post-it Note was stuck to it. She smiled as if remembering something she had forgotten to do, then tapped it."

Jim looked at Monroe. "Waiting for someone." Jim turned back to Mary. "A man eventually left with her. Did you see him?"

"Well, just before she left, I was serving some people at the other side of the room and saw a man standing next to her table. I thought he was just giving her a weather update or something. By then, it was snowing hard."

Jim crossed the room to the table Ms. Tanaka had occupied. "Show me exactly where you were when you saw this man. How was he dressed?"

Mary took a dozen steps to her left and called out: "I was at this table. I thought he was just passing by because he wore a ski jacket, blue, and had a black toque on."

"And you wouldn't have seen him from other places in the room because of this pillar," Jim said.

"No . . . well, not from the routes we take back and forth to the kitchen."

"Anything distinctive about the jacket or toque? Would you be able to identify this man or describe him?" Monroe asked.

"Not really. He was faced away from me. A jacket and toque like that is pretty common here on the mountain. But clearly not that young, sort of thick-looking, not a snowboarder from his shape or dress. Nobody was snowboarding anyway because there wasn't enough of a base . . . well, nobody except a few gonzos looking for places to do jumps."

Jim made a note of this. "Could the guy in the jacket have escorted Ms. Tanaka out of the restaurant?"

Mary shrugged her shoulders. "I didn't see them leave. Shortly after I saw the man talking to her, they both were gone."

"One more thing," Monroe said. "Did she seem frail? Any trouble walking or standing up?"

"She was elderly. Limped a little on her way to the restroom. But she walked well enough. Clearly not a hiker. Wrong shoes."

❖

"You don't look pleased," Monroe said as he and Jim stepped onto the deck.

"I don't like it. I want to know more about Mr. Blue Parka and Black Toque. The obvious thought is that he leads Ms. Tanaka off in the wrong direction with the intent to abandon her in the storm."

"Leaves her to freeze with only a light jacket," Monroe said. "But why? Surely not to steal a bit of cash. And if she was waiting for him, what's their connection? I wonder if the young snowboarders saw anything."

"We'll try," Jim said. Then he looked over at Constable Hudson and waited for her to finish a phone call.

"It was Mr. Morton," she said. "He's seriously distraught. He just checked the music academic safe and it's empty. Ms. Tanaka's violin has been stolen. Only he and Ms. Tanaka had the combination. She had it written on a Post-it Note."

Monroe looked at Jim. "She still had it when she paid the server."

"Hudson, check Ms. Tanaka's wallet again." Hudson took a step then turned and added, "Morton said he made her promise to memorize the combination and destroy the note. He thought she didn't take it seriously, told him it was Canada. Sounded like he was almost crying."

Jim shook his head. "An innocent. Foreigners have this idea about Canada."

"Of course, the combination could have been copied from the Post-it Note," Monroe said.

"Yes. But with all that snow falling, that seems unlikely. . . . And he would have been in a hurry."

Hudson returned walking quickly. "No Post-it Note in the wallet or anywhere in the purse."

"Thanks. It's what I expected. Be sure the wallet and the purse are bagged. We'll check them. Oh, could you go down and start reviewing surveillance tapes from the gondola and its staging area from last Friday? We're looking for a man in a blue parka and black toque. He would have come up around 6:00 and gone back down around 7:00. Try to get a glimpse of his face or anything else that will help identify him. Also try to get identities of the young snowboarders. Maybe they saw this guy."

"Pretty generic look," Monroe said. "What was he up to?"

"Looks like he was after the violin. Sets up a meeting. Tanaka trusts him. He takes her out into the snowstorm far enough away from the Skyride that she can't get back. He pushes her or she falls into that hollow where she's stuck. She's cold, disoriented, frail. He checks her purse, gets the Post-it, takes her cash, and tosses the bag. Trying to make it look like robbery. Then back to the Skyride, into his car, and to the academy to open the safe and grab the violin."

"He got the violin that Friday, Saturday, or Sunday," Monroe said. "He knew his way around the academy and knew she had the combination to the safe."

"The snowstorm was crucial," Jim said. "A crime of opportunity and someone with inside knowledge. How did he know she had the combination, for example? Whoever did this is a cold-blooded sonofabitch."

29

Tuesday morning Monroe headed to the kitchen to get the coffee going and out of habit checked his computer for appointments. Meetings, student appointments, and a squash date with Jean-Michel: wiped out now.

Well, he wasn't going to hide away because Davis—or Spelt—didn't want him on campus. He could meet Jean-Michel as planned and sit in his office for a while in case one of his students came by. A glance at the local news online caught him by surprise. Damn, there was a photo of him standing behind Jim on Grouse Mountain with the caption: "Police Investigate Death of Japanese Musician."

Before getting on his bike, Monroe called Warren to meet up at The Buzz before his squash game. He wanted to keep things as normal as possible. And normal it was as Mrs. Rigetti waylaid him on the lane behind her house. "Hello, Professor Monroe. I heard about you on the radio. That you're on leave. Something about neglecting duties to do police work. I don't believe it. But then there you are again in the news this morning. Are you also investigating the death of that poor Japanese lady? Years ago, you know, Marco and I heard her play with the symphony."

Monroe decided to tell Mrs. Rigetti what he had been doing. He tried to explain why he had to find out why Eliot died. She listened, wide-eyed and with apparent sympathy. As he spoke, she kept reaching out and patting him on the arm. He concluded with a request: "Could you let me know if you see anything unusual in the neighbourhood? If you do, only tell me. Don't say anything to neighbours or even to Marco, in case it could put one of them in danger."

"What do you mean by 'unusual'?" she asked.

"Could be a car parked on the street with someone just sitting in it. Or a person who comes to the door, pretending to deliver a package or offer a service."

She clasped her hands in front of her. "Oh, my. Now that you mention it. A man came to your house yesterday and walked around with a clipboard making notes. He looked a little strange, was wearing a mask and examining each window. I asked him what he was doing and he said he was preparing an estimate for cleaning the windows. Said he specializes in removing mould in the insets surrounding the frames, which was the reason for his mask."

"Mould? I've never noticed," Monroe said. Besides, I wash my own windows."

"Well, I didn't like the sound of mould so I asked him to do an estimate for me, too. He didn't seem to like that. Said he had to keep to his work schedule and would come back later in the week. I asked for his card, but he pretended he had forgotten them."

"Did you happen to notice his car?"

"I did indeed. It was a white van with license PLB 203. 'Please leave bags, two or three.' That's how I remember things."

Monroe grabbed a pen from his pocket and wrote it down. "That's great. What did this man look like?"

"I couldn't tell too much. The mask covered his nose and mouth and he was wearing one of those hats with a visor. Otherwise, dark hair, olive skin, a beard, youngish, say in his late twenties. Oh, and his cap was red but I don't remember what was on it."

You're a wonderful observer. But be careful."

Mrs. Rigetti beamed at Monroe as he turned to pedal down the lane and out into the street. "*You* be careful," she called out.

A few minutes later, Mrs. Rigetti's comment resonated as a passing white van nearly clipped him with the side mirror. Farther along, he saw a what could be the same van parked a hundred metres or so up a side street. A rag tucked around the license plate covering everything except for 3 at the right edge. Could this be the same vehicle Mrs. Rigetti saw? *Following me now or what?*

At The Buzz, Monroe was just getting his coffee when he saw Warren about to take a seat at the usual place by the far window. "Not that seat, Warren. I've reserved it."

"What?"

"Reserved. You sit on the other side so I can keep my back to the room. Trying to be discreet," he said in a low voice.

"They haven't banned you from campus, have they?"

"Not directly. But I'm keeping a low profile. But they can't stop me from writing and research. I'll be using the library and I may want to be in my office once in a while in case a student comes around. I'm even meeting Jean-Michel at the gym for a squash game in a little while. Life goes on . . . sort of."

"Including trips to Grouse Mountain?"

"You, too, huh?"

"Well, it's obvious. There you are hovering around another police investigation. What *were* you doing?"

"I tagged along with Jim after meeting him for coffee. Spelt had just given me word of the suspension."

"And now you're looking into another death?"

"Not really. It is interesting, though. Looks like a man in a toque walked the woman from the bistro to the Expo run and then abandoned her. He must have been after a violin she planned to donate. He got the combination to the safe at the Music Academy from her wallet and stole it that night or on the weekend." Monroe tapped the table and pursed his lips. "Anyway, I'm off to meet Jean-Michel."

On the way out, Warren did a double take upon glancing at one of the side tables. "Turner," he said.

Monroe followed Warren's gaze. *Hanging out with Renwick,* he thought.

Monroe and Jean-Michel managed to extend a few spirited rallies but too many were cut short by unforced errors. It had always been that way. Each lacked the killer instinct. After a hard-won point, one or the other would let up and the score would stay close.

"Pretty aggressive out there today," Jean-Michel said. "I couldn't get position in the centre. All those balls hugging the walls and dying in the corners."

"You did all right. You were digging them out. Some good drop shots."

Jean-Michel shook his head. "I need to get out more often, got winded too quickly. I'll be better next time." He paused, shifting his voice from jocular to serious. "By the way, what's the deal about your suspension?"

Monroe shrugged his shoulders. "Don't know. Triggered by that *Norwester* article."

"A poor attempt at satire and a doctored photo. No one took it seriously."

"Well, someone did. Now it goes to a committee."

"Can't believe they're going to waste time on it."

Monroe slid his racket into his bag. "It's window dressing."

"Meaning?"

"Public relations. Spelt told me as much. The university needs to appear to be doing something, anything. Pressing the back-to-normal button after Eliot. And certainly do everything to avoid calling it a murder. Which I didn't do, by the way."

"But hang a faculty member out to dry over something like this?"

"Hell, yes. *Especially* that. We're the *last* ones they'll stand up for. It's a wonder I wasn't put in handcuffs and escorted from campus."

"I don't get it. Spelt was supposed to be the faculty's man."

"What a joke." Monroe kicked at one of the lockers. "Ouch . . . Spelt *said* he was pressured by Davis. You know, restore order, show that the place isn't in chaos with people killing each other."

"To me it looks like panic. Someone on the board must have second-guessed it."

Monroe shrugged. "I hope so."

"I can understand why Spelt, Davis—whoever it is—could be nervous," Jean-Michel said. "But using that article as a pretext. . . . I wonder what the student reps said. Or Kerr."

"I'd like to ask her," Monroe said. "But she's pretty close-mouthed."

"But face it, today's coverage of the woman on Grouse doesn't help. You look pretty intense in the photo, like you'd like to get your hands on the culprit."

"I'll admit it. Another needless death. A kind person, trusting, wanting to help others. I didn't even know someone was taking a picture. But you're right. It didn't help me. You're the third person today who's mentioned it." Monroe paused. "But I keep wondering, why kill in order to steal a violin, if that's what it amounted to?"

Jean-Michel shoved his squash racket into a bag. "You're too curious for your own good. I agree, though, it seems unusual. If it's like stealing art—something valuable but traceable because it's one of a kind—everyone knows it can't be sold on the open market without provenance. Your only buyers are rich and unethical people. It would be the same for stolen instruments, except way smaller than for art."

"Makes sense," Monroe said. "Private buyers hang stolen pictures in their mansions. Out of sight. Yet right next door. Musical instruments, I think, must be played rather than stashed away."

"Probably," Jean-Michel said. "I know I wouldn't be able to keep an instrument in some secret closet. I can't really see anyone bothering to steal something in league with a Stradivarius and not play it. And a real musician wouldn't play it in secret. Not if they're like visual artists, who won't buy stolen paintings. We respect the art even when we don't much like each other."

Monroe nodded slowly. "Sounds nice but it doesn't nail anything down."

"I suppose not." Jean-Michel zipped up his bag and hunched the strap over his shoulder. "By the way, do you think a woman would kill the violinist that way?"

Monroe smiled. "Not necessarily."

"Me neither. It's the guy in the toque."

"Yes," Monroe said. "But a woman could end up with the violin. Couldn't she come on stage with the lights dimmed and play such an instrument?"

Jean-Michel shrugged his shoulders. "Not respectful."

Monroe threw up his hands. "Hope you're right."

30

Monroe and Jean-Michel shared a companionable silence on the walk to the quad. At Stirling Hall, Jean-Michel nodded toward the entrance. "Come in for a minute? I've got something to show you. I'll make us some coffee."

"Great. No coffee, though. I need water, the colder the better."

Jean-Michel unlocked the door, turned on the lights, and waved toward the sink. "Help yourself. See if there's a clean glass in the cabinet. Or wash one that's on the counter. Jean-Michel wasn't making eye contact now as he slipped off his jacket from the locker, looked it over, and gave it a shake. He did it mechanically. Monroe could see that his mind was migrating elsewhere. He eyed the jacket carefully, as if the entrenched wrinkles in the linen encrypted some lively moments from his past.

Monroe didn't know the half of it, but over the years had pieced together enough to be impressed. Jean-Michel had been in full bohemian mode on the Côte d'Azur in the '90s. Painting in his studio by day and playing a decent jazz sax by night in small bars in Nice. On campus, that jacket somehow pointed to its owner's different trajectory from other academics.

Suddenly, Jean-Michel was somewhere else. From the jacket pocket he had pulled out a small, folded paper, carefully opened it, and studied it. "An old note from the old days," he said. Never wanted to throw it away. Maggie Lynch. Scribbled her name on a notepad from the Negresco Hotel where we were playing. Her phone number, can't quite make it out. There's a six and a three . . . or is it an eight? Must have been in a hurry."

"I'll bet you were." Jean-Michel didn't say anything but continued to study the paper. "A long time ago," Monroe added. "Why still in your pocket? Don't you take the jacket to the cleaners once in a while?"

"Of course, but the note comes out first. Then it goes back. It's an heirloom, a might have been, a no second chance." Jean-Michel's voice had become a little dreamy. "Don't you have a few of those?"

Monroe thought of his father's old briefcase. Or that baguette Eliot promised to the dog. And some others,. "A lot, now that you mention it. But no reminders in my jackets."

Jean-Michel gave Monroe a pat on the shoulder. "I'll be right back, got some purchase orders to drop in campus mail."

❌

By the time Jean-Michel re-entered the gallery, Monroe was on his second glass of water and parked on a bench in front of a mini-exhibit of six landscapes by Ross Penhall. "Impressive, aren't they?" Jean-Michel said. "We have them till November."

"Good. I'll come back and look at them again. On loan from private collectors, I see. Hoping to acquire them for the permanent collection?"

"Working on it. The advancement office and I think Mrs. Kerr is involved. But look again at the beach painting here on the easel next to my office." Jean-Michel flicked a switch and a spotlight brought the painting to life. "I already told you it could be by Gerald Murphy. I'm sure of it now." Monroe placed himself five or six paces back and, without a word, began to take it in, his eyes roving from three children in the foreground at the edge of the water—blue, clear, and inviting—in contrast with a lifeless grey of hotels or buildings of some sort looming behind. "Strange juxtaposition of those children and the buildings."

"Yeah, there's a message there. I've just got the report after X-raying it. I was hoping to find the artist's signature under some of the thick paint laid on to give texture to the sand."

"And?"

"No luck. But almost as good, the X-ray showed a kind of inscription. It was scribbled quickly in big letters as if an afterthought, and then painted over."

"And?"

"It says *adieu*."

"Goodbye," Monroe muttered. "What's that supposed to tell us?"

"Well, in French, *adieu* is permanent, forever. Not *au revoir*, see you later."

"Go on."

"It goes with something else." Jean-Michel reached for a file folder on his desk and pulled out a sheet of paper. "Have a look. This was under an extra flap of the backing paper added when, or maybe after, it was framed. I noticed it when I was getting the painting ready to send to X-ray."

Monroe took the paper and sank into the Binning chair at one side

> Dow's sketch from '36. His last. Both boys dead then. Told
> Joseph to destroy it but he kept it for Honoria. A. MacLeish,
> June 13, 1947.

Monroe handed the paper back to Jean-Michel. "You've lost me. Who's Dow?"

"My question too. Obviously a nickname. I started going through MacLeish's published letters."

"And?"

"Dow is Gerald Murphy. His daughter Honoria called him 'dow-dow' when she was a kid and it became his nickname. She is one of the children on the beach. Once you home in on the Murphys, the rest can be filled in. Most importantly Murphy's loss of his sons, Patrick and Baoth, who died so young."

"That's what the inscription is about?"

"Yeah, look at the timing. One of the boys died in '35 and the other, from tuberculosis, in January '36. Murphy travelled to Europe that same year on business and went to Antibes. He was putting his house, the famous Villa America, up for sale. While there, he must have had the impulse to pick up his paints again after not touching them for five or six years."

"Like an obituary for their life there," Monroe said softly.

"In Antibes, the children were the centre of things for Murphy and his wife, even though the rich and famous were around a lot for parties and dinners."

"Who is Joseph?"

"He was the gardener and caretaker," Jean-Michel said. "I think, when MacLeish says that he kept the painting, he means that he kept it safe during the war."

Monroe frowned. "Or that he kept it even though Murphy told him to destroy it?"

Jean-Michel leaned against the wall. "That too. Then MacLeish, the close family friend, shows up and Joseph has a way to get it to Honoria."

"Without Murphy knowing," Monroe said. "And MacLeish keeps the painting to pass it on when Murphy dies. I wonder why Murphy painted over the inscription."

Jean-Michel said: "Well, look at the *way* he covered it up. A hasty scribble. I think it fits with his decision to destroy the painting. The painting itself, remember, was more a sketch than a finished work. I think it's a view of the beach next to Villa America. The buildings are symbolic, fate ready to pounce."

"Still . . ." Monroe stopped, vaguely skeptical but not sure why. "You must be right," he continued. "I'm only speculating. But having read a little about Murphy, it seems he tried not to wallow in despair. Depressed, yes. But worried more about his wife. She was close to a complete breakdown after the second boy died."

"Bravo." It was a voice behind them and a familiar one. Jean-Michel and Monroe turned in unison to see Mrs. Kerr standing just inside the entrance. "Impressive progress. I look forward to a full report. May I suggest, though, one additional point? Or maybe I've interrupted."

How interesting, Monroe thought.

Jean-Michel said, "Not at all. Please go on."

"It's a detail but an important one. The figure in the background leaning on the rake. My dear husband Lloyd was obsessed with him and believed it amounted to both signature and inscription. I would say you have confirmed it. It is Murphy himself. From the first, Lloyd was fascinated by the way the composition divides into a kind of triptych, each painted in a different style: the children in a golden glow, full of life, self-absorbed, in the moment; the buildings looming behind drafted—yes that's the word—as geometric abstractions in Murphy's modernist style, precise, impersonal, overbearing, threatening. But just stuck there out of context, if you will, and now we see from Professor Sevene's researches why."

"Yes," Monroe said. "Villa America: life as art with style, elegance, spontaneity, taste, and those beautiful children at the centre of it. Everything before them, all the possibilities. But forces are at hand, normalized as backdrop, yet symbolic of forces that pounce and crush life at any time. Like the sketches from the Middle Ages used as designs for works destined for stained glass or tapestries."

"Right," Jean-Michel said, "always with a story line or a moral lesson."

"Pretty obvious here," Monroe said.

"Too obvious for Madame Murphy," Jean-Michel said. "Reason for Murphy to cover his inscription and tell Joseph to destroy it. It's too brutal a representation of what they had lost."

Kerr stepped closer. "I think you're right. That's where the third element of the composition figures in."

"The figure with the rake . . . Murphy," Monroe said.

Kerr nodded. "Exactly. Lloyd insisted that this figure was a kind of Greek chorus, the seer who knows things, things he doesn't want to see."

Jean-Michel said, "I remember Lloyd saying something like that. And we know now that Murphy used to rake that beach every day because the tides carried a lot of seaweed in. So there he is, a Sisyphus eternally tidying the beach for his children and friends. It is endless, nature can't be tamed, part of being alive."

Monroe nodded. "I see that. The figure is small yet it exudes a kind of wisdom. The eyes, look at them, they're engaging the viewer as if with the message to live life fully while you have it, clean the beach, take care of the children because it can all end in an instant. I want to spend some serious time with this painting."

The three remained quiet until Monroe broke the silence. He said, speaking to no one in particular, "*Adieu justement*. And now we know the artist and the painting's provenance." He looked at Mrs. Kerr. "I suppose you would know how Lloyd found it."

"Indeed I do. He found it in a small gallery in Northampton, Massachusetts, while on a business trip to Boston. About thirty years ago. Part of the estate of MacLeish that ended up in a local antique shop. A curator of the gallery at Smith College was interested just because MacLeish is a big name locally, but the college was slow to release funds. Lloyd saw it and paid the asking price, no questions asked."

"How much?" Monroe asked.

"It was $1,200. A lot at the time but he believed until the day he died that it would prove to be important."

"I wonder why the painting ended up in a shop when it had been part of MacLeish's estate," Monroe said. "It was supposed to go to Murphy's daughter."

"Maybe she didn't want it," Jean-Michel said. "Too painful. And I think he wanted to keep it on his own wall right to the end."

"Why do you say that?" Monroe asked.

"MacLeish owned Murphy's greatest painting, *Wasp and the Pear*, and when Murphy was dying, he offered it to the Museum of Modern Art in New York. They agreed to add it to their permanent collection but he specified that it remain in his possession as long as he lived. As Murphy was dying he told him that *Wasp and Pear* would be going to the MoMA."

"Is this documented?" Kerr asked.

Jean-Michel glanced at some notes he had next to the painting. "The part about the MoMA is in a letter MacLeish wrote in September 1964, less than a month before Murphy died. An old friend saying goodbye. But yes, the beach painting got lost in the shuffle when MacLeish died. MacLeish's wife, who outlived him by a couple of years, was then about '90. Who knows how his personal effects, those not specified in his will, were dispersed."

Kerr looked at Jean-Michel. "Dispersal, always the fate of things that mattered to people. Thank you for your research. We will cherish this painting and keep looking at it for what it tells us about life. Peter Eliot didn't have time to find out and Lloyd only had a premonition. It is the future of the gallery and I don't mean just because it has value."

"Is the painting what you and Eliot had argued about the week before he died?" Monroe asked.

Kerr sighed. "Argued. Well, I suppose. How did you find that out? My position was that, thanks to Lloyd, Northlake had an important painting. But we needed to put minimal resources into authenticating it. Peter supported the gallery in general but was pressuring me for a new donation that could start a campaign to endow it."

Monroe nodded. "So mainly a difference in tactics."

"Yes. And I took it more personally than I should have. When the Board of Governors was voting on the new president I asked if they would support some reasonable effort to authenticate it. Eliot was positive, enthusiastic; Spelt guarded and bureaucratic. So Eliot got my vote and I told him he was bound by a moral obligation."

Jean-Michel looked puzzled. "Wait, so it was your vote in exchange for his support for the gallery?"

Kerr said, "It amounted to that, yes. Peter was a political man, understood the workings of give and take. And it turned out—this is in confidence—my vote was the deciding one."

Monroe nodded. "Well, it turned out well. At first I thought he was an outsider parachuted in by the minister. Later, I realized he had a vision for this place and that he and the minister had disagreements. The gallery was part of it."

"I'm not clear about the details of that," Kerr said. "He did tell me, though, that a donation from me as soon as possible to start the endowment project would help him counter pressure—that's the word he used—from the minister and the premier."

"Pressure," Jean-Michel said. "That must be why my research leave to authenticate Murphy's painting was cancelled. Spelt signed it but it must have come from higher up."

"Of course, to put pressure on me," Kerr said.

"Fortunately, it came together quickly with the X-ray and finding the note by MacLeish in the backing. Once I knew Murphy did the painting and its provenance it was obvious that it was his last. The others are all in major collections, in the Whitney and the MoMA in New York, for instance. Yale University, Murphy's alma mater, recently acquired and restored one."

"That puts us in very good company, now doesn't it?" Kerr said.

"There is still a question to be answered," Monroe said. "Is it possible that you were so angry at the way Eliot changed the terms of your deal that you found a way to remove him?"

"Don't be silly. I was angry, yes, but better the devil you know. Peter had to adjust our plan on the fly. I wasn't aware of the pressure he was under by the minister." Monroe glanced at Jean-Michel, who had stepped to one side and was looking intently at the brush strokes on the largest of the Penhalls, an abstract vineyard scene ablaze in glorious yellow sunlight.

31

Monroe's next stop was to see Luce at the dean's office. When he entered, Margo Johnson looked up and smiled. "She's just back from a meeting with *el presidente*."

"Thanks, Margo." Monroe rapped on Luce's door, which was ajar, and poked his head in. She jumped up and embraced him. "I didn't expect to see you here." She glanced at Monroe's sports bag. "Squash? But no racket."

"Borrowed one from Jean-Michel."

"Ah." Luce paused. "So how're you doing?"

"OK, I guess. Waiting it out now." Monroe wanted to change the subject. "I like the sign. 'Dean of Arts,' in brass too."

"Fake brass. But it's better to be on the inside where you're listened to than locked out in the street. Take your turn, guard against the creep of self-importance, and then go back to the trenches."

"I agree in principle but may not get the chance now that they're trying to ditch me."

"You'll be back. Your students are up in arms. But maybe you made yourself a target with a big-foot approach."

"You think? A bigger foot of someone higher up is stepping on me. A PR move to pretend that everything is back to normal."

Luce looked toward a photo in her bookcase. She was standing with hiking buddies on a sub-alpine trail holding the hand-woven toque her Uncle Charles had worn to the summit of Mount McKinley. Her heirloom, Monroe thought.

"True, it's not logical," Luce said. "If it's a message that everything's in order, they should *encourage* and protect you. You're not the main event, the police are. So why you? Unless you're threatening someone."

Monroe shook his head. "But who? Jim said that, too, but I doubt it. I can't see that I'm getting anywhere."

"Well your text messages have told me quite the opposite. Pieces of the puzzle, although I don't see how they fit together. You figured out what Mildred was doing. You found out about Turner's conflict with Eliot. You discovered that Hans Meyer and Eliot were investigating something. Maybe the thing would be to find out more about that. And what about Mrs. Kerr? Do you trust her?"

"I'm not sure. Jean-Michel has identified a painting she and Lloyd donated. Rare and wildly valuable. She walked into the gallery when he was telling me about it and admitted to some sort of deal to vote for Eliot in the BOG in exchange for his support for the gallery. Then he changed the plan, pressed her for a donation to start an endowment drive. To protect the gallery from pressure from the minister. She was annoyed but had no plan B that was any better."

"Well, that valuable painting could do it, no? Sell it and there's the solution."

"It might have been. But Kerr is ambitious, wants to build a permanent collection around it. She identifies with the pathos behind its creation and thinks Lloyd's finding it symbolizes his genius to discover overlooked gems. Meanwhile, the minister was holding the gallery hostage in exchange for Kerr's support on a vote in the BOG"

Luce shuffled some papers and looked toward the window. "Such a tangle. Kerr all worked up, thinks only of the gallery, worried about the minister, imagines Eliot stabbed her in the back because he has to think of the university as a whole. Then the sideshows of Turner, Spelt, Mildred, and whatever Eliot had Meyer working on."

"And there's Meyer's van. Whoever blew up is seriously dangerous. Completely different style than switching a muffin. Which may yet prove to be an accident or misadventure."

Luce leaned forward in her chair. "I doubt it. With the chess match starting, someone saw you moving a couple of pawns and the countermove was to get you off the board. The article made you sound a little crazy."

"It worked," Monroe said. "I don't think a student wrote it. But it captures the way they talk about us in the pub or on rate-your-professor."

"It circulated quickly. I suppose the chancellor had to do something. It *was* Davis, wasn't it, who made the decision?"

"That's what Spelt said. He was sympathetic, offered travel money for research while things were getting sorted out."

"Really?" Luce looked skeptical. "Are you supposed to be on campus now?"

"He didn't say. I've got editing to do so a research trip isn't right now anyway."

Luce looked at her watch, then gathered several folders and a pad of paper to put into a shoulder bag. "I've got a meeting, *mon cher ami—another* one—in five minutes. It looks to me that you're making progress, even if it's complicated."

"Maybe a little. Anyway, I'm off." Monroe stood, picked up his bag, leaned across the desk to squeeze Luce's hand, and left the office.

At the door to the corridor, he saw Margo trotting toward her desk with a stack of folders. He stepped back. "Margo? Luce once told me that you and some of the staff had a running joke about Evan Spelt's travel. Can you tell me about it?"

Margo glanced to one side as if to make sure they were alone. "Well . . . yes, we did joke around a little. Office banter. I think I started it."

"But it's based on *something*, right? Do you have any specifics or could you get some? Maybe later today or tomorrow."

"I suppose I could look in the files." She paused. "The ones I have access to. Some may be confidential."

"I'd be surprised if this were confidential. But if anyone asks, just say it's background information Inspector Martino asked for."

"It'll be all right," she said, smiling. "No one will see me."

"You might as well avoid mentioning me. Could be a red flag with my suspension. Can you give me an idea of how this office banter might go?"

"This will sound petty. It might start with some mention in the news about darling Chiara and her next solo appearance. Nothing against her. She's a talented kid. It's more Dr. Spelt bragging about her all the time. It's true, the media keeps track of her pretty closely since she won that contest for young musicians in Toronto a couple of years ago. So, just mentioning Chiara gets us started. Silly stuff along the lines of here we go again: the local sweetheart off on another junket. And then Dr. Spelt's grand announcements about whatever is coming down but he never ever shows any interest in our kids."

Monroe was surprised at the bitterness that had crept into Margo's voice as she continued. "We're expected to jump for joy at every scrap of news about Chiara. So when he's not around, we play the game of connecting his travel on *university* business with her travel to classes or concerts. It could be a coincidence, but it seems like a pattern. There is always an official story, something about a meeting or conference. Once I compared where he was going against where Chiara was appearing, and they happened to be fairly close."

"Interesting. Details?"

"Chiara went to Pittsburg for something with the youth symphony there and Dr. Spelt travelled at the same time to Cleveland. That's what he said. I wasn't suspicious or anything because I thought the two cities weren't close, but Marlene Harris checked and found they are two-and-a-half hours apart by car. At lunch one day we debated whether this was close enough for Dr. Freeload—we call him that sometimes—to be faking his trip. It was pretty silly but by then our game had some momentum. Something more interesting than the usual chit chat about neighbours from hell and schools screwing up our kids."

"It would be good, Margo, if you could find records of Spelt's trips. An itinerary, confirmation of airline tickets or hotel reservations. Even just one or two would be helpful."

32

◼

Monroe left the office feeling better. Talking to Luce had reassured him and so had the possibility that Margo might find something of interest about Spelt's travels. In the quad Monroe squinted toward the far end, where light reflected off the library windows. He recognized Spelt accompanied by two figures, one with a camera perched on his shoulder. *Looks like a walk-about with a couple of reporters to show the campus functioning normally.* As he watched them, he saw Spelt swing his head behind and to the side as if half checking for trouble. When he looked in Monroe's direction, Monroe worried Spelt may have just seen some. But Spelt was shortsighted. Monroe nevertheless turned his head away. That's when a hand on his shoulder shook him out of his trance.

Monroe whirled around and faced Warren.

"How'd the game go?"

Monroe glanced down at his gym bag. "Splendid. Forgot all about my suspension for a while. Oh, some news. Jean-Michel has identified a painting in the gallery as a Gerald Murphy. Rare and valuable."

"Good . . . although I don't know this artist. What are you doing now? Hanging around campus for a while?"

"Well, I need to stop by the library and I'm going to sit in my office with the door open in case one of my students drops by."

"I was wondering about the stuff from Eliot's office in my lab. I'll need the space eventually. They took the computer, why not the rest of Eliot's stuff?"

"Well, it's only been"—Monroe paused—"three weeks. Jim might want to look through it again before this thing is finished." Warren looked doubtful. "More importantly," Monroe continued, "do you want to jump into the investigation again?"

"Sure, what's up? I should mention that Sheryl James, my chair, told me it would be unwise to be seen with you."

Monroe laughed out loud. "Now you. *Unwise*. Is that what she said?"

"Yes. I suppose she thinks I could be suspended like you."

"Or someone told her to pass on the message."

"I could ask her where it's coming from. She seemed embarrassed. Tried to make it sound casual."

"These department heads. Sounds like Jake, although in my case it was already a done deal." Monroe watched a couple of chickadees bouncing around on a pine tree for a few seconds. "Look, Warren, she's right. Someone *is* watching me. And they've seen us together. Possibly talking in The Buzz or when we questioned Mildred. They might think you're nosing around too much."

Warren flashed a sneaky smile. "I like it," he said. "Noticed, for a change."

"Yeah, but don't push it. You're good with the computer and you can work out of sight at home."

"On what, for instance?"

"A couple of things. I'd like to know more about Spelt's travel. The staff in the dean's office think that his travel on university business coordinates with Chiara's trips."

"It may just be good planning. Nothing wrong unless the university's covering Chiara's expenses."

"It's worth checking. Margo Johnson is pretty sharp. It's mainly coming from her although it's true she's not a big fan of Spelt. But he has expenses. What if he has dipped into university funds?"

"Well, if it came out it, it would make the university look hapless, unable to manage itself. And promoting a thief to be acting president is worse. It would ruin him and make the chancellor and BOG look like idiots. Where should I look?"

"Not sure," Monroe said. "I'll see what Meyer has from looking into the records of the Dean's Research Fund."

Warren frowned. "Ask him then. What do you need me for?"

"You could check into Chiara's pattern of travel. Go back a couple of years to when she won the competition in Toronto. She was twelve or thirteen. Remember it?"

"Sure. It was a big deal."

"Well, that's our starting point. After that, she got invitations to appear with some orchestras and fellowships to attend master classes."

"Right," Warren said. "I'll just check for articles in the *Sun*. But what would Meyer do with this?"

"Simple accountant stuff. Look for correlations."

"What about university procedures?"

"I think they keep a closer eye on faculty than administrators. Meyer will sniff out faked invoices and the like. I'm not saying it will be easy. But with the authority deans have it would be possible to piggyback onto another grant. A memorandum to travel to a conference or to fund graduate students to work as research assistants would do the trick. Funds would be dispersed without a lot of paperwork or second-guessing. It's considered a perk for administrators."

"How do you know this stuff?"

Monroe paused as if caught off guard. "Not sure I do. Maybe I picked some of it up from Luce when she became associate dean. It's not a secret, but not exactly out in the open. Maybe I'm being unfair."

"Maybe a grey area. Not spelled out but a matter of judgment, trust, good faith."

"Crossing those lines would have been enough to get Eliot riled up. Cancer implies sickness of character."

"Well," Warren said, seeming to warm to the scenario, "scamming travel expenses over two or three years isn't an accidental slip-up. What else do you want me to check into? You said a couple of things."

"Remember we saw Turner sitting with Renwick, the IT guy, in The Buzz this morning? I'd like to find more about what those two have in common." Monroe looked toward a dishcloth perched at the edge of the counter. How about this? Renwick is something of a weasel, he can be intimidated. What if Jim sent Ravi to have a word with him?

Warren said nothing but smiled.

Monroe took out his phone and tapped out a message to Jim. Then he glanced toward the far end of the quad and saw that Spelt was now heading back their way with his two companions. Even from this distance he could see the smiles. Everything seemed friendly and normal. Except, of course, for his own situation.

33

Monroe unlocked his bike, strapped on his gym bag, and pedalled past student residences toward the path that circles the lake. He wasn't paying much attention until, at the student residences, he heard familiar voices. On a patch of grass in front of Greenlaw Hall, he saw Rob and Farshad tossing a frisbee. "Hi, Professor," Rob called. "Are you back, then?"

Monroe stopped. "Not quite." He gave a little laugh trying to sound confident. "Soon, I hope. But email me if you've got any questions." They nodded nearly in unison, with sympathetic expressions.

"This suspension, it's so ridiculous," Farshad said. "A case of scapegoating. Rob and I have started a petition."

"I appreciate that. A lot." Monroe paused. "Hey, there is something you guys could help me with. A general question about social media. What if I'm trying to get a list of a performer's appearances or concerts? Is that the sort of thing you would find on Facebook?"

"Maybe," Rob said. "But access might be screened unless you're a friend."

"Except," Farshad added, "a performer might have a website or a fan page on something like Instagram."

Rob turned toward Farshad. "We—or I, if Farshad's too busy—could help you check someone out."

"Thanks," Monroe said. "I might check back with you but I should be able to take it from here."

Getting back up to speed, Monroe made a mental note to phone Warren when he got home. He could check Chiara's fan page or website—she must have one—to get her travel info.

At a fork in the trail Monroe took the gravel path to the Beaver Lake loop, which passed by the rowing club and the Vancouver Music Academy. Near the main building, Monroe stopped to watch a couple of tall, muscular guys put a rowing shell into the water. As they began to glide into open water, he admired the converted mansion, now the VMA, where young musicians from the region came for advanced training. As he was about to resume his ride, an older Subaru station wagon moved slowly toward the parking area at the academy. The car door opened and from it emerged a shock of grey hair, spiking erratically, perched on the tall, pencil-thin frame of Alex Morton. *He must be seventy-five,* Monroe thought, *and looks pretty spry. Music must be good for you.*

Without thinking, Monroe called and pedalled closer. Alex squinted his way and gave a tentative wave, seeming unsure who had greeted him. At the car, Monroe removed his bike helmet and introduced himself.

"Ah, yes, Professor Monroe. Call me Alex. We've met, I recall, but briefly at one of those Town and Gown occasions." Morton grimaced.

"I don't much like them either. I also attend your recitals when I can. Always impressive."

"Thank you. In fact, I'm rarely aware of anyone in the audience. The music absorbs me, trying to play as the composer intended."

"Oh?"

"Well, it's true. Performing a Beethoven sonata is never routine." Morton glanced at his watch. "Did you want to see me about anything in particular?"

"I'm helping Inspector Martino investigate President Eliot's death. Not directly, just a kind of liaison with the university. He wanted me to ask about Chiara Spelt's trajectory as a musician."

"Evan Spelt himself is the man for that question. He keeps a close watch over his daughter and, as chair of our board of directors, on those of us who teach her."

Surprised, Monroe managed a bland expression. "Chair. I had no idea. How does he do it? All the more reason not to bother him when he's so busy."

Morton cracked a sly smile as if pleased to be in on a conspiracy. "Well, just between the two of us, he sometimes doesn't always get it done."

Monroe nodded but said nothing.

"Too much on his plate, especially now that he's president." Morton shook his head. "Last Friday, for instance, he didn't arrive at our annual fundraiser until everyone was leaving. I wasn't too pleased. The snowstorm, he said. By the way, is this something for his investiture ceremony? I suppose I should attend."

"Oh no, there won't be one. Not now. Spelt is *acting* president. The university will need to do a formal search before appointing a new president. Spelt likely will be a candidate."

Morton, shaking his head, leaned against his car. "Yes, yes. Procedures. Quite correct. And there are the circumstances of dear Peter's death—a decent flute player, you know—to sort out."

"Flute player? I had no idea. . . . But back to Chiara—"

"Right. You wanted to know about her trajectory as a musician. She's become a bit of a celebrity, especially since winning the Montreal Allegro Competition. Allegro, you know, means quick and bright, a style that naturally fits young musicians. Unheard of for a cellist to win. The cello is a soulful instrument. A pianist, playing a first or third movement of a Mozart concerto, almost always wins the Allegro."

"Wasn't there a complaint about awarding her the prize? Something about a divided jury and a bribe paid to one of the judges?"

"Yes, a bit of silliness. One of the jury complained she got unfair advantage by playing Haydn." Morton laughed. "Rubbish. Harder, not easier, to win with Haydn. As for the bribe, I doubt it. Nothing was ever proven."

"This was two years ago? In October?"

"Maybe a bit less. But I'm not so good on dates."

"What were your early impressions of Chiara?"

"A natural. Gifted and motivated. Unusual that she wanted to play the cello from the word go. I remember asking her why and she had seen a film of Jacqueline du Pré playing the Elgar. Imagine, just like that."

"But I thought she took piano from you."

"Oh, they all do. The piano is the foundation. Students learn harmonics, texture, pacing, articulation to sensitize them to nuances of compositions. With Bach, melody, harmony, and counterpoint can be in play all at the same time. We start with chords, the modulation of the left with the right hand on the keyboard. It's physical but not athletic. Not *only* athletic. Learning to touch the keys translates to the brain and feeds back again to the fingers. A huge part of the brain, you see, is delegated to managing the hands. So we give a lot of time to piano. Some conservatories—I won't name them—can produce a kind of robotic perfection in students who study only their instrument and can play all the notes with facility but woodenly, without learning to modulate touch or experiment with playful touches, and thus lack intuitive range that finds passages of angst, sorrow, and regret or of joy and optimism . . . but I'm going on now—"

"No, I'm interested. And Chiara has developed this?"

"She's getting there." Morton chuckled. "Of course she's not Jacqueline du Pré but neither am I Murray Perahia."

Morton thought for a minute. "Musicians develop at their own pace and some stop developing. Abruptly, almost over night. But a few go to levels the rest of us can barely imagine, much less get to. Usually, they make that journey alone after surpassing all their teachers. We don't pressure them; we don't know how they get there. I've tried to explain this to Evan Spelt, but he seems to think he can push Chiara to some higher level."

Monroe started to thank Morton and back away as if to resume his ride, then stopped. "I read about the Japanese musician who was donating that valuable violin. What a tragedy—"

"Aiko Tanaka. Just awful, we're devastated. She was a dear friend, a gifted violinist. But an innocent, a trusting soul, and I worried about her. I wasn't able to reach her on the weekend so I called the bed and breakfast where she stayed. I just don't know what to say . . ."

"Do you think the violin can be recovered? Inspector Martino told me it was stolen over the weekend."

Morton's face fell. "That was partially my fault. I changed the combination in our safe where it was stored. Only Aiko and I knew it. I made her promise to memorize it but apparently she didn't get beyond keeping it on a note in her wallet."

"Would anyone have known the note was there?"

"Well, the office staff knew about it and some of our students might have known because it was seen as a little joke."

"Is it possible that someone overheard some of this joking?"

"Well yes. Parents come to pick up their children and chat with staff. I think the board was meeting that day."

"Could you ask your staff to make a list of people who were around that day? Oh, and one more question about Chiara before I go. Is it the case that a new instrument can make a big difference in a young musician's development?"

"Of course. Chiara outgrew her old instrument and has been using one on loan. It has made a big difference. Her playing in the upper register has been more refined. But now she must get a new instrument. The loan period is about to run out. Her father has consulted me and I've recommended an instrument made by Samuel Zygmuntowicz. One of the best. Isaac Stern and Joshua Bell have used his violins. Modern instruments can be excellent. Even Jacqueline du Pré started using a modern cello toward the end of her career."

"What would one of these modern instruments cost compared, say, to a Strad?"

"Oh, not that much. Thirty or forty grand for a new one but triple that for one with a distinguished provenance. Stern's violin, for example."

34

■■

At home, Monroe threw together a Greek salad with plenty of feta and slathered it with olive oil from the Brofferio villa near Florence. Monroe eyed the half-full bottle with the hope that Carlo might send another bottle soon. Pulling a chunk of Manchego from the cheese drawer, he put it on the cutting board with yesterday's baguette.

As Monroe ate, he looked at the matrix of leaves, vines, and grapes outside his window and watched a flock of bushtits flitting in and out. He thought again about his conversation with Alex Morton. Would he remember to get that list of people at the academy who might have known about Tanaka's note with the safe combination in her wallet? Monroe had started to text Jim to follow up on it when Jim phoned. Ravi would be coming to campus to talk to Renwick, Jim said, and could also stop by the Academy.

Monroe closed the paper. Forking a chunk of feta and pushing it through a pool of olive oil, he thought again about Spelt's travel. Possibly Margo and her colleagues were only letting off steam about a boss they weren't fond of.

Now what? Monroe reached for a pad of paper and began to brainstorm. He wrote *Spelt travel* in the middle with a circle around it. Then to the sides: *Chiara, Margo, Warren,* and *Meyer,* all with lines connecting to Spelt travel. Two quick raps on the back door interrupted him.

It was Warren. Monroe motioned him in as he flicked open the lock. "What's up? Hungry?" Monroe waved toward the table. "Bread and cheese and Greek salad. Check out the olives. Calamatas from Petros's uncle's orchard in Spitakia. Or coffee."

"Coffee's fine. I'm not staying long. Just on my way home and wanted to give you the dope on Chiara's travel. Six guest appearances with orchestras since she won the competition in Montreal. Some bragging online about trips for master classes. Maybe not all of them. Her teacher at the conservatory might know for sure. Is it important?"

"I don't know. Could be. At least we've got the concert dates. I can ask Alex Morton if necessary. In fact, I just ran into him on the ride home."

"Hope he's OK."

"Very funny.

"So you took the scenic route and chatted with him. I thought he was . . . uhh . . . preoccupied . . . in his own world."

"A bit, maybe. Once you get him talking he's sharp. Devastated about the Japanese woman on Grouse. She was a friend. I asked him about Chiara."

"And?"

"'Talented kid' and all that."

"Oh, I've got some news. I asked Myron Scott, our genius PhD student, to look at Eliot's hard drive to see if we missed anything. He found another hard drive embedded in the main drive."

"What?"

"An odd mix according to Myron. Pretty advanced with several gatekeepers but the passwords are amateurish. Some pretty obvious, one his social insurance number backwards another his grandfather's middle name and birth year. Also, the files were encrypted. Probably some off-the-shelf program. He thinks he can break it. But from folder titles it's mainly his correspondence with Mrs. Kerr and the minister. Also something labeled 'University Renewal.' Anyway, Myron's working on it."

Monroe rubbed his forehead. "Renewal? Why be secretive about that?"

"Probably just keeping it under wraps till it's ready," Warren said.

"That must be. A lot of politicking going on behind the scenes. Stuff we didn't imagine. For one thing, Kerr cast the deciding vote for president in the BOG meeting after making a deal with Eliot."

Warren blinked. "She admitted that?"

"Yup. But it won't be on the record. Once there's a majority, there's usually a motion to make it unanimous so that becomes the official version. I'm not sure it's worth trying to find out more from Kerr. What would I ask her?"

"I'm surprised you got this much. She always has a little smirk on her face as if she's got all the cards."

Monroe didn't respond. He was trying to think. "Whatever else was involved, her throwing the presidency to Eliot had everything to do with the gallery. Something visionary, improve the collection, better links to the art history program. But to get that done she has to live another day. Which means a new term or two on the BOG."

Warren nodded. "Her vote for Eliot in the BOG and dealings with him as president fit."

"Politics again," Monroe said. "And her next move was, and is, to secure another term on the BOG. It's all a little fuzzy because also in play were Eliot's plans to oppose the minister's project to expand applied science, engineering, and industry-linked programs at the expense of the humanities, liberal arts, and theoretical sciences. To a degree, maybe, but not at the expense of the gallery and the arts. Kerr and Eliot were allies but his game was more complicated and her game fell apart when he died."

"For Kerr, I would think it would come down to trying to lock down the gallery so it couldn't be touched," Warren said. "And leave humanities, history, and political science to sink or swim."

35

What was wrong with him? Monroe awoke late Sunday morning thinking not about Eliot's death but Ms. Tanaka's. Why was she left on the mountain to die? The theft of the violin was one thing, a motive. But why kill her? So strange that she'd gone alone to the mountain.

Monroe decided to clear his head by walking. After only one coffee he pulled on a fleece and started out. After a half hour he found himself in Warren's neighbourhood. *My best sounding board,* he thought, as he cut through a small park where some small kids were playing on swings. A parent, looking bored, gave him a wave, which he returned distractedly before stopping himself and really looking at those happy faces swinging high in the air and then falling back to earth with squeals and laughter.

He covered the rest of the way by cutting through the woods. Warren looked surprised when he opened the door. "What are you doing here? It's Sunday."

"I know. I'm out for a walk and thought I'd drop by."

"I don't think so. You're not the dropping-by type."

Monroe smiled. "I am. But I also need to talk about Eliot."

"Again? I'm getting tired of this. I have a report to write." Warren looked at the table with some papers on it. "OK, what is it?"

"Spelt."

"Yeah, what about him?"

"I think he's a suspect."

Warren stared at Monroe. "Well, maybe, but there are others. OK, he's self-important, unlikable, and he *possibly* cheated on his expense account. I don't much *like* him. But that's not enough. You should talk about it with the inspector, not me."

"I know it's hypothetical. And I haven't worked it all out. That's why I want your opinion."

"OK. I'm having another cup of coffee. Want some?"

Monroe nodded. As Warren got up to pour the coffee, Monroe shifted in his chair and pulled out his notebook, although he didn't open it. "First point. Whoever killed the Japanese tourist, their motive had to be—"

"Stop. I thought we were talking about Eliot."

Monroe rubbed his palm over his forehead. "We are. But maybe there's a connection—"

"OK, go on."

"Think about it this way. First, we have Eliot's death; second, Hans Meyer's camper blown up; third, I'm suspended from teaching and offered a trip to anywhere; fourth, Hans is put on PTSD leave; fifth, Ms. Tanaka dies on Grouse mountain."

Warren just sat there for a minute with a sour look on his face. "Yes? And this adds up to something?"

"Tanaka again. A clear motive: the violin."

"Well, it's worth a lot of money. Robbery gone wrong."

"Yes, but think it through. Tanaka agrees to meet someone she trusts at an odd place like Grouse Mountain. That person knows about the violin, that it is in the safe at the academy, and knows Tanaka has the combination to the safe. Spelt, as chair of the board of the academy and father of Chiara, fits the description of such a person. He arrives late, it's beginning to snow hard, and he says they should get off the mountain and talk in the city. On the pretext of walking her back to the gondola, he walks her *away* from it. He tires her out enough that she's a bit out of it, sits her down next to the tower, and tells her he's going for help. But first he grabs her purse—she's not paying attention now—and takes the note with the combination to the safe. He also takes her cash and tosses the purse into the salal then walks to the gondola, rides down the mountain, and drives away. He then goes to the academy to make an appearance at the annual fundraiser. He is late, the meeting is breaking up. Alex Morton is annoyed and doesn't quite believe his excuse of being delayed by the snow. Either then or on the Saturday or Sunday, Spelt opens the safe, and takes the violin. He plans to fence the violin for big bucks to pay for Chiara's new cello."

"Well, it's a nice story but—"

"I know. It's still rough. But I have motive and opportunity. He missed the meeting."

"Just because he was late for the fundraiser doesn't mean he was on Grouse with Tanaka."

"True. But he could have been. Is it enough for Jim to question him? Pressure him for an alibi?"

Warren looked doubtful. "He'll say he was stuck in the snow.

❖

Fifteen or twenty minutes later Monroe resumed his walk. He cut through the playground again and sat on a bench next to a grass field. Quiet here, he thought. A good place to think. But then his phone rang. It was Jim.

"Breaking news. Last night I sent Ravi and Hudson to Renwick's house with a couple of uniforms and flashing lights. No problemo getting him to talk. His version is that it was Turner's idea to do the hatchet job on you. Turner took the photo and wrote the text, Renwick Photoshopped it and sent it to the school paper. It was Turner's revenge because he thinks you derailed his institute with Eliot. Can you believe it? You guys play for keeps. He had gone to Spelt about it and Spelt put him onto Renwick. So Spelt was in on it unless Renwick is lying. He said he thought of it as a joke, claims he does freelance work like this all the time, mainly designs and prints business cards for faculty and staff. Turner paid him $300. Gotta go now, another meeting . . . Yes, I know it's Sunday."

Monroe's "thanks" came too late; Jim had already hung up.

❖

Monroe resumed his walk, his pace comfortable but his mind chattering. He was almost surprised to come in sight of the familiar cluster of shops at Nelson Cove. It wouldn't hurt, he thought, to pick up some sourdough multigrain at Spurling's Bakery. He didn't recognize the white SUV parked in front but as soon as he stepped inside he realized it belonged to Howard Davis.

"Chancellor," Monroe said. He was aware that he was speaking more loudly than normal and his tone was not exactly friendly.

Davis, peering through the tunnel of a grey Northlake U. hoody, smiled.

"Hello, Professor Monroe. I see we share excellent taste in bread."

Monroe pulled back from the edge of incivility and muttered something about the multigrain hearth loaves made with natural yeast. Only two were left in the display case.

"How are you keeping?" Davis asked. "I imagine the suspension isn't doing you much good. Or your students. The whole thing is ridiculous, if you ask me. The board should never have agreed to it."

Monroe did a double take. "I don't understand. I was told it was your idea."

Davis frowned. "Who told you that? The opposite is true."

"Evan Spelt told me, explaining that you were concerned about the public perception of things on campus."

Davis shook his head. "Well I can't say too much about the BOG's meeting, but it was contentious and a close vote and Evan spoke most eloquently to the point you just mentioned. The public perception of it. Evan is doing a good job, of course, but perhaps is still a little insecure these first days—"

"You mean the board was not of one mind?"

"I've probably said too much already. But I'm a rough and ready kind of guy who believes in straight talk. And you deserve to know something. Officially, of course, the session dealing with your suspension and Hans Meyer's PTSD leave were in camera, confidential, as are all discussions about university employees. I can assure you, though, it was professionally handled and suspension was agreed on reluctantly and by a narrow vote."

Davis picked up his bread, three baguettes in a single large bag that he tucked under one arm. "Believe me, Professor Monroe, I wish you the best and, to say the least, I'm not pleased to hear what you just told me. I will try to see that you're reinstated as soon as possible."

36

※

On his way home, Monroe thought about Spelt. Somehow, using Turner and Renwick, he was behind the dirty trick to justify his suspension. And probably getting Meyer off campus, too. Way more extreme, though, if blowing up his camper was part of it. Worth it to destroy Meyer's research? Surely Turner and Renwick were not part of that. What would they know about explosives? What about that character Aziz who was cleaning the carpet in Eliot's office? Does he fit in somewhere?

It was nearly midnight when Monroe decided to turn on his computer to look for a Banyon in Chicago, the name Mildred blurted out Monday. He tried various spellings and the internet didn't yield anything "Thomas and Robert Banyon" appeared in connection with the Chicago Symphony Orchestra. They were patrons and supporters who had endowed the Nicholas Banyon concert-master position in 2002, in honour of their late father, a composer and musician. They identified themselves as *brokers of fine string instruments.*

※

The Vancouver International Airport was relatively quiet for mid-morning on a Monday. Monroe looked down at his boarding pass, registered that it was October 18, his father's birthday, and wondered if his flight to Chicago would leave at 10:30, as promised. He had a carry-on bag and not much else. Just before boarding the plane, he texted Jim: *at YVR and headed for Chicago, be in touch later. Monroe.*

On the flight, Monroe pulled out his notebook. Under the heading

"Banyons," there was a phone number, and the details he'd found online. If Spelt had a meeting with them, he was possibly shopping for a new cello for Chiara. That's all he had. Not much. Ideally best not to go nosing around without a local contact. As the plane approached O'Hare Airport, he mulled over his next move.

Nothing came to mind but the obvious: check into a hotel, the Bayshore, a block from Lake Michigan. He tried Jim's cell, but he didn't pick up. He then walked over to Michigan Avenue, where, next to the Art Institute, the Symphony Center was located. At the door he could hear the muffled sounds of the orchestra rehearsing. Several people in the lobby were looking around. From a guichet a man in owlish glasses made eye contact. "Help you, sir?"

Monroe knew he looked like a tourist but didn't care. "Is that Maestro Muti rehearsing the orchestra?"

"No, sir. It is Sir Simon Rattle, here this week as guest conductor." His blasé expression became animated. "The orchestra's energized. Can you hear it? We haven't heard Beethoven's sixth since 1991, when Maestro Solti conducted it."

"Any seats left?"

"Just a few singles." He peered at a computer screen. "One good one, row 19, seat 103, the centre of the orchestra section. There are fourteen others but all in the upper balcony. This one is $135."

Monroe whipped out his wallet, paid with his Visa, tucked his ticket away. "By the way, I'm trying to locate a gentleman named Banyon who is a broker of musical instruments. Do you know of him?"

"Of course. The Banyon brothers. Big supporters of the orchestra. You must be looking for an instrument yourself. Let's see, if you go to—"

"Thanks, I have a number I got online." Monroe stepped away and dialed but the number was no longer in service. The clerk, still observing, called out "for their current number, check the bulletin board at Roosevelt University's Music Conservatory. It's just up the street."

At the conservatory, Monroe walked into a high-ceilinged foyer with students clustered in a half dozen small groups. He approached a threesome: a tall young man with thin arms and thick hair, an equally tall woman with poor posture holding a violin case, and a middle-aged man in a threadbare jacket with elbow patches. They were talking but seemed bored with each other. When he asked for directions to the bulletin board, Thin Arms spoke up quickly in a reedy voice. "Down the corridor, sir, on your right past some practice rooms. It's in what's supposed to be a lounging area. You'll see why no one goes there." His companions smiled knowingly.

Monroe soon saw what the young man meant: the bulletin board was next to a broken-down sofa and a battered coffee table with old magazines and papers scattered about. Worse even than a dentist's office. He worked his way around the board clockwise until he finally came to the Banyons's business card— embossed, minimalist, classy— askew at four o'clock on the overcrowded board. It read *Thomas and Robert Banyon, ancient and modern violins, violas, and cellos. By appointment only*. No address but a different phone number and Monroe jotted it down.

It was now after four. Monroe made his way to the park behind the Art Institute thinking he would make time to view their collection of Impressionists. But neither did he have time to loiter about as if on holiday. For one thing, he couldn't afford too many nights at the Bayshore even though, by Chicago Loop standards, his tiny room was cheap at $320 a night.

He shivered as the wind coming off the lake cut through his light jacket. Just then he heard his phone ring. "Ah, Jim. Just a minute I'm putting it on speaker. It's a bit chilly here. I'm sitting on a bench by Lake Michigan."

"What the hell are you—"

Monroe interrupted. "Feeling free as a bird. I checked into the Bayshore Hotel. Write it down. *Muy caro, amigo*, in case you want to cover my costs."

"Forget it. Just tell me what you're up to."

"I'm trying to track down the Banyon brothers. They're dealers in high-end instruments. I think they sold Spelt a cello."

"So what? We're trying to find out who killed Eliot."

"I know. I think the violin could get us there."

Jim was silent and Monroe waited. "Are you still there?"

"Thinking. What in the hell do you mean?"

Monroe laughed. "I've got an idea that Spelt stole the violin in order to get a cello for his daughter. And he may be behind Eliot's death and my suspension as well. I know you've been busy with opioid trafficking. Rightly so. Since I'm suspended from teaching, I'm—"

"We need evidence. I think you might be a bit over your head. Look, there's a guy who may be able to help. His name is Roosevelt King. He runs the gang squad on the Chicago Police Force. He knows the city. I've met him a few times at conferences, a good guy. He can help keep you out of trouble."

"Thanks, I'll call him. I've got to go now. I'm freezing and my battery's about to give out."

"Don't do anything crazy. Call me tomorrow."

⊞

Back at the hotel, Monroe plugged in his phone and called the number he copied from the bulletin board.

After two rings, a polite, business-like voice answered. "Banyon speaking."

"Mr. Banyon, I would like to set up a consultation."

"Of course. And what is it you're interested in?"

"My name is Bruce Monroe. I'm a professor from Northlake University in Vancouver and I'm in Chicago only for a few days. I'm seeking your help with some research I'm doing. It would only take a few moments of your time."

"I see. Well, today is not possible. My brother is out of town and I have an engagement tonight. I have time tomorrow, the 19th. Shall we say 10:00 a.m.?"

"That would be fine."

"We're at 914 Wagner, a small street near Clark and Roosevelt. Ring the bell at the gate. Goodbye, Professor Monroe."

Monroe googled the address and saw that it was only a few blocks from the hotel. He checked his watch and decided it was probably too late to phone Roosevelt King. Besides, he was hungry and by tomorrow Jim will have spoken to him.

At the reception desk Monroe played the tourist and asked straight up for advice on a restaurant. The clerk eyed Monroe's clothing: a fairly casual jacket, no tie, and a Mountain Equipment hooded coat. "Miller's Pub on Wabash Street is a good bet. Go out the front door, turn right and then left at the first street. Straight ahead five or six blocks. Prices are good and a selection of beers on tap to die for." His eyes glazed as he mentioned the beer. "Best to get there early because folks going to the symphony—not counting the after-work happy hour crowd—will be there. Even some members of the orchestra. They're not that well paid, you know."

Monroe glanced down at his boat shoes and figured he had been categorized with the not-well-paid types. Walking briskly, he was at Miller's in ten minutes. He found a small table next to the wall and picked up a menu. Too many brews, mostly craft beers with odd names. He finally took the easy way out and ordered a Stella.

As he studied the menu, he was torn between white fish almandine and a regular burger, thick-cut fries, and coleslaw. Glancing up, he made eye contact with a dark-haired woman in a black dress, alone but with a violin case propped on an adjoining chair. She was picking at a plate of white fish. It looked pretty good although she seemed distracted. Monroe smiled and she returned the smile but then looked away.

The waiter returned and plunked a frosty glass in front of Monroe, who eyed it gratefully. "Decided yet?"

"Yes. I'll have the regular burger. But with feta and avocado. And apple pie for dessert. And bring me an espresso, please, with the pie."

The waiter scribbled down the order with a nod of approval and turned quickly away. But somehow, in the process, he upended the chair from the adjoining table. The violin flew into the air. Monroe jumped forward and caught it. In doing so he tipped over his beer, which splattered the lady with the violin.

"I'm so sorry," Monroe said as the woman wiped off her dress.

"Nonsense. You saved my violin. The dress will survive."

The waiter standing by looked sheepish. "It was *my* fault. Just a minute and I'll clean everything up." He picked up the fallen chair and removed the soaking tablecloths as well as the lady's plate, and ran off. In a minute he was back with two busboys, one mop, fresh tablecloths for the tables, and a clean towel for the woman. A manager then arrived and told the woman and Monroe that their meals were on the house. "We will bring you a fresh order of sole as soon as possible, madam, and please bring your cleaning bill to me."

When all was back to normal, Monroe lifted his beer to the violinist in a kind of sardonic toast as if to say, *Well, I guess we survived it.* She smiled and raised her water glass. "Thank you again for your quick reflexes. My name is Eleanor Schwartz. I play in the violin section of the CSO. I would like to offer you a ticket to one of our concerts."

"Bruce Monroe. I'm glad to meet you. In fact, I'm already attending the concert tonight." Monroe reached into his pocket and flipped open his wallet. "Row 19, seat 27."

She paused briefly to picture that location. "That's a great seat. Maybe a complimentary ticket some other time then. I'll look for you tonight. I think you'll enjoy the concert. We're excited that Maestro Rattle is here." Eleanor looked at her watch. "I must be going."

Monroe nodded. "Of course . . . uh, if you're not busy after the concert, would you like to meet for a coffee or drink? I'm afraid I'm only here for a day or two checking on a little mystery. Maybe you can help me."

Eleanor shrugged her shoulders. "I doubt that, but I'm intrigued. Come down to the front of the concert hall and I'll pack up my stuff and meet you there."

By the time Monroe's burger arrived he had finished his beer and was thinking he should have another. The waiter set his plate down and once again apologized for the earlier mishap. "They've added some new tables last week and I'm still getting used to them," he said.

"No harm done," Monroe said.

"Another beer?"

Monroe paused. "Yes, one of your craft beers. What about Goose Island?"

The waiter nodded approvingly. "One of my favorites, brewed ten blocks from here."

At the concert Monroe looked for Eleanor as the members of the orchestra began to drift to their places. When she saw him, she gave him a smile and a wave and then settled into her seat, flipped open the score, and ran through some short passages. She was two rows behind the concertmaster, which seemed to put her five down from the top spot, if that was an indication of the orchestra's hierarchy.

An older woman in braids sat down next to Eleanor and the two of them started an animated conversation, pointing to the score with spurts of playing as if reviewing passages requiring special attention. Monroe settled back, his eyes flitting between the musicians taking their places and people laying claim to their seats. In due course the lights dimmed and the crowd hushed.

The concertmaster appeared and moved toward his place in short quick steps in shoes that seemed to be too tight. Violin in hand, he gave a lord-of-the-strings bow before facing the orchestra as the oboe sounded a clear A and everyone tuned their instrument. A few seconds later, Sir Simon Rattle strode out, his curly grey hair not quite out of control, but close, a frame for his still youthful face. His expression was relaxed yet serious, conveying to orchestra and audience anticipation for the encounter with Beethoven. The members of the orchestra beamed with pleasure as they watched his every move and the audience only reluctantly stopped their applause.

And then Sir Simon dropped the baton and Monroe let the opener, Wagner's Tannhäuser Overture, take him away. From time to time he became aware of the directions and facial expressions the maestro, turning from side to side, used to pull from the orchestra the sounds he was seeking. He zoomed in on the cellos and on Eleanor and the violins even more often. It was impressive as a warm-up. Then the two massive E-flat major chords opened the first movement of the Beethoven. It was a rocket launch, music that shot one into a higher orbit. Monroe was spent when the symphony ended. The audience brought Sir Simon back six times and members of the orchestra beamed as if they knew they had come together in a special way.

Eleanor appeared after most of the audience had filed out. Monroe looked at her closely. "You look beautiful," he paused. "I mean, younger . . . energized . . . not . . ."

Eleanor smiled. "Not what? You're blushing, you know."

Monroe shook his head. "The concert was amazing. . . . It transformed you, all of us."

For a second a flicker of sadness came into her expression. "I've heard that before. Not so nicely put, though. The music courses through me. Playing in a great orchestra, playing Beethoven, it's better than a religious experience. It *is* one. And then, so I've been told, I revert to being plain old me."

"No way, not plain. Just back down to earth. I was in a trance myself." Monroe heard himself prattling on and thought it was time to take a deep breath. "Here, let me carry your violin." Monroe smiled. "Trust me with it? I won't drop it."

"I trust you," Eleanor said. "You rescued it in the restaurant. For tonight, I'm thinking of a quiet place called Santa Barbara. We can have a conversation there and you can tell me about this mystery you mentioned. Leo, one of the owners, plays jazz piano. He's mostly self taught, a genius, really. We were at the institute together until he dropped out. He developed a problem with his left hand and opened this bar with his aunt. He's recovered now. We've played duets a few times when I've drunk enough wine."

"Like Grappelli and Oscar Peterson."

Eleanor rolled her eyes. "Oh, to be in that universe."

At the bar, a tall man with high cheekbones, a sharp nose, and curly black hair rushed over to greet them. He embraced Eleanor and then, before she could introduce Monroe, stuck out his hand. "Leo Santini. You're coming from the concert, no? How was it?"

"Bruce Monroe." Before Monroe could get another word in, Eleanor blurted out, "Brilliant, you're going to love it."

"Simon Rattle conducting Beethoven? My idea of a peak experience." Leo sat Eleanor and Monroe down at a choice table. "The usual?" he asked Eleanor.

She smiled and nodded her head. "I'll get it started while you"—he looked at Monroe—"check the menu."

"Leo knows that I'm always hungry after concerts. I always get the same thing: an omelette with emmental cheese shaved on top and parsley and the house Chardonnay." On Leo's next pass, Monroe ordered the same and two glasses appeared almost immediately.

Taking his first sip, Monroe looked over at Eleanor's violin. "It must be an expensive instrument. You seem to keep it in sight at all times."

"We all do. It's a good instrument . . . good enough. My parents helped me buy it, but it wasn't that expensive."

"Mind if I ask how much? I'm curious because a colleague of mine might have contacted the Banyon Brothers about a cello for his daughter. Do you know them?"

"Not personally. They're known to sell beautiful but expensive instruments." Eleanor glanced toward her violin. "Mine cost $30,000, counting the bow and the case. It came from a dealer in Scotland."

Monroe nodded. "And what did you get for that?"

"Well, its provenance is a little uncertain, but the people at Martin Swan, where I bought it, think it was made by a Frenchman named Langonet who modeled it on a Bergonzi design. I love it, actually. It's very smooth, projects well, and is especially pure in the high registers."

Monroe's eyes widened. "Bergonzi. Carlo Bergonzi." It was more an exclamation than a question.

"Yes. Stradivari's associate. You've heard of him?"

"I sure have," Monroe said. And then in a rush he told Eleanor about Ms. Tanaka's death and the theft of her Bergonzi violin, about Eliot's murder, about his suspension from teaching. She listened intently without interruption. "I could go on," he said, "but the main thing is to see if that Bergonzi violin surfaced here in Chicago. I have an appointment tomorrow to see one of the Banyons."

Eleanor shook her head. "The Banyons, from what I've heard, wouldn't touch an instrument like that. A 1737 Bergonzi inscribed to Stradivari would price this instrument in the stratosphere."

38

The next morning, Monroe showered and took his time with a plate of huevos rancheros, a double order of multigrain toast, and a pot of mediocre coffee in the hotel dining room. Then he walked toward the Banyons. He was a little early so he sat on a bench at the edge of a pocket park and called Jim.

"Been in contact with Roosevelt yet?" Jim asked.

"I'll call Roosevelt when I'm done."

"Better call him now. I just spoke to him. He said the Banyons aren't very talkative. Not to strangers. He's willing to help."

"OK, but it's short notice. What's his number again?" Monroe jotted it down and called.

King picked up on the second ring. "King speaking."

"Hello, Sergeant. It's Bruce Monroe from Vancouver. I'm about to—"

"Ah, Monroe. Just spoke to my buddy Martino. He said you wanted to see the Banyons. Let's put it this way: they can be prickly."

"Jim said you offered to facilitate if that's the right word. But I'm supposed to be there at 10."

"Ouch. In seven minutes. OK, I can do it. Go ahead, I'll be there in ten."

At number 914 Monroe pressed a buzzer outside an iron gate and within a few seconds it clicked open. He entered a Japanese garden, stepping on stones that curved through a half dozen vine maples underlaid with mosses. Two stones—splendid specimens of greenish basalt, one rounded and the other pointed—played off one another as they rose a couple of feet from a gravel bed to set off the space as a complete miniaturized landscape.

At the door, a large man peered at Monroe through round, wire-rimmed glasses. He was thick and firm looking, like a tightly stuffed sausage, his

175

expression that of a well-fed owl barely tolerating an unwelcome interruption.

Yet he flipped a switch to turn on the civilities. "Come in, Professor Monroe. I am Thomas Banyon." Banyon extended his hand. "Please," he said as he gestured toward a room down a corridor. "My office." When they were seated, he said, "My brother, Robert, is in Hungary this week. May I offer you a coffee?"

"Thank you, yes."

Banyon pushed a button on the side of his desk and almost immediately an undernourished-looking young man with a receding hairline entered the room with quick, short steps. "Alexi, would you be so kind . . . two coffees, please." He looked at Monroe. "Espresso straight up or do you prefer something in it?"

Monroe caught the tone of disdain at the idea of contaminating coffee. "Yes, please. Straight." He didn't mention that Roosevelt King would be arriving momentarily.

"Use the beans that arrived yesterday," Banyon called out as Alexi left the room. Looking at Monroe, he explained: "One of our associates arrived last night with beans roasted thirty six hours ago in Vienna. They're at their best now, and will be used up in three or four days."

Monroe looked around a spare but tastefully furnished room. The spacing of the furniture bespoke a Japanese aesthetic. Bookcases, one filled with leather-bound books, lined one wall. Several trees, a palm, and a good-sized lemon, stood near a leather sofa next to large, floor-to-ceiling windows overlooking a private garden.

Banyon shifted in his chair. "How can I help you, Professor? You are a professor of history, perhaps?"

The two questions, seeming unrelated, caught Monroe off guard. "Yes, history. Of the Spanish Empire in the Americas, mainly. How did you know?"

"I observed your eyes lingering on the history section of my humble collection. They passed quickly over more technical imprints." Alexi arrived with two espressos on a tray and set them before Monroe and Banyon. As he turned to leave, a bell rang and Banyon flashed a look of annoyance at no one in particular. "The gate, Alexi. Send them away."

Banyon remained silent as he took a sip of his coffee. He seemed to be listening for anything untoward at the front door. Monroe was relieved, thinking that Roosevelt King had arrived. Alexi's words "This way, sir" announced the intruder and King stepped into the room. Banyon flipped the switch again and flashed a welcoming smile. "Sergeant King. Welcome. May I present Professor Monroe? What brings you here?"

Roosevelt King, a serious physical presence towering over both Monroe and Banyon, shook hands and then took a seat. "I'm here in support of Professor Monroe, Thomas. The Chicago force is cooperating with the Royal Canadian Mounted Police on a case they're working on. I hope you don't mind my dropping by."

"You're always welcome, Roosevelt. Robert and I owe you a lot. We were nearly ruined by those thugs running that protection racket until you put them away."

"They were a vicious bunch." Roosevelt paused as if to reshelf a bad memory. "Well, it's probably best if Professor Monroe explains how you can help him."

Monroe waited for Banyon's nod of assent and then went for it. "As part of a murder inquiry, I've been helping Inspector Jim Martino. He wanted me to ask for some details about a cello my colleague Evan Spelt may have bought from you."

Banyon raised an eyebrow. "There's not a lot to tell. It's a beautiful instrument made by Samuel Zygmuntowicz from Brooklyn. It is suitable for a musician of the highest level. Some think his instruments are as good as those made by the old masters in projection, dynamic range, and articulation. At this point, I suspect it's a better instrument than a young musician like Dr. Spelt's daughter needs, but she will grow into it. It will teach her to play to a level of refinement and passion that a lesser instrument cannot support."

It sounded like a set speech. "You make it sound like it's alive."

Banyon didn't respond directly, but a hint of a smile crossed his face as if it would be a waste of time to explain. "The instrument in question was evaluated by several musicians, including Roland and Almita Vamos at the Music Institute. Their judgment is impeccable, more than enough for any buyer."

"And what would one pay for such an instrument?"

"It's a matter of public record. This one cost $32,000 and we found a bow for less than $8,000 and a relatively inexpensive case. The total cost was $40,000, a little more with evaluation fees. A bargain."

"I suppose," Monroe said. "That's a good deal of money on a professor's salary."

"Well, I understand he is a university president."

"Yes, *acting* president, and only for the past couple of weeks. Before that, he was dean of the faculty of arts."

"I see. Well, with all due respect, this is beside the point." Banyon picked up a folder at the edge of the desk, opened it, and flipped through it. "I can only tell you that Dr. Spelt paid for his daughter's instrument with a certified cheque. Now, if you gentlemen will excuse—"

"Issued by which bank and branch?" King asked.

"Wired directly to our account at the HSBC branch on Madison Street."

King nodded. "Just down the street. But you didn't see where the money originated?"

"No," Banyon said. But he looked uneasy. "Is that all then? I'm expecting a phone call from my brother in just a few minutes."

"One more thing," Monroe said. "Would you know what sort of price range one could expect to get from a 1737 Carlo Bergonzi violin?"

Banyon did a double take. "From 1737? The year Stradivari—"

"Died, and it's inscribed to him, by the way."

Banyon threw out his hands, palms up. "Sky's the limit. Such a violin at auction in good condition should fetch a million dollars. At least. Depends on the buyer. A collector who views it as a work of art—one of a kind with that inscription—might pay twice that."

"What if that violin is stolen property?"

Banyon pushed his fingers together and then studied them. "Well, that's different. Your territory, Roosevelt. We, of course, don't deal in stolen property, so I can't say. Auction houses require evidence of provenance. So obviously the number of buyers would be limited. In truth, it would likely be handled by organized crime."

Monroe closed Banyon's gate and he and Roosevelt stepped onto the sidewalk. "Let's go for a coffee," Roosevelt said. "Basil's Coffee House is only a couple of minutes away." When they got there, Monroe saw a crowded hole in the wall with about fifty bikes outside. Inside, most of the seats were taken. It was pretty obvious who the students were. "My usual table's free, over in the corner. Most of the traffic's for takeout."

They sat down and Roosevelt said, "I'm really glad to meet Martino's friend. I got him to admit that you guys were quite the pair on your high school football team."

Monroe laughed. "Small potatoes . . . fun, though. You look like a *real* athlete. Linebacker, maybe?"

"Long time ago. University of Michigan. The injuries piled up. I was lucky to get out of it without a concussion." King shifted in his seat. "Did you notice that Banyon seemed a little embarrassed when you asked which bank issued the cheque?"

"Yeah, he didn't seem to know."

"Coffee?"

"Sure." Monroe turned to look for a waiter. But King had already made eye contact with a guy at the espresso machine. "Americano OK?" Monroe nodded and King flashed two fingers. The barista gave a thumbs-up, and in a couple of minutes brought two fresh cups to the table.

"He's good," Monroe said. "No messing around."

"Yeah, that's Basil. I busted him once for B and E. Just a kid then, sucked in by one of the gangs. We made a deal, got him away from the hood and into one of the colleges. He's never looked back. Has a talent for business, works his butt off." King looked into the distance as if mulling over a bunch of other Basils recruited by gangs, then shifted gears. "So what else can I do for you? On the phone Jim was mainly picking my brain about gangs and drug trafficking."

"He would. A lot of fentanyl getting on the street in Vancouver, even some weed laced with it, kids, street people dying. A constable shot on stakeout. I'm helping with a death at the university. Maybe two."

King raised his eyebrows and took a sip of coffee. "Why you? I can see you're not a cop."

"Couldn't help it. Became an obsession. Completely unofficial. I'm a kind of liaison to clue Jim in about the campus and its quirks. Then I was suspended from teaching. Supposedly because I was nosing around too much and not doing my job."

King nodded. "Tough one. But why are you in Chicago?"

Monroe took a sip of coffee. He hadn't prepared anything and didn't want to waste King's time. "I'm trying to find what happened to a stolen violin. Following the money trail, you see—"

"I get it, that million-dollar violin," King broke in. "It was stolen and you think it could have financed the cello you were asking about?"

"Yes."

King shook his head. "Something doesn't fit. If you're saying that an inexpensive cello—relatively inexpensive—was exchanged for the violin, I don't think so. The Banyons wouldn't do a deal like that. They're honest and decent. They've even paid for music lessons for some street kids. Thomas Banyon would never accept cash. No way, he's a money launderer."

"Not knowingly perhaps. But what about that money wired to his account?"

King tapped his fingers on the table as he thought. "Yes, just maybe. If someone fenced a million-dollar violin at about five cents on the dollar, that could cover the cello. That's the going rate for a lone wolf dealing with organized crime. And they're the only ones who could get a violin like that out of the country."

King reached into his pocket and pulled out a small note pad and a stick pen. "Let's see if I can find out about that certified cheque." He pushed the notepad toward Monroe. "Just scribble the name of the guy buying the cello."

Monroe wrote for a moment then stopped. "And the date. Let me think, I was suspended on the 11th and that day Banyon phoned to tell Spelt he had an instrument and set up an appointment for the next day. About that time, then."

King sent a text. "It's going to Bosko, our best research guy. He's good and he's fast." He leaned back in his chair. "The truth is," he added, "we're unlikely to find this violin. If the mafia boys got it, it's already gone. First stop, probably Russia."

"What about Hungary? Banyon said his brother, Robert, is there right now."

"Robert Banyon flogging a hot violin in Hungary? No way."

Monroe nodded. "How does the mafia acquire a violin like this?"

"Something this valuable they usually steal directly. Normally, they're not interested in the junk from pawn shops."

"But what happens when a pawn-shop guy hits the jackpot and knows it's too hot to handle?"

"It's possible, but rare. Most of them have a contact who passes the word. If it's worth enough, they'll give the messenger a peanut and the pawn broker a few grand. The model for this is art theft, where guys in turtlenecks who know how to fast-talk newly rich financial-sector types can end up being complicit."

Monroe didn't reply. Another dead end, it seemed. He took another sip of coffee and watched King, who had picked up his phone and was speaking softly. "OK," he said, as he put the phone down, "we're in business. I told you Bosko's fast. An account was opened on October 8 under the name The Elgar Project, Inc., with a deposit of $45,000. The deposit came as a certified cheque by Lodestone Collectables, Limited. The Elgar Project, in turn, transferred all 45K to the account of Banyon Brothers."

Monroe rubbed his chin and squinted into the distance. "So—"

"Wait. There's more. Lodestone no longer exists, can't be traced. It was a shadow company. Bosko also looked at the Banyon Brothers account and found that on October 12, the day after the 45 grand went into their account, they issued a cheque back to Mr. Spelt for $3,620 with the notation 'in trust for The Elgar Project.'"

Monroe scribbled the numbers on a napkin. "OK, that's $41,380. It covers the cello and bow. So Lodestone Collectables—"

"Somehow, your guy gets the violin into the hands of organized criminals. The big boys pay 45 grand for it and run the money through one or more shadow companies. Lodestone ends up with it, passes some to the Banyons, and they'll sell it for a million or more. Good businessmen. Meanwhile, your suspect—Spelt, isn't it?—gets a decent instrument for his daughter and has no direct contact with the money except $3,000 or so. I've got to run now. I'll let you know if I find out more about the Banyons."

39

Monroe watched King walk away. He was finished in Chicago now; he had enough to ask Spelt a few questions. Time to book a flight home but he might as well nose around a little first. Why not check a few pawnshops? Maybe he'd get lucky and find one that had been approached about the violin. He pulled out his cell and came up with a list of seventeen.

He headed for the cash register. "I think I owe you," he said to Basil.

"No way." Basil flashed a smile. "Whatever Roosevelt King and his friends get is on the house. I wouldn't be here if he hadn't got me straight."

"Well, thank him for me next time." Monroe pulled a ten out of his wallet and tucked it into a tip jar with the sign *instant karma*. "I can use some of that."

"You've got it now. Hey where're you from . . . Canada?"

"Yup, Vancouver. You've got a good ear."

"I've got a cousin in Toronto."

Monroe didn't think he sounded like someone from Toronto but let it slide. "If you were to pick some high-end pawnshops, where would you start? I'm trying to track down information about a violin that was stolen in Vancouver."

"High end?" He laughed. "Not likely. But try the east side."

Three hours later, Monroe had found three violins, all badly in need of repairs and so with no trail back to a person of interest.

Eleanor would have had a more expert opinion. Monroe phoned her to see if she wanted to meet for a drink or dinner before his flight. She picked up right away and Monroe told her about the meeting with Roosevelt King and his tour of the pawnshops. "There is a person," she said, "an estate liquidator, who sometimes posts notices on the bulletin board at the music academy. He has sold some decent violins to students. His name is Percy Black or Blackman. I'll try to contact him."

They agreed to meet at Leo's at 5:00. Until then, Monroe decided to relax on a bench in the park next to the Art Institute. As he sat there, he started to feel drowsy. His hotel room had been so noisy the night before. The garbage trucks began banging bins around at 6:00, 4:00 a.m. Vancouver time. At most, two or three hours sleep. The circadian rhythm completely messed up. A kind of sadness weighed on him now that Spelt's link to the violin was coming into focus. He could be a thief *and* a murderer, a man without pity or compassion. And yet a family man. How does that work? *Be sure before dumping it on Jim,* he told himself. *And run it by Warren.*

That was the last thing he remembered thinking until something struck him on the leg and woke him from a sound sleep. Looking down he saw a soccer ball coming to a stop several paces away. A kid, about ten or twelve, wearing a Chicago Fire Department T -shirt, looked concerned, and from a distance yelled, "Sorry, mister."

Monroe smiled, stood up quickly, and kicked the ball to the kid. "Hey, nice pass," the kid said, and he kicked it back to Monroe as if inviting him to join him and his buddy. Monroe wanted to but instead he gave the kid a thumbs-up and said he had to run.

When Monroe entered Leo's, he needed a few seconds before he could see anything in the darkened interior. Discreetly in the background the sound system was playing a soft but edgy version of "Danny Boy" by Bill Evans. He hadn't heard it in years. Monroe spotted Eleanor about halfway down the narrow space. Next to her sat a man with wire-rim glasses, a thin layer of brown hair pulled back from his forehead, and a Van Dyke beard trying to cover a weak chin. Eleanor smiled.

"Sorry I'm a little late," Monroe said as he kissed Eleanor on the cheek.

"Mr. Black, Bruce Monroe," Eleanor said.

"Percy is fine," Black said, as the two men shook hands. Leo, meanwhile, had appeared with a glass and a plate of calamari. "Is the house pinot grigio OK?" He pointed to the carafe of wine sitting on the table. "California, Paso Robles."

Monroe nodded and Leo poured. After some small talk, Black pulled out a small notebook. "Eleanor tells me you're trying to track down a violin—a Bergonzi, no less—that was stolen in Vancouver and may have ended up in Chicago."

"That's right. I've talked to Thomas Banyon and a sergeant in the Chicago

Police Force and have visited eight or nine pawn shops."

Black shook his head. "Nice try, but a Bergonzi wouldn't find its way into a pawn shop. Those guys are good at spotting stolen property. They avoid high-end stuff that calls attention to itself. If something's suspect, they may take a chance if it's small enough to keep out of sight and show clandestinely."

"That's *exactly* what the sergeant said. But I gave it a try."

"Fair enough. We all dream of winning the lottery. Even *I* check the shops once in a while and have a standing order with a couple for first refusal to pick up something that can be restored. But I work mainly with estate sales and have stumbled onto a few treasures that had been sitting in dusty attics."

"Any chance you can help me then?"

"Well, there is one thing. Let me see . . ." Black leafed backward in an old-fashioned paper agenda. "Last Sunday, October 11. A guy contacted me who had seen my website. We met at the airport, Starbucks in concourse C. He said he had an eighteenth-century violin from Italy in mint condition and would take $200,000 for it. I asked if it could be a Stradivarius and he said he wasn't sure."

Eleanor leaned forward. "I wonder how he knew it was eighteenth century. Did you ask to see it?"

"I did. He claimed it was already on a connecting flight and that he could show it to me when he returned to Chicago the next week. He said his grandfather told him how old it was."

"Sounds a bit sketchy," Monroe said. "Where did he get this violin?"

"He didn't say exactly. His grandfather, who could play, bought it in Japan after the war when he was part of the occupying forces."

"Roughly late 1940s, then. What did you think?"

"I was suspicious. And the guy didn't look right. And his name—here it is, Ronald North—didn't fit with his looks."

"Provenance would have been a nightmare to establish," Eleanor said. "All that upheaval in the war. And after."

Black put his wine glass down. "Well, he didn't try. He stuck to the story that it had sat in an attic all those years. He inherited the old man's house and was liquidating his stuff."

"What about the other point? That the guy didn't look right for his name."

"He looked like a guy from the Middle East. Or possibly Iraq or Turkey. Maybe even Latino. Big beard, outgoing, a huckster style. Not well dressed.

English wasn't his first language. That name Ronald North and the story about a grandfather in US-occupied Japan who supposedly settled in Boston so many—"

"Hold it. He said he was from Boston?"

Black frowned. "I'm not sure he *said* it. But he was wearing a Red Sox cap. And I think he said the connecting flight was to Boston."

"So, just to get this straight," Monroe said. "This guy looks Middle Eastern in a vague way, had a beard, and wore a Red Sox cap. Was he short—maybe five foot seven or so?"

"Yes to all of the above." Black checked his watch. "Look, I have an appointment in thirty minutes," he said and he started to rise.

"One more thing," Monroe said. "At what point did you tell him you were not interested in the violin?"

"Well, just before he left to board his plane. I told him the provenance was too sketchy. He wasn't happy. He even asked if I would be interested if he dropped the price. I just laughed."

Monroe and Eleanor, at Leo's insistence, stayed for steaming plates of lamb fricassee and Monroe ordered a decent ordinaire, a Cabernet Sauvignon from South Africa's western cape. After eating, Monroe walked Eleanor home. "You seemed to recognize the man Black was talking about," she said.

"It's possible. It might be a man who has been hanging around the university. But what an odd story. I don't know why he was going to Boston or how the violin could already be on a connecting flight. Could have been part of his cover story."

Monroe stumbled a little as they walked and Eleanor linked arms with him. "You're almost asleep on your feet," she said. "Come up for a coffee."

Once there, Monroe collapsed in a chair and Eleanor, flitting about, showed him the music she was working on: The Devil's Trill.

"Play a little of it, would you?" The coffee tasted bitter and he only took a couple of sips.

Eleanor smiled and picked up her violin. She looked at the score, and played A above middle C as if turning up with an orchestra. She laughed nervously. "Why are young female violinists so beautiful?" Monroe muttered as if to himself as Eleanor played her first note.

■

The next morning Monroe awoke in what he guessed was Eleanor's bed, because her violin case was propped on a chair and next to it his clothes were neatly folded. How did he get here? What had happened to last night's plan to catch a red-eye back to Vancouver? Eleanor entered the room holding a tray with two cups, a pot of coffee, and a plate of croissants. "Good morning. You fell asleep on me. I didn't even get to the slow movement."

"Sorry."

"It's OK. It's not like people falling asleep in a concert. You were out; I tried to wake you, finally got you on your feet and to the bed. Coffee?"

"Yes, please." Eleanor poured a cup, then pointed to a pitcher of milk and a sugar bowl, but Monroe shook his head.

As she leaned over to put the cup on the side table, Eleanor's robe flopped open a little and, Monroe, without thinking, reached for her and pulled her onto the bed.

She laughed. "Careful, I almost spilled the coffee."

She scrambled under the covers, shrugged off her robe, and turned into him.

"Coffee," Monroe whispered, "is no longer a priority."

40

◼

Later, after showering, they sat down with a fresh pot of coffee, a plate of scrambled eggs, and the croissants that had been waiting patiently. Between bites, they reached out for the occasional hand squeeze, and Eleanor rifled through some sheets of music. Monroe enjoyed the moment and their easy compatibility.

Eleanor looked at her watch. "Unfortunately, I have a lesson. Ten o'clock at the Music Institute. Every Wednesday."

"The 20th already. I thought I'd be home by now. Glad I'm not."

Eleanor nodded her head. "Calendar's on the wall behind you. Pictures from a great Canadian painter."

Monroe turned around. "Alex Colville, how did I miss it last night?" Monroe stared at it. "Over three weeks now since things came apart. The president of my university was killed on September 28."

"But you're doing something about it." Eleanor picked up the music and tucked it into a folder but then returned to her filing cabinet. "You can stay tonight, if you want."

"That would be grand but . . . we'll see." Monroe checked his messages. So many of them.

Jim had sent one yesterday offering to pick him up at the airport. He said Hudson had found out that Spelt had been at the academy during the kafuffle over Tanaka and the safe combination.

Luce wrote that she would be in South Hadley, Massachusetts, for a few more days. "Maybe longer," she added, "something on offer, it's big. Maybe time to put my money where my mouth is." So Luce is surely considering a new job in a new place. Monroe pictured her as president of the excellent Mount Holyoke College. What a turn of events. She'd be a great catch for Holyoke. And a massive loss for Northlake.

Warren uncovered something of interest, he said, but didn't say what it was.

And Roosevelt King sent an attachment of Bosko's report for his records. Monroe opened the document and saw King's notes: *$45,000 deposited to the Banyons' account on October 11, from Lodestone Collectables International issued by Cayman Islands National Bank. Before that it had bounced from Cyprus through the British Virgin Islands. Likely Russian money. The $3,620 transferred to Evan Spelt's Visa account was change, so to speak. Lodestone, a shadow corporation, disappeared after this single transaction.*

"A shadow corporation," Monroe said to himself.

Eleanor looked up. "What did you say?"

"Shadow corporation. The money that bought the cello from the Banyons came from an account in the Cayman Islands that no longer exists."

"Something illegal?"

"It *must* be. Possibly money that originated in Russia, probably because it went through Cyprus. Then on to the British Virgin Islands and the Caymans. I think it means the mafia bought the stolen violin to resell it for big bucks to some unknown buyer. Mr. Spelt used the 45K that it went for to pay for his daughter's cello at 42 something with three grand change."

"So what do you do now?" she asked as she slipped on her coat and picked up her case.

"Well, I've got to get back to Vancouver. I need to close in on the person who killed our president."

"Be careful. You know how to get in touch." Eleanor pressed a card with her email and phone numbers on it into Monroe's hand. "When you leave, just pull the door closed and it will lock itself." She kissed Monroe and started out the door but, turning in mid-stride, gave him a dazzling smile. "Remember, you haven't heard the slow movement of the Devil's Trill yet." And then she was gone.

Monroe felt the silence close in as he poured the last of the coffee. He then booked a 7:30 flight on Air Canada to Vancouver and sent a message to Jim that he would arrive at 10:14. Just in case his offer was still on.

He got up, dumped the dregs of his coffee into the sink, and rinsed the dishes he and Eleanor had used. He closed the door and checked that it locked itself. He made his way to the street and noticed some finches frolicking in shrubs fronting the sidewalk. Getting ready to fly south, those guys. Ready for a change.

Like me, he thought, as he remembered Eleanor's smile as she left. Like Luce, mulling another job offer.

As he walked toward the hotel, he realized that he was close to Banyon's house. On impulse, he turned onto Wagner Street and found himself at the gate. Monroe pushed the button several times before a voice crackled out of the speaker.

"Yes. Who is it, please?"

"Bruce Monroe. We spoke yesterday. Do you have a minute?"

A silence underscored reluctance, then a weary "I suppose so." The latch on the gate released and Monroe walked to the front door and waited. Finally, the door opened and the round head with the owlish glasses peered out. "I'm in the middle of something, Professor, so this will have to be brief. Come in."

Monroe entered and Banyon ushered him to his office, which, except for a couple of sheets of paper and a fountain pen on the desk, looked the same as it had the day before. "I'll come right to the point," Monroe said as his eyes strayed momentarily to a shard of croissant that had flaked off and stuck to Banyon's lapel. "Sergeant King's associate ran a check on your bank records and found that $45,000 was deposited to your account on October 11, and on that same day you transferred $3,620 to Evan Spelt's Visa." Monroe opened his notebook and took his time to find the page he was looking for. "Here it is. That means he paid $41,380 for the cello and bow."

Banyon frowned. "Yes, that's what I told you."

"So this squares with your memory of the transaction?"

Banyon pressed the fingers of both hands together. "Yes."

"One thing worries me. The $45,000 was issued from a Cayman Islands account. It no longer exists. In other words, the money that paid for the cello likely came from an organized crime syndicate."

"What?" Banyon's owl eyes flitted left then right as if he was looking for an answer. "All I know is what Dr. Spelt told me. A charitable foundation had granted his daughter up to $45,000 to purchase an instrument. I gave him our bank account information at the local HSBC branch so it could be deposited. It's up to the bank, of course, to verify that such funds are legitimate. The only restriction from the foundation, Dr. Spelt told us, was that the instrument be purchased from a reputable dealer—we are clearly that—and be evaluated by a qualified third party."

RICHARD BOYER

Monroe checked his notes. "Roland Vamos at the Music Institute."

"Yes, Roland and his wife signed off on it and their son, a talented cellist, played it and considered it a fine instrument."

"I think the Chicago police may want to double check the paperwork on that. What about the $3,620 you put back in Spelt's Visa account?"

"Well, he said he was going to return it to the foundation along with our invoices and a copy of the Vamos' assessment. And I think he was planning to deduct his travel expenses."

"I see." Monroe stood up. "Thank you for your help. By the way there's a crumb on your left lapel." Banyon swiveled his head, found the culprit, and flicked it away.

41

At the Bayshore Hotel, Monroe changed into his last clean shirt. He paid his bill and left his bag at the reception desk. He then sat down in the lobby and, from memory, sketched the face of Aziz. He wasn't much of an artist, but the beard and prominent nose looked about right. He stuck a Red Sox cap on him and roughed in clumps of hair hanging over the ears and down his neck. He studied it for a couple of minutes and it was passable. Monroe checked Google Maps for pawnshops and saw quite a few he hadn't yet been to. He had time to kill and could check some even if Black thought it was a fool's errand. In fact, maybe it was a thankless chore. He really wanted to go to the Art Institute and look at Seurat's A *Sunday on La Grande Jatte*. It had been years since he had seen it.

Duty first. He decided to follow up on Roosevelt's suggestion to try Armour Square on the south side and took a taxi. His first stop was Mario's Palacio, a shop filled mostly with junk but it had a glass case holding some decent-looking watches and jewelry. Mario, a rotund, mustachioed, middle-aged man, barely glanced up from a clock he had disassembled on a battered partner's desk.

Monroe pulled out his drawing. "Did this guy come into the store a week or so ago? Maybe asking if you'd be interested in a violin? An expensive one."

Mario squinted at the drawing without getting up. Then he picked up a pair of glasses, stuck them on, and laboriously got to his feet. He stared at the drawing for a minute. "You drew this?"

"Yeah."

He nodded. "Even I can see you're not the second coming of Raphael. No offense."

Monroe smiled. "I'm a history teacher."

"Good for you. I like history, World War II. Why do you want to know?"

"Well, he might have been trying to peddle a stolen violin."

Mario yawned. "Not good. He must be a bad boy."

So it's the runaround. "Listen, Roosevelt King said you were a straight shooter. I spoke with him yesterday."

"King said that?"

Monroe tried to look sincere. "Yup."

Mario hesitated as if thinking things over. "A guy looking something like that did come in. He had the Red Sox hat on and had scruffy hair same as you sketched. Said he had an old violin, worth a lot, made in Italy. You got his nose, mouth, and chin with that scraggly beard about right, by the way. Maybe you do have a bit of talent. He had an accent. But not like yours."

"Well, if it's my guy we're both from Canada, but he just got there. Then what?"

"I said I might give him a grand for it if it was in good shape."

"And?"

"He got all hot and bothered. This little squirt. He said the violin was worth a million bucks and he was looking for at least fifty grand. I figured it was hot."

"So you don't do stolen stuff?"

"You kiddin'? Not with Roosevelt King around. Besides, a grand's my limit for cash flow."

"So what'd you do?"

"I told him to forget the pawn shops. For something in that league, you go to DiVito's bar and to talk to Tony. Guys with expensive stuff go there."

"You mean stolen?"

Mario shrugged. "No one asks."

"So if my guy here"—Monroe tapped his drawing—"got big money for his violin, he might have made the deal at DiVito's?"

"Indirectly. It's a hangout where information gets passed."

"Do you think the mafia might have—"

"I don't know. They're out there, of course. If they did, it's long gone."

Monroe thanked Mario and went outside. The idea of going to DiVito's crossed his mind, but he dismissed it. It would be a waste of time. Only a sophisticated sting operation could work its way through whatever maze started there. Roosevelt would know it exists. *Looks like Aziz got lucky.*

The Art Institute cafeteria seemed to have screened out loud talkers. A lot of people sat alone with a book and their plate of food. Monroe picked out a ham and cheese on a less than stellar Portuguese bun, ordered a coffee, and found a table next to the far wall. He pulled out his notebook. After a minute or two a middle-aged man walked in surrounded by several young people. He was in charge, talking with gestures and now and then to demonstrate postures and body movements that complemented bowing actions.

"That's Roland Vamos, in case you were wondering. Greatest violin teacher in the world. Along with his wife."

Monroe looked at the guy clearing dishes from an adjoining table. "He comes here with his students. We have way better coffee than the music academy next door. Roasted in small batches by an Australian dude on the south side."

Monroe kept an eye on Vamos talking to his students until they were settled at a table at the other side of the room. Then he approached him. "Mr. Vamos. Excuse the interruption. I know you're busy, but may I ask a quick question?"

Vamos's face remained neutral. He was cordial. "Yes, of course, if it is quick."

"I understand you examined a cello that was sold to Professor Evan Spelt, who purchased it for his daughter."

Vamos nodded. "That is correct. A good instrument, perfect for a young cellist, although I can't speak to its exact fit as I haven't seen the young lady play."

"It's possible that the funds used to purchase the cello came from the theft of a valuable violin. The thief may have been involved in a homicide."

Vamos didn't answer right away. "Let's talk over there." He motioned to a table where no one was sitting. "And who are you, sir?" he asked "A policeman, perhaps, or federal agent?"

"Neither. I'm a professor. I have no official standing but am assisting the inspector investigating this. Here, I've talked to Roosevelt King of the Chicago Police and to Mr. Thomas Banyon."

"And you're wondering if I might have run across the violin? Could you describe it in more detail?

"Yes, it's a Carlo Bergonzi dated 1737, and inscribed to Stradivari."

"Quite touching—the year of his death. That would make it attractive to a collector of a certain kind. But not to most, of course, if it's stolen property. Bergonzi made splendid violins. Perhaps only fifty or so known ones are still alive and well. But to answer your question, yes, I was asked but declined. I was too busy and didn't like the way I was approached."

"What do you mean?"

"Well, it was secretive. Someone from Lodestone Collectables—something like that—called and offered $10,000 to place a value on it and confirm its authenticity and my report was to remain confidential and anonymous. I was suspicious. I've never heard of them. And I don't do anonymous."

"Sounds like a lot of money. Is that a reasonable fee?"

"God, no. I test instruments for sound but have no interest in assessing them for rich collectors who don't play. My fee is a few hundred dollars."

⁂

Same old dead end, Monroe thought, as he left the cafeteria and went upstairs to sit for a while in front of Seurat's *A Sunday on La Grande Jatte.* He found a bench and began to look at the stiff figures locked in a diorama. It was a time capsule, 1884, Paris, a park in the middle of the Seine. A day off work. But no one makes eye contact, no smiles, no interactions. Except the little girl in white looking back at you. Everyone else locked in solitude and staring toward some distant nothingness. *No church-going for this group,* he thought. *It's irrelevant; they gravitate to the park, a brief respite from the noise, drudgery, dust, and overcrowding of factories and tenements. Stunned and disoriented.*

"Waldemar thinks this is a pick-up scene and the women are prostitutes," said a nearby thirty-something woman, a smirk on her face, packed into tight-fitting clothing of clashing bright colours.

"I don't care what he thinks," said her companion, a younger woman in a blazer and skirt. "I see people trying. They don't know how to connect anymore. Not even with their dogs, those pitiful little things on leashes. It's alienation. Karl Marx could have painted this—if he could paint."

She's got a point, Monroe thought, remembering the energy and dignity of the dog on Cypress Mountain.

The other woman paused, as if surprised at the reference Marx. "Well," she said, "Waldemar's an art critic. And besides, I've seen the musical *Sunday in the Park with George.*"

"Hooray for you. Just leave me alone."

With silence restored, Monroe returned to his thoughts. How did Seurat do it? he wondered. A message from the past that speaks to us now, a place and a context—a specific park and day, the industrial age, familiar yet mysteriously generalized, stylized, mannered to convey a larger message. Alienation? Despair? Modernity?

38

◼◼

Home but still on Chicago time, Monroe was up early the next day. Over coffee, he reviewed his notes and decided that the priority was to look into the links between Aziz and Spelt.

It would be good to talk to Mildred again. He phoned her in the president's office and asked if Spelt was around. She told him the coast would be clear at noon, when he had a lunch meeting.

◼◼

Monroe parked his bike near the gym. He was a little early so he sat on Lloyd Kerr's bench among the Japanese maples. From there, he could see when Spelt exited the building. When Warren came into view, walking slowly with his nose in a book, he called out.

"What are you doing?"

"I'm back from Chicago. Going to talk to Mildred as soon as Spelt leaves."

"And?"

"Well, too much to tell right now." Monroe looked across the quad. "There he goes. I'm off. Want to come?"

"Sure."

◼◼

Mildred looked up with a little smirk, but it looked forced. *She's trying*, Monroe thought. *Maybe to cover that she's worried.*

"We won't keep you. You're probably hoping to get away for lunch."

Mildred shook her head. "Not anymore. Too much to do." She nodded toward a brown bag at the corner of her desk with a look of distaste.

"I want to know more about Spelt's relationship with President Eliot. When did Eliot start looking into the Dean's Research Fund?"

"Well . . . early in August. Right after I returned from a weekend in Tofino with my niece. Mr. Eliot had gone over some letters that President Bancroft never got around to dealing with. I'm not even sure he read them. But I did because I filed them. Financial Services, by the way, noted some instances of funds improperly accounted for. When Mr. Eliot saw this he called Dean Spelt in and told him he was concerned."

"Is that all? Concerned?"

"Well, more than that. That he intended to check further although he specified—that's what he told me later—that he wasn't accusing Spelt personally."

"And Spelt wasn't happy?"

"He went ballistic from what I heard here in the outer office."

"And from then on you used a code in the agenda book for meetings between Mr. Eliot and Meyer?"

"Not right away, but soon after. From then on, relations between Mr. Eliot and Dean Spelt were not cordial. No smiles, no handshakes."

"After this, do you remember a time when Spelt came to Mr. Eliot's office and was left alone? Maybe only for a short time when Mr. Eliot stepped out to ask a question or get a file?"

Mildred seemed surprised at the question. "No . . . I don't think so, but I'm out of the office now and again."

Warren caught Monroe's eye.

"Or they could have met early, before I arrive," Mildred added.

Monroe flipped through some pages in his notebook. "I'm also interested in this man Aziz who was cleaning the carpet the morning after Mr. Eliot died."

"Yes. I remember him."

"Did he do an estimate first?"

"Yes, he did," Mildred said. "Introduced himself and gave me his card." She reached for a well-thumbed agenda booklet and began to leaf through it. "We no longer use this, everything's on line now. Here it is. Thursday, September 23, at 1:15: estimate to clean carpet. I also wrote, *contract worker sent by Facilities*

Services, that's what he told me. Mr. Eliot was out of the office at his monthly meeting with the deans."

How convenient, Monroe thought. "And Mr. Aziz went into Mr. Eliot's private office."

"Oh, yes. He had his clipboard and measured both the inner and outer offices. Took only about ten or fifteen minutes."

After the meeting with Mildred, Monroe and Warren went to The Buzz. A couple of chess players had just vacated their table. "Ham and cheese OK?" Monroe asked? "I'm buying."

"That's a miracle. I'll take it."

Once they had their food, Warren asked, "What did *that* accomplish?"

"Talking to Mildred? Trying to nail down the timing of when Spelt felt threatened."

Warren stared down at his sandwich for a moment. "OK, Spelt doesn't like getting second-guessed. You're thinking motive?"

"Well, think about it. Spelt was seriously worried from early August. I should have gotten the exact date when Mildred got back from the Tofino trip. Eliot starts investigating the fund and Spelt has a fit, so Eliot starts to use a code to set up the meetings with Meyer. Then on September 23, five days before Eliot gets muffined, Aziz shows up and does an estimate for carpet cleaning. Spelt sends him on a day when he knows Eliot will be away from his office. His real job is to find Eliot's EpiPen and sabotage it."

"Ah, so at that point we've got a murder plot."

"Right. Aziz was told to say he was sent by Physical Plant. He's outfitted with a business card, possibly done by Renwick in IT at Spelt's behest. Mildred doesn't blink an eye because contract workers do a lot of these jobs now. I'll check on this one with Physical Plant. By the way, Aziz was also in Chicago trying to fence that violin stolen from Tanaka. That's another connection with Spelt. Let's get creative here. What if Aziz blew up Han's camper? What if he's Spelt's all-purpose dirty-tricks guy?"

"I don't know. Those types must be expensive."

"Right, and I don't think Spelt has that kind of cash flow. Or connections. We need to find out more about Aziz and how Spelt knows him."

Monroe nodded and picked up his phone. "Jim, I think it's time to bring Aziz in for—" Monroe grew silent, his face ashen. "Yeah, thanks, let me know."

Monroe looked at Warren as he ended the call. "Aziz may be dead. They're pulling a car out of Howe Sound north of Lion's Bay right now. A sign on the door says carpet cleaning."

43

Monroe felt upended. Aziz was a key piece for connecting the dots. "Now what?"

"Could it be an accident?" Warren asked.

"I don't know. But it's still important to figure out how Spelt and Aziz were linked. I'll give you a call." Monroe grabbed his half-eaten sandwich and hurried away.

On the way to the dean's office, he stopped at facilities management. Bob Walker was standing near the front desk, shuffling papers. "Monroe, aren't you supposed to—"

"Be suspended. Yes but still asking questions. And I have one for you."

"Sure, ask away."

"Can you check your records for a contract carpet cleaner you sent to the president's office on September 23 to do an estimate? He was in the offices on the 29th, the day after Eliot died, cleaning. Said that maintenance sent him an email work order to proceed on the basis of the estimate."

Bob looked surprised. "Sounds odd. We usually do those jobs in house. I'll check." He paged through a book of maintenance duties scheduled in September. "Nothing. We didn't send anyone. Who was the person who came?"

"A guy named Aziz: young, bearded, personable, maybe from the Middle East."

Bob shrugged his shoulders. "Never heard of him. We didn't send him."

"Thanks, Bob."

At the dean of arts' office a few minutes later, Monroe looked around to see if Luce had returned yet. "Any word from the dean?" he asked Margo.

"Still away. She extended her stay until next week. So, you know me, I'm the nosey type. She scribbled the word interview on her calendar for the day after she left and she had plane reservations for Boston."

Monroe sat down. *It's happening. She's going inside. The world where MBAs—they can't help it, it's like a religion—manage universities as if they're corporations. Unless... could it be true? They're moving to something else: fairness, equity, curiosity, and openness.*

Margo looked concerned. "Sorry. It's not what you wanted to hear. But I do know she's sick of the mess this place is in and is pretty depressed that Spelt is now president. You would know. She's so able and wants the chance to lead her way."

Monroe nodded. Margo began to fiddle with some papers as if to give Monroe time to process the news about Luce. He cleared his throat, to give himself a little time.

"Margo, on an unrelated note, I have a couple of questions. Did a young man named Ahmed Aziz, supposedly a carpet cleaner, come to this office when Spelt was dean? He's bearded. Sometimes wears a red baseball cap. Late twenties. Speaks with an accent. Friendly, outgoing, confident."

Margo paused and rested her chin in her hand. "Well, there is a person who might be a rough fit: bearded, no hat, but dresses in a suit. He phones ahead—if it's him—asks to speak to the dean but never identifies himself. I thought he may have had business dealings with Dr. Spelt because they were sort of formal with each other. Shaking hands on arrival, that sort of thing. The dean met him several times at the door and ushered him into his office quickly. He usually carried a small case that, I assumed, had files in it. Business-like, you know?"

Monroe was puzzled. Business-like wasn't exactly the Aziz Monroe remembered. Maybe a good actor, though. "It could have been Aziz. Do you think Spelt has any information on him in his office?"

"It's possible. He puts everything into files. Both of the filing cabinets have been moved to the president's office. If it's confidential, it could be in a locked metal box in one of them. I walked in on him once when he was putting a folder into it, and he was annoyed, told me to knock before barging in."

"Barging in? He said that?"

"Yeah, he made me feel like a kid."

"OK. I'm going to his office now. I want to find that box. Message him, will you, and ask him to stop here on his way back from his lunch meeting. Tell him it's urgent. When he gets here, make something up."

"Thanks a lot."

"You can do it. Say Luce is interviewing for another position. Whatever you can think of. Then call Mildred to sound the alarm."

"You're going to owe me one," Margo said with a grimace. "I don't know what you're up to, but—"

Monroe gave a wave and hurried away.

At the president's office, he told Mildred that he needed to check for something in Spelt's office. "It's about Mr. Eliot's death," he said. "Stay close to the phone because Margo's going to warn me when he's on his way back. Tell me when she calls."

Mildred looked worried. "No one's supposed to go in. Not even me."

"He'll never know," Monroe said as he entered the office. He went to the file cabinets and opened the bottom drawer of the larger one. There were no folders, just a metal box about twelve inches square. It was locked. Monroe took his keys out and prodded at the lock, but even his bike lock key was too thick. Maybe a paper clip would work. He slipped one off some papers on the desk, pulled it open, and poked the wire around in the key slot. Nothing, no feel at all for the mechanism inside. He thought of taking the whole box but couldn't risk Spelt finding it missing.

What is in this box? Maybe Jim could get a search warrant? Too slow. Think. Where do you hide a key? He crossed to Spelt's desk and looked in the top drawers. Nothing. He was out of ideas.

Wait. Margo said Spelt files everything. Try it. He looked under S for "secret," "special," or "strongbox." Then A for "Aziz."

The phone rang in the outer office. He stepped to the door. Mildred gestured for him to get out.

Monroe ran back to close the file cabinet. But a final idea, check K for "Key." And there it was. *Of course, hide things in plain sight.* In an envelope inside the file, he found a small key that he jammed into the lock. It opened. Inside, he found a thick envelope labelled "Aziz." He grabbed it, relocked the box, and returned it to the bottom drawer. As he stepped out of the office, Mildred pointed to the Lester Pearson Conference Room. Monroe ducked in just as he heard Spelt's footsteps approaching.

44

Once Spelt had passed, Monroe cracked the door open. He felt something poking his leg as he leaned against the doorjamb. Reaching into his pocket, he found the key to Spelt's strongbox. *Damn.* Mildred, meanwhile, sidled up to the door. "He's angry," she said in a soft voice. "Something about Margo Johnson wasting his time and not giving a damn what Lucile Drummond does. I'll let you know when the coast is clear."

Monroe nodded and stepped back into the conference room. He took a seat at the table and opened the file on Aziz. It was a series of government applications for immigrant status for his father, mother, and younger sister, Amira, age fourteen. He had just unclipped a packet of notes between Aziz and Spelt when the door opened.

"Go now," Mildred said. "He's on the phone talking to Mr. Davis. Usually stands at his window and looks out on the quad. Hurry."

Monroe left the building, slipped the file into his backpack, and unlocked his bike. On the way home he was passing by Gunderson's when he remembered that his fridge was empty. After the little escapade in Spelt's office he wasn't exactly hungry, but he knew he would be soon. So in he went for a few basics. As he came out, Margo Johnson's daughter flagged him down. He had met her once or twice while she was waiting for her mother in the dean's office.

"Sorry, Professor Monroe. You seem to be in a hurry. Just a quick question: I'm cooking dinner for three friends from the cross-country team—salmon, but trying to decide between Sockeye and Coho."

"Well, you can't go wrong with either. I'd go for Sockeye myself, but any wild salmon should be fine."

"Thanks, I figure you work at it more than most. We see you biking and running in the neighbourhood. It seems like you're a good influence on other faculty."

"Influence, really?"

"Yeah, even President Spelt has taken up jogging. Following in your foot-steps, I bet. Chiara had to bus it today because he went out at some ungodly hour, she said. Mom and I picked her up at the bus stop."

❖

Monroe carried a Granville Island Pale Ale to his desk and opened Spelt's file on Aziz. The government forms Aziz had filled out provided information about his family in Iraq and why they should be granted refugee status in Canada. Aziz's notes to Spelt Monroe arranged chronologically. They started in early September. At first Aziz had been deferential, somewhat timid but increasingly his notes had become urgent, desperate even.

They had a deal. Spelt promised to get Aziz's family into Canada and help sponsor them for permanent residence. In exchange, Aziz had been doing certain jobs, unspecified, for Spelt. But Aziz's family was in danger and the refugee process had either been delayed or never started. Finally, Aziz had threatened go to Howard Davis, whom Spelt claimed was a co-sponsor for Aziz's family. That was in his most recent note, undated but with a reference to his "successful" trip to Chicago.

Monroe took another sip of his ale. Just then, the doorbell rang. Mrs. Rigetti, he thought. Maybe with a welcome-home carrot cake. Instead, it was Jim.

"Ah, come in. We need to talk. Get you a beer?"

"Thanks, no. On duty. I was close by and thought I might catch you. We've made positive identification of the guy who went into Howe Sound this morning. At the Bear Rock turnout. It's Aziz."

Monroe had expected this but felt sick to hear the confirmation.

❖

At the kitchen table, Jim had poured glasses of water and was waiting for the news to settle. "It was a stolen vehicle with a removable sign. Vinyl, magnetized and attached to the door. You OK?"

"Yeah." Monroe walked to his office and retrieved the folder he had been reviewing. "It had to be Spelt. Start with motive." Monroe gave the folder a pat. "Spelt made a deal with Aziz that he—possibly with Davis's help—could get his family out of Iraq and into Canada. Refugee status, permanent residency, citizenship, eventually. His family in danger, Aziz was desperate, agreed to do anything in exchange. From these notes, nothing was happening and Aziz was increasingly worried, swimming in murky waters doing Spelt's dirty work. It doesn't specify the jobs here, but at least borderline criminal. I suspect Spelt was stringing him along from the beginning and may have threatened to black-mail him."

"What do you mean?" Jim asked.

"Well, think about it. Report him to the police. One, when he gained access to Eliot's office as a carpet cleaner in order to disable Eliot's EpiPen. Two, when he set the explosives on Meyer's van. If he did. But I'll bet we find that Aziz was trained for that in the Iraqi army. It's possible he didn't know Meyer and Mildred were supposed to be in it when it blew up. Three, when he fenced the violin in Chicago he may not have known it had a connection to Tanaka's death."

Jim nodded. "Going to see Davis means that he expected the deal to be hon-oured. But if Davis isn't really part of—"

"If he isn't part of it, then Spelt can't let that meeting take place."

Jim nodded. "We're thinking the same thing."

"So Spelt sets up an early meeting at Bear Rock on the Sea to Sky highway. He announces to his family last night that he's beginning an early-morning jogging regime so off he goes. He meets Aziz at Bear Rock before there's traffic on the highway, pushes him and his truck into Howe Sound, and shows up at his office around 6:30 or 7:00."

"How do you know about the early-morning jogging?"

"Jennifer, Margo Johnson's daughter. She and Margo picked up Chiara at the bus stop and they learned it from her."

Jim nodded. "Good. And how'd you get hold of this folder?"

"Ah . . . yes, thanks for asking. There may be a small problem. I snuck into Spelt's office and took it out of a locked box he keeps in his file cabinet."

Jim scowled. "Holeee. . . . You call that *small*? A good defense lawyer would love this. No search warrant. Look, make copies and put it back as soon as you can, and we'll try to get a search warrant and find it ourselves."

45

Jim couldn't stay, but agreed to meet Monroe later at the Cactus Club. By then, Ravi would be done searching Aziz's place.

When he arrived, Monroe spotted Jim holed up in a quiet area away from the bar and TV sets. As soon as he sat down, a server named Marie, one of Monroe's former students, showed up with a pint of pale ale.

"I told her it was for Professor Monroe and her face lit up. No messin' around. What the hell, you know everyone in this burg or what?"

"Just a fluke." Monroe raised his glass. "Cheers."

"Well, to get you back to a local brew after the Chicago excursion."

Monroe smiled. "It was only a small sample, called Goose Island. Pretty good."

"You need to catch me up on your trip and other developments," Jim said. "But first, you should know that Hudson took an anonymous call a couple of days ago saying we should be looking at Lucille Drummond. "She received a promotion when Eliot died, and now she's apparently leveraged that into a job offer to head a university in Massachusetts."

Monroe said nothing for a long minute. "This is nasty, a stupid, mischievous call done by someone with a twisted mind."

"Anonymous callers come up with stuff like this all the time. Have you seen Meyer since Chicago?"

"Not directly. But this from Mildred. Eliot found a file of faculty complaints from his predecessor's time. Applications for research funds, modest ones for start-up projects, were getting turned down without a sniff. Or taken up with sketchy accounting for how money was spent. Eliot called Spelt in and told him he was investigating it. Spelt hit the ceiling and shortly after, Eliot had Mildred use a code to schedule meetings with Meyer in the agenda."

"So to keep the investigation out of Spelt's sight." Jim caught Marie's eye and pointed to his empty glass.

"Yeah, a little late for that. But Eliot took Spelt's defensiveness as a red flag, convinced that he and Meyer were dealing with a cancer."

Monroe looked up as Marie came with another beer for Jim and they ordered their burgers.

"Anyway," Monroe continued, "Meyer has now tracked down the grantees—some of them this past week—and asked them for details about their research projects. Six didn't know what he was talking about; four retired faculty received funds for research they had completed and published years ago. Same with the regular faculty, except three of them admitted outright that they were in on the scam and had agreed to falsify research expenses in exchange for $500."

"Admitted this to Meyer? This is good work."

"He had the goods—printouts with discrepancies redlined. Or in some cases, warned them about identity theft for purposes of fraud."

"Some of these people come pretty cheap," Jim said. "Do you have names? We need to bring them in, get statements. The university may want to press charges."

Just then, Jim's phone buzzed. He listened, eyes down, with an occasional grunt. Then he looked up. "Ravi. He found a few things of interest at Aziz's place."

"Such as?"

"Well, a bad-news good-news story."

"As always." Monroe's voice was muffled because he had taken a bite of his burger.

"Someone got there first. But they were in a hurry."

"And they missed something?"

Jim nodded. "Most importantly, Aziz's discharge papers from the Iraqi army. He was a specialist, munitions and explosives, private first class. The paper was tucked into a leather-bound copy of *The Travels of Marco Polo* on a bookshelf next to an old TV."

"Marco Polo, eh? You never know when a classic will come in handy. Anything else?"

Jim nodded but remained silent as Marie glided to the table with a square platter heaped with guacamole and corn chips. "I asked Pete for some extra for an important professor and his friend," she said.

"I'm coming here with you more often," Jim said.

"A fluke," Monroe said again. Marie left with their thanks. "This makes Aziz the suspect for blowing up the van."

"I'd say so. He was seconded to the Americans and received a commendation from a Colonel Michael Matthews. It was attached to the discharge paper. It probably helped him get out of Iraq. He must have figured it would be easier to get his family into Canada than the States."

"That's it?"

"One more thing. An email from his father. Dated a week ago. ISIS thugs hanging around who knew Aziz had worked for the Americans."

Monroe frowned. "Written in—"

"Arabic. Ravi knows enough to get the gist. We'll get a native speaker to do a translation."

"Where'd he find it?"

"Tucked into a beat-up *Vanity Fair* magazine in the bathroom. *Vanity Fair* and Marco Polo. Eclectic taste—"

"At least for hiding places."

"Yeah, we should check all the books and magazines. Probably Ravi's already done it. So Aziz got in over his head. Criminal stuff to get his family out of danger."

"Whatever it takes—"

"And he believed Davis backed it."

Monroe shook his head. "I wonder if Davis knew anything about it. I'll ask him tomorrow—unless you want to."

"You do it," Jim said. "Under guise of university chit chat. He may talk more freely if the police aren't in his face." Jim scraped up some guacamole with the final piece of his burger. "I should go. But first give me a little report on Chicago. Did you and Roosevelt accomplish anything? From your phone call, it sounded like you were sidetracked over that old violin."

"Not sidetracked." Monroe almost smiled. "I had a hunch that Spelt snatched the violin and, one way or another, caused the death of the Japanese woman on Grouse."

Jim started to speak, but Monroe cut him off. "I was in Spelt's office when Mildred walked in and reminding him of his meeting with an instrument dealer in Chicago. I began to think he could be planning to use the violin to pay for a new cello for his daughter."

"And?"

"Well, I located the dealer, a guy named Banyon, who sold Spelt a cello for almost exactly the price that the violin went for. I couldn't track down the violin itself but found two people approached by someone who fits Aziz's description—one a pawnbroker who said he was flogging one for $50,000."

"But it was worth around a million."

"But not as stolen property. Aziz likely made contact with the mafia. Then, mysteriously, a certified cheque for $45,000 went into Banyon's account drawn on a Cayman Island bank account owned by Lodestone Collectables. Roosevelt King's colleague tracked down the details."

"Ah, and the company was dissolved immediately, right?"

"Yes, and that paid for the cello."

"So where does that leave us?"

"Well, the violin is long gone and untraceable. Probably in Russia or Eastern Europe. But the money checks out. What do you think? Time to bring Spelt in?"

Jim looked at his watch. "Damn, almost 7:00. Meeting in half an hour. Every bloody Thursday since the big push to get fentanyl off the streets. It's everywhere, sneaking across the border, in containers coming into port, and opiates are even getting pilfered from hospitals. On Spelt, let's hold off a few more days. I want to be sure we've cleaned up the loose ends. For one thing, we need to be sure we've found everything Aziz left behind. I'll go through Aziz's apartment again. And you need to get Spelt's documents back. Don't forget the copies. Let's hope he hasn't missed them. And we'll get those people down to the station who were involved in the research fund fraud."

46

The next day, Monroe parked his bike out of sight in a rack next to the gym and headed for Warren's lab.

Warren was working with three students on one side of the lab next to a kind of maze with rats in it. But he walked quickly to the doorway. "Kind of busy right now. What's up?"

"Can you help me out?" Monroe handed over Spelt's folder with the material on Aziz. "Could you return these originals to Mildred? Ask her to sneak it back into the locked box in his file drawer. Here's the key." Monroe handed Warren the envelope with the key to the box. "Remind her it goes into a file folder labeled 'Key.'"

Warren gingerly reached for the folder. "What a concept. I take it Spelt didn't give it to you."

"I borrowed it. To clarify Spelt's links to Aziz. Look it over. But don't let him see you."

"Wait. You're getting ahead of me. Is this the character who had the accident on the Sea to Sky?"

"Yes, but no time now to fill you in. Except unlikely it was an accident." Monroe glanced at the students next to the rat maze. "Just get it to Mildred as soon as you can. I'd do it but don't want to be seen in that building. Not today."

Monroe hurried out of the lab and stepped into the quad. To his right he saw Jean-Michel coming out of Sterling Hall. They met at Lloyd Kerr's bench. "A good spot," he said with a little gesture of his head in the direction of the president's office. "In case someone's monitoring for shady characters."

"And snapping photos."

Monroe nodded. "That, too."

"So what are you doing?"

"Right now I'm trying to find out more about that carpet cleaner in the president's offices the day after Eliot died. It was still a crime scene. It wasn't the maintenance people who sent him. I think Spelt did."

Jean-Michel shuffled his feet. "Too bad. Missed a curve on the Sea to Sky? I saw the picture. Nice enough guy, kind of depressed, worried maybe."

"You had contact with him?"

"A little. He came into the gallery a few times. Seemed to like the Murphy painting. He sat for long periods looking at it."

"Recently?"

"Well, yes. A couple of days ago. Let's see, Wednesday, two days ago, when Mrs. Kerr stopped by."

"How'd he look? Nervous?"

Jean-Michel shrugged his shoulders. "Hard to say. Sort of withdrawn, weighed down as if worried or something."

"I'm glad you told me. He might very well have been distracted. Got a few errands to run now. Catch you later."

Monroe had caught sight of Kevin Renwick with a coffee in hand moving toward the academic computing offices. On a whim, he followed him, but by the time he entered the building he was out of sight. He walked down the corridor to his office and banged on his door. A voice called out, "Enter, all ye who dare."

Monroe stepped in. "Hello, Kevin. I guess you remember me."

Kevin didn't answer right away. Instead, he picked up a toothpick and pretended to examine it. "What do you want?" he said finally.

"Well, I suppose you've heard the news of the so-called carpet cleaner who died yesterday. His name was Aziz and, like you, he was working for Spelt. But he became a little too uppity."

Monroe noticed Kevin's Adam's apple bounce up and down as he swallowed, but he remained silent. "I think you knew him, made some business cards for him for the carpet cleaning business, no? The police will find the evidence on your computer. Spelt's idea? Aziz's death wasn't an accident; it was murder. Since you occasionally do Spelt's dirty work, you may want to think about it. The police will want to talk to you after I tell them how you operate around here."

"What do you mean?"

"Cut the innocent act. Nice little charade that Spelt played out for me in his office when he pretended to chew you out and told you to give me access to Eliot's files. But he made a small mistake. He asked his secretary to phone Kevin Renwick—he knew your last name. It rolled right off his tongue even though he pretended that he didn't know you. Mildred had you on speed dial because she often calls you for him and she had you on the line in seconds." Monroe knew this could be an exaggeration but figured it was close enough.

"I'm not sure I know what you're talking about. Yes, I have helped Dr. Spelt a time or two with computer problems, but that's all. It's my job."

"And of course that includes the article in the *Norwester* with the doctored photo of me and Hans Meyer. Turner may have started it, payback because he thought I criticized his project, but Spelt pulled it all together. A way to get me off campus and to stop investigating Eliot's death. I don't know who took the photo but Spelt knew your skills to Photoshop it. And Turner to write the text. No doubt you and Turner had a little fun working together on the Clouseau part. The odd thing is that Sellers did those films in the '60s—pretty old for a guy like you. Sound about right? It'll all be on your hard disk for the police tech to sort out."

Kevin squirmed in his chair , then picked up a pen and studied it as if it could supply him with an answer. "I love those Pink Panther movies," he said softly. "Sellers was the best, so many great roles, Chauncey Gardiner . . ."

"Look, Kevin, you need to focus. Your admiration for Sellers pushed you into some deep waters. What you and Turner did will be the least of your problems. As the police unravel this mess on campus, they'll find you in the thick of theft and fraud in Spelt's scheme to embezzle university funds. But that's not the worst of your problems. They might charge you with accessory to murder."

Monroe stood up. "I suggest that you act quickly. Get a lawyer, get on your bike, and get yourself down to the police station. Tell Inspector Martino every-thing. Just go, and don't tell anyone where you're going."

47

Monroe got to Chancellor Davis's office at about 11:45. A portly woman with a stern expression sat behind a wooden plank that seemed to function as a kind of rampart. Monroe tried a friendly approach. "Hello, I need to speak, just for a minute, to Mr. Davis."

The receptionist barely looked up. "Mr. Davis is *very* busy right now."

"Aren't we all?" Monroe walked by her, rapped once on Davis's door, and entered. Davis, seated at a large desk, looked up with a frown and pushed some papers to one side. At the desk, Monroe remained standing to admire an impressive grouping of Robert Genn landscapes on the wall behind. "Peace River, no?" Davis glanced behind him before answering. "Right, and now the bloody dam is going to flood the valley . . . unless we can stop them."

Davis stood and extended his hand. "But I'm sure you didn't come to discuss my paintings or environmental concerns. Sorry, Professor Monroe. Time is short; I've got to be at the Teahouse at 12:00. University business. How can I help? Can we do this quickly or shall we set a time to meet?"

"It'll be quick," Monroe said. "On leave, I've continued to think about Eliot's death and . . ." Davis looked disinterested, had already glanced a couple of times at his watch. *He thinks I'm obsessed*, Monroe thought.

"I need to clear up one thing," Monroe continued. "Were you ever approached by Evan Spelt to co-sponsor as refugees to Canada the family of an Iraqi man named Aziz?"

Davis looked surprised. "What an odd question. And coincidence. I'd never heard of the man until he made an appointment to see me. Helen cancelled it when she read in the paper that he had died in an automobile accident." Davis jumped to his feet and stepped quickly to the door to the outer office. "Helen, was it next Monday that a Mr. Aziz was coming to see me?"

"I'll check," she called out. Davis drummed his fingers on the door as he waited. "Yes," she said. "Monday at 10 o'clock."

"Did he say what it was about?"

"Ah, no. I wrote 'personal' and 'urgent,' his words."

Davis closed the door and returned to his desk but remained standing. "Look, Monroe, I know the suspension has upset you. But for your own good, give this stuff a rest, will you? You're not yourself."

Monroe nodded. "Just one more thing. I should tell you why Aziz considered his meeting with you urgent. ISIS thugs in Iraq threatened his family. Spelt promised him that he and *you* would sponsor their entry into Canada as refugees."

"But I knew nothing about that." Davis sank into his chair and slumped forward. He finally looked at Monroe, really looked as if searching for some indication that this was not true.

"Thank you, Mr. Davis," Monroe said. "I'll leave you to your luncheon."

⬛

A half block away, sitting on a bench, Monroe replayed Davis's reaction. He was genuinely surprised, egotistic perhaps but straightforward. Decent in his way. Monroe thought about his opposition to the Site C dam. *He's in shock now even if he thinks I'm a little crazy.* Monroe dialed Jim. Constable Goodwin answered and put him on hold for six or seven minutes before Jim came on.

"Well, you took your sweet time," Monroe said. "I just spoke to Davis. Aziz had an appointment to see him next Monday, something urgent. But no details on what it was about."

"Got it. Spelt was on his own with Aziz. Look, I'll get back to you. We're pretty busy now. A hit and run a while ago. One of yours, a guy on a bike with university ID."

"What's his name?"

"Goodwin, hand me the sheet on the H&R. . . . Thanks. . . . It's Renwick, Kevin Renwick."

"Shit. I talked to him a while ago. Told him to go to the station and make a statement. He's one of Spelt's collaborators. Spelt used Renwick and Turner to work on my suspension. When did Renwick get hit?"

"About a half hour ago, we got a call from a woman walking her cat. Yeah, cat. She found him. We're looking for witnesses, but it's a quiet street. Cyclists love it. Hit from behind and thrown down the embankment on Hemlock just before 3rd Street. He's at Vancouver General now with a concussion, dislocated shoulder, broken left femur, and cracked pelvis."

"Damn, you won't be able to talk to him for a while."

"Looks like it."

"Can you keep an eye on him?"

"Bit tough. We're short of staff right now. I'll leave word at the hospital that he's not to have visitors unless they're family."

"Anything more on Aziz?"

"A little. Ravi went through his wallet again and found a small scrap of paper at the bottom of one of the card slots. Here it is: RBC/6278."

"PIN for an ATM card?"

"I don't think so. He banks at VanCity and the number doesn't check out."

"Let me know when you figure it out."

Monroe noted the number in his notebook and then dialed Warren but cancelled the call before it rang because an old beagle limped up to him, pushed his nose against his leg, and, at the same time, lifted his front left paw. "Hey, old fella. Got a problem?" Monroe noticed that the dog had no collar or ID. He stood stoically as Monroe held his paw and found a piece of glass embedded in it. "Ouch, you need to see a vet." Monroe looked at his bike. "And someone with a car to take you." He dialed the SPCA and a woman said someone would be there in ten minutes. The dog, meanwhile, settled down and Monroe sat with him, quietly collecting his thoughts, until a white van pulled up.

The driver, an athletic fifty-something with brilliant blue eyes, jumped out. He went down on one knee in front of the dog. "Let's get you into the back here and to the vet." He gently picked up the dog and placed him on a kind of mattress. Monroe gave him a pat and the dog licked his hand. "Thanks, mate," the driver said. "We'll take good care of him."

Monroe handed him three twenties and his card. "It's all the cash I have, but I'll cover any fees. Call me if you don't find the owner."

"Will do. We usually know within a day or two."

Monroe sat back on the bench and took a deep breath. He felt flat. At least he had helped the dog. But poor Aziz, not so lucky. Davis not even aware that he existed. And Kevin. Not exactly evil but not an innocent either. A kind of trickster with a sketchy moral compass. That fixation on Peter Sellers, where did that come from? Still . . . rough to think of him in intensive care right now.

48

Monroe kept an eye on the van until it rounded the corner and then rang Warren again. "Did you get the folder back to Spelt's office?"

"Not yet. About to go now."

"OK, could you ask Mildred if she knows where Spelt has been for the past couple of hours? And ask her if Kevin Renwick from the computing centre phoned him this afternoon. Call me. I'll be on campus in about twenty minutes."

Monroe was nearly there when Warren phoned back. He leaned his bike against a tree before picking up. "The folder's back in the metal box, locked up, and the key's back in the file folder. I was fast, man. Mildred said Spelt left about an hour and a half ago, right after Renwick phoned. Oh, there's something else a little odd. Spelt borrowed Mildred's Firefly. You've seen it. Little old beater, 1980-something vintage. His car was being serviced, having snow tires put on and then an urgent errand and a meeting with the Dean of Graduate Studies. He promised to fill the tank for her."

"Big deal, hardly uses any gas. Hard to imagine him driving a car like that. Coffee at The Buzz in fifteen?

"OK, see you then."

Monroe cut through the quad and slipped into the parking lot reserved for administrators. In it, he saw Spelt's grey Passat. He got off his bike and felt the hood. It was cold. Then he checked the tires: all weather. Peering into the interior to read the sticker on the windshield, he saw that the car had last been serviced in August.

"Hey, what are you doing?" A young guy dressed in a campus police shirt stood straddling his bike at the rear of Spelt's car.

"Evan . . . President Spelt gave me a ride this morning and I thought I left something in his car. It's not on the front seat where I would have left it. Want to see some ID?" Monroe didn't wait for a reply but had already flipped open his wallet, where his faculty card was on display.

"Thanks, Professor. Just checking. We're supposed to be on the lookout for people breaking into cars." Monroe pedaled off, but when he glanced back, he saw that the young man was writing something in a notebook attached to his handlebar.

Monroe stopped by an acacia tree and phoned the police number. Constable Hudson picked up and he told her to tell Jim that somebody should inspect Mildred's car for accident clues and Spelt's fingerprints for today's hit-and-run case.

In a far corner of The Buzz, Warren gave a wave and pointed to a coffee sitting in front of an empty chair. Monroe sat and looked at the cup. "Good initiative, Warren."

Warren leaned forward on his elbows. "Now what? I read the stuff in that file, but what good is it now that Aziz is dead?"

"Not much. I think he may have been ready to talk. He must have told Spelt he was going to see Davis. Signed his death warrant."

Warren nodded. "Now Spelt's in the clear."

"Maybe not. What if Aziz left a record of what he had been doing? He was smart, would have had some insurance if he threatened to see Davis."

"So you think he hid something that incriminated Spelt?"

"He might have. But maybe not in the apartment. It was ransacked before the police got there. Ravi found only one letter and his military record."

"That's a big deal," Warren said.

"Yeah, and we should keep looking. . . . Oh, I didn't tell you there was a scrap of paper in his wallet that must mean something."

"What's on it?"

Monroe checked his notebook. "It says RBC 6278."

"Easy. His ATM password with the Royal Bank of Canada."

"That's what Jim thought. It doesn't check out. Aziz banked at VanCity."

"And?"

"Not much in that account. He was sending regular wire transfers to Iraq."

Warren glanced at his watch. "Department meeting started five minutes ago."

Monroe frowned. "On a Friday?"

"To confirm the short list for the new appointment in ethno-psychology."

"When are the candidates coming to campus?"

"The first is next Friday, the 29th."

"Swell, perfect for an ethno-Halloween."

Warren didn't crack a smile. "Not funny."

Monroe finished his coffee then headed for the exit. Outside, Monroe moved to an area a little off the crisscrossing paths planted with blueberries and Oregon Grape, and texted to remind Jim to send someone to campus to confirm Spelt's alibi for midday when Renwick was run down and, again, to do a forensic examination of Mildred's Firefly. *He'll be annoyed that I'm repeating myself,* he thought.

When he looked up from his phone, he saw Mrs. Kerr heading his way. "What a surprise," he said.

"I might say the same. I take it the silliness of your suspension is still under review? I'm only on the BOG and no one has told me anything."

"Yes, unfortunately. The committee hearing on it doesn't take place until next week, Friday the 29th."

"Well, I think I will bring it up at our next meeting. I understand that your students will be presenting a petition to get you back before the term ends."

"That's gratifying. I don't have much confidence in the process. Getting rid of me was a fix from the outset. Spelt organized it and got Fred Turner from political science and Kevin Renwick in IT to do the newspaper story. Renwick's now in hospital, run down on the way to give a statement to the police."

Mrs. Kerr's eyes widened. "So you think . . ." Her voice trailed off. "You confronted this person?"

Monroe changed the subject. "At least you have the good news about that painting by Murphy, thanks to Jean-Michel."

"Oh, my . . . yes." Her face beamed as if she was suddenly ten years younger. "As you know, it vindicates Lloyd. He was sure about it. I've just been closeted with Dean Erickson in Graduate Studies for the past couple of hours to brainstorm how to leverage it to build our program in art history."

"I hope it happens. By the way, was President Spelt in on that discussion?"

"Good heavens, no. We'll go over his head if necessary. The BOG is ready to overrule him if he squeaks." She paused to listen to the clock tower. "Do rats squeak or only mice? I must be going."

Monroe walked toward the administration building deep in thought. *Did Spelt really have a meeting with Erickson as he'd told Mildred? Should check. Otherwise, he has no alibi for when Renwick was run down.* If only Aziz hid something that could be used. And if Spelt planted that muffin meant for Eliot, how and when did he do it? He sat down in an alcove near the dean of arts' offices and pulled out his notebook. Checking his notes, Monroe began to set out a chronology of events.

1. *Eliot dies on September 28.*

2. *In August, Eliot tells Spelt he is investigating complaints about the dean's research fund. Meyer involved. Spelt not happy.*

3. *Meyer finds indications of malfeasance. Lack of accountability, indication of theft? Eliot calls it a cancer.*

4. *Letter from Eliot's doctor (dated August 30) telling him to renew his EpiPen could have been on Eliot's desk in one or more meetings with Spelt.*

5. *Aziz accesses Eliot's office (September 21) to estimate carpet cleaning.*

6. *Eliot's investigation of dean's fund motive for Spelt? Spelt believes his career is over, unless he can get rid of Eliot. Aziz's "estimate" (September 21) is really a ruse to get into Eliot's office and sabotage his EpiPen.*

7. *With the pen ruined, a switch of Eliot's muffin (September 28) would be fatal.*

Monroe stood up and went into the dean's office. He saw Margo at the copy machine in the back and gave a wave. She came to the front.

"Hello, Bruce. What can I do for you?"

"Hi, Margo. Bear with me. I'm trying to go back to September 28th. Do you recall anything about Spelt's schedule that day?"

"*That* day." She sighed. "I'll check the scheduler." She sat down at her computer. "OK, here we are. Red ink: no appointments 2:00 p.m. because the dean has meetings downtown. There's a notation that I put in: 'C recital at 10.'"

"Meaning?"

"Normally that Chiara should get to the academy by 9 and Spelt would be driving her. Make something up in case he gets a call."

"Got it. Anything else?."

Margo tapped a few keys and looked at her screen. "Well, it wasn't as simple as the entry here. Chiara got here around 8:30, all dressed up and ready to go, but she hadn't eaten. She went down to Food Services to get something. Spelt seemed impatient. Finally, she got back a little after 9:00, running a little late, but not outrageous. She'd lost track of time because she had been talking to Nicole."

"And Spelt was annoyed?"

"Well, he had gone to look for her and wasn't back himself. When he got here he said he wouldn't be able to go, that she would have to take a taxi, and he was going to see Bob Getty."

Monroe looked surprised. "Getty in English?" Those two had barely spoken since Spelt cancelled their search for a new appointment in Canadian literature.

"I was surprised. We knew they haven't been on good terms. But off he went, still dressed as if he was going to the recital."

"In his raincoat?"

"Yes, and when Chiara and I left to catch her taxi, he was standing in a cluster of people near the English department."

"At the cart?"

"Near it, I'd say. Closer to the front of the student aid office."

"And talking to Getty?"

"No, he was off to one side with Professor Ellis, gesturing as if trying to make a point. She and Luce talk here sometimes. They celebrated a couple of weeks ago after she won the teaching award."

"OK, switch gears, something general. What did Spelt think of President Eliot?"

Margo frowned. "Well, that's a loaded question. He didn't say that much, but we knew he didn't like him. Everyone knew he expected to succeed Bolton as president. When Eliot was named he was here and he—uh—"

"Disappointed?"

"Well, that's putting it mildly. I overheard the term 'political hack' way out here in the outer office when he was on the phone."

"But then he resigned himself?" Monroe asked.

"Um, more like he was smoldering. And it became worse six or eight weeks ago when President Eliot told him he would be investigating the management of the Dean's Research Fund."

"And you gathered up the records for this investigation."

"Everything we could find. Mildred took the files to Financial Services to be checked against receipts and reports they had received directly."

"And Spelt knew you were doing this?"

"Oh, yes, he knew it was coming. But I think he thought it would be pro forma. With Mr. Meyer involved it looked serious."

48

◼

At the English department a student was coming out of Linda Ellis's office and another was waiting to go in. Monroe asked her if he could butt in for a quick question, and she smiled and said of course. "Honest," Monroe said, "it'll be short."

"Linda, quick question. Your student kindly let me jump the queue. I feel like I'm on the run like the fugitive or something. It's an old TV show and movie."

Linda laughed. "I remember the movie. By the way, the young woman in the hallway is Angela Delany's friend. They talk a lot, and ideas from Angela in your course have sometimes filtered into my tutorials."

"Oh, I like *that*. Supposed to happen, no? OK, here's my question. Do you remember anything about September 28, the day Eliot died?"

Linda paused. "A sadness, sense of loss. Not sure what else to say."

"Of course, but I'm asking about something more mundane, when the cart was here. Margo said she saw you and Getty talking."

"Oh, that. Just commiserating about losing our new appointment. He blames Spelt. He's fed up with chairing and keeps telling me I should be the next chair because I can fight the *beast*—his word—to a standstill. I take it as a joke. It's not much of a sales pitch."

"Did you see Spelt at the cart that day?"

"I'm afraid so. He and Bob had words. Spelt said something about our enrollment numbers and Bob said—I'm quoting—'fuck you, you little worm.'"

Monroe nodded. "Bob can be pretty direct. Anything else?"

"Bob walked away and Spelt drifted to one side and became interested in the muffins on the cart. Trying to save face, I thought. And he looked awkward in that raincoat. One of our students said he was probably on his way to flash someone at the Stanley Park tennis courts."

Monroe smiled. "Could have been right."

✖

"Come in, Bruce," Bob Getty called in response to Monroe's tap on his half-open door. "What's up? Still in purgatory?"

"Yes, in a way. The hearing's next Friday."

"A complete joke. This place is going to rack and ruin with the likes of Spelt running the joint. What's with the secrecy? A big deal to ask a few questions about what's really going on?"

"Apparently not. Lately I've been poking around full time. Not sure they had *that* in mind."

"Finding anything?"

"Hmm . . . maybe yes. I think a break may be coming soon. I just wanted to check on what you saw in this corridor on September 28th. The day Eliot—."

"Yeah, yeah. The day he died. A Tuesday, three weeks and three days ago. I remember stuff like that. What I had for lunch yesterday? Not so much."

"That morning, Margo Johnson saw you talking to Linda Ellis near the cart."

"Yeah, probably. I talk to her every day. She's right across the hall, has ideas, a sense of humour, good judgment. With any luck she'll replace me as our next chair."

"What about Spelt that day?"

"Ah . . . you mean my little outburst. He was clucking about our enrollment numbers being a little down this semester. And then complaining about an opinion piece by one of our students in the *Norwester* about university administrators proliferating."

"This to justify cancelling your appointment?"

"In a roundabout way, yes. Managerial speak. Can't stand it."

"What happened after your . . . outburst?"

"Let me think . . . I remember wondering why he was sticking around, studying the muffins as if they were rare specimens. Then he ups and sticks one in his pocket, no wrapper or anything, tosses some money into the box, and takes off toward his office."

"Pocket of his raincoat?"

"Yeah, a nice one but too big for him. Some sort of heirloom, I think."

"Thanks, Bob." Monroe hurried down the corridor toward the president's offices. He asked Mildred if Spelt was in and she said he had just stepped out and should be right back.

"Good. Where does he keeps his raincoat?"

"On a peg just inside his office. Actually, he asked me to take it to the cleaners some time ago." Mildred kept a straight face. "I forgot."

Good one, she's getting snarky. Monroe stepped into Spelt's office, grabbed the raincoat, rolled it, and tucked it under his arm. "If he asks about it, you have a ready-made answer." Walking down the corridor, he texted Jim: "Send someone to my house, ASAP, to pick up something for forensics."

With his head down, Monroe nearly ran into Jean-Michel.

"Distracted? Still thinking about the Aziz business?" Jean-Michel asked.

"Yeah, off and on. But something has been bothering me since we last talked."

"Such as?"

"Well, the way he was in the gallery the other day."

"What's the problem? A lot of people come in and look at the paintings."

"Yes, but you said he kept looking around as if waiting to be left alone or something. Can we go into the gallery for a minute?"

"Sure. I was heading back there anyway."

Once there, Monroe set the raincoat aside and approached the painting. "You haven't moved it?"

"Nope. This is where it was."

"And he pulled a chair up and sat where?"

Jean-Michel settled at a spot six or eight feet from the painting. "Here."

"Am I imagining it or is the painting not quite level?"

Jean-Michel looked carefully. "Possibly. Someone could have brushed against the frame, although we ask people not to get too close."

"Could you take it off the wall for a minute?"

Jean-Michel gave Monroe one of those is-this-really-necessary looks. He lifted the picture off the wall and held it up. "Satisfied?"

"Not quite. Check the back."

Jean-Michel turned the back of the picture toward Monroe and they both saw it at the same time: a bronze key taped to the edge of the frame. Monroe looked at it closely without touching it. "Don't see a number on it."

Jean-Michel looked puzzled. "What the hell—"

"Tell you later. Stick the painting in your office and don't touch it."

50

The quad was deserted and Monroe glanced at the clock tower, expecting it to be close to 4:00 but it was just hitting 3:15. A single bong confirmed it right on cue. Friday afternoon's early exodus was well advanced and no one was around. Monroe parked himself on the Lloyd Kerr bench among the maples and, for a minute, watched an energetic clutch of chickadees poke around for seeds and crawling things. He pulled out his phone. "Jim, can you talk?"

"Yeah, but make it fast. Some border patrol guys here. What's up?"

"It looks like Aziz taped a key to the back of a painting in the campus gallery. Probably on Thursday, about the time he set up a meeting with Davis. It could be the key to a safe deposit box."

"Timing is good, maybe about his dealings with Spelt."

"That's what I was thinking. By the way, did any of Aziz's neighbours see anything?"

"No. The woman in an adjoining apartment heard noises. But that's all. Anyway, great work. I'll send someone to collect the key and dust it for prints."

"It's in Jean-Michel's office in the gallery. Have you followed up on Mildred's car yet? Or talked to Renwick?

"Easy, can't do everything at once. Renwick's still in a coma. But we got a fleck of paint off the bike. We'll see if it matches. Anything else?"

"Not right now. I'll try to send you some files later today or tomorrow if Hans Meyer is far enough along."

"Files?"

"Yeah, the stuff Meyer was looking into about the Dean's Research Fund."

"OK. As soon as you can. Oh, yeah . . . you texted about something to pick up at your house?"

226

"Right. Spelt's overcoat. I have an eyewitness who saw him put a muffin into one of the pockets on the morning Eliot died. I think it was Eliot's muffin that he had switched for one with peanuts in it."

"You've got the raincoat?"

"Yes, I took it out of his office. . . . Uh oh. I know what you're going to say. Tampered evidence. A lawyer would say I planted the crumbs."

"At least that, old buddy. Unless we picked it up ourselves, the prosecutor wouldn't touch it. You're a bit of a loose cannon, you know."

"I know . . . in too much of a hurry again, I guess. Well, couldn't Mildred testify that Spelt put it on a hook in his office and it hasn't been moved since? She forgot to take it to the cleaners."

"Hmm, a lawyer would cross-examine Mildred and tear her apart. Has the raincoat ever been out of her sight since Eliot's death? That sort of thing. In effect, you just stole the guy's raincoat."

"At least Spelt's documents are back in his file box and I have copies."

"Good. As for the coat, I'll go through the motions on the coat with a receipt signed by Constable Hudson. We'll leave it with Mildred and she can forget about it unless he asks for it. I'll arrange for a search warrant now, so we can find those documents in his file."

"Thanks."

"I'll pick up the coat around dinnertime at your place. Forensics can compare it to our analysis of the allergy-free muffin from three weeks ago."

Monroe didn't say anything, feeling frustrated with himself. Spelt was his man, but he was contaminating the evidence like a rank amateur.

⚎

At home, Monroe rang Meyer, who picked up on the fourth ring.

"Meyer, Monroe here."

"You're back."

"How'd you know I was gone?"

"I stopped by your house and your neighbour came through the hedge and told me."

"You're lucky she didn't call the cops. How'd she—"

"She saw you getting into a taxi. You had a small bag and she inferred a short trip with only carry-on."

Monroe laughed. "That's what she said? She's good."

"I could use her in my office."

"Why'd you come by?"

"I had an update for you. . . . The investigation is pretty well done."

"You *know* where the money went?"

"Most of it."

"Excellent."

"How about we meet tomorrow?" Meyer asked. "Your house. I need to get out of here. Is 10:30 OK? You academics up by then on a Saturday?"

"Take it easy. We're not all layabouts. And check your email tonight. I'm going to send you what we've found on Spelt's travel expenses. See what you think."

"Glad to be doing something. I'm getting bored with this leave crap."

"Just be careful. Don't go for a stroll in the neighbourhood and keep your files out of sight. Our killer has been active in the past couple of days."

Monroe put the phone down and splashed a little wine into his glass. He then dialed Warren, who picked up after one ring.

"What do you want? I'm just back from Ambleside observing a couple of red-winged blackbirds in the swampy area by the soccer pitches. Beautiful, still singing and calling to each other like it's breeding season. Now Winston's here."

"Winston?"

"The neighbour's golden retriever. Boswell buddy."

"Oh, what a pair. His people traveling?"

"Yeah, Hawaii. I'm his second home anyway. Now he's wondering why you're bothering us."

"Meyer is coming by my place tomorrow at 10:30. Can you show him what you've got to link Spelt's travel with Chiara's. If it does."

"OK, I've pretty well got it in my head. A half dozen guest appearances and some master classes. Not that extensive."

"And look for something Margo may email you if she comes up with anything. See if it adds to your spreadsheet. Oh, one more thing." Monroe thumbed his notebook. "Here it is. I got it from Mildred that Turner came to see Spelt right after me the day I was there. Same day that the Clouseau photo was taken. Looks like Spelt organized it with Turner and Renwick."

"Oh, clever. Not too surprising, though."

Monroe picked up his glass and swirled the wine. It would be good to have a pal like Winston around. His neighbours only had cats. He remembered the beagle with glass in his paw. Stoic, patient, wise, trusting. He yawned, suddenly aware that he was losing his focus and was tired. The wine didn't even taste particularly good.

Just then there was a knock on the front door. It was Jim. "I don't have much time. Another shooting in Surrey."

Monroe nodded. "I'll get the coat. It's in a bag in the kitchen."

"I could use a glass of water," Jim said.

"Help yourself."

Jim picked a large glass from the cupboard and ran the cold before filling it. "Any news from Chicago?" Monroe asked

"Nothing new. I called Roosevelt to thank him for his help. But no leads on the violin or the shell corporation that paid for the cello. But none expected."

"What about Mildred's car or Aziz's? Pushed into the drink?"

"Probably. The car went in motor running and in drive. Aziz was hit with a blunt object, a board or a baseball bat. It didn't kill him though. Died from drowning."

"Supposed to look accidental?"

"Yeah, but botched. . . . Unless they expected the blow on his head to look like it was caused by the wreck. Whoever did it took the trouble to get the car in gear but had to get up to enough speed to break through the barrier. I think we'll match a few flecks of paint from Aziz's rear bumper with what we found on the front of a '75 Ford 150 pickup truck that went missing for a few hours that morning from Horseshoe Bay."

Monroe didn't answer but felt a wave of frustration. Another near miss. The truck would be checked, paint would be found, but nothing would link it to Spelt or whoever pushed Aziz over the embankment. Mildred's car running Renwick off the road might prove to be different if Spelt's prints were on it. His raincoat probably useless in front of a judge.

Stop thinking about it, you screwed up, Monroe told himself. Jim, meanwhile finished off his water and picked up the raincoat. "I'll be in touch," he said with a tired smile.

51

Monroe slept poorly and was up early. He made a coffee and went to his desk to look at his manuscript. He made a few editorial changes but half-heartedly, second-guessing changes he had made. He checked his email and read a note from his brother Ben asking him to come to Barcelona. He was trying to find out what happened to their grandfather who had gone to Spain in 1937 to fight for the Republican forces in the Spanish Civil War. The idea appealed to him, but for now he had his hands full. The phone rang and Meyer, obviously annoyed, announced that his car had a dead battery.

Monroe said he would come to his place. Afterward, he could go for a run around Stanley Park and so put on some nylon pants and a sweatshirt. After lacing up an old pair of Asics—past their prime but still comfortable—he poked his head out the front door. Warren was standing in the street with Winston, giving him a pat, pointing toward James Crescent.

"Telling him to go home?"

"Yes, you point and say, 'Go home *now*.' He understands 'home' and 'now.' But he's a social creature." Warren pointed and repeated his command, but Winston didn't move, instead he looked at him and wagged his tail.

"Look, we've got a change of plans. Meyer can't drive. Dead battery. I'll drive us to his place. We can drop Winston off on the way."

Meyer's front garden looked neglected, more so because someone had done a half-hearted weeding job in one of the front flowerbeds. Warren pushed the doorbell and the door opened. "Doing a little gardening, I see," Warren said.

Meyer frowned as he looked out. "I hate gardening. Especially this time of year. My wife does it. Come in, please." Monroe was surprised to hear the word please. "This way," Meyer gestured. "A fresh pot of coffee on the kitchen table. Sorry for the last-minute change in plan."

Monroe did a double take. *Please? Sorry? What's with Meyer?* As they walked toward the kitchen, Monroe noticed some framed engravings on the wall that looked to be urban lithographs of nineteenth-century cities. Meyer noticed that Monroe had paused to look at them. "All Munich," he said. "My family's home. A sister, an engineering professor at Technical University of Munich, still lives there, although she travels all the time giving lectures." He laughed. "She got most of the brains in the family."

At the kitchen table, Monroe saw a couple of spreadsheets ready to be inspected. Meyer motioned toward the coffee pot at one side. "Help yourselves."

Monroe filled a cup and passed it to Warren and then poured a cup for himself. "What have you got here, Meyer?"

Meyer smiled and pointed to a spreadsheet. "This one deals with the Dean's Research fund. It documents all the funds I was suspicious about. In column A, I've listed sums awarded to grant recipients, and in column B, the amounts ending up in one of Mr. Spelt's accounts. The sum of B equals 93 percent of A, which tells me the recipients, some of them, received a small kickback in exchange for the use of the name."

Monroe looked at Warren and then back at the spreadsheet. After staring at it for a couple of minutes, he said, "OK, I see twenty-seven names on the list, some getting several grants. Ah, Bob Milton from business administration. I don't think he publishes much. And some others of the same ilk."

"That's the idea," Meyer said. "There were two categories of recipients. The first I call conduits. They receive, say, $10,000, deduct three to five percent, and forward the remainder back to Spelt's private account. Sixteen names fall into this category."

"And the others?" Warren asked.

"The others were faculty who didn't apply for funds and never received them. The cheques were sent to a post office box care of Mr. Spelt and he simply endorsed them with an account number, no name, and deposited them straightaway into his account. I should say 'accounts'—he had several."

"How did you get into Spelt's accounts?" Monroe asked. "Isn't this illegal?"

"Not for me," Meyer said. "My niece has top-level EC security clearances and can quietly check accounts in Canada too because a lot of Canadian banks have partners or direct operations in Germany. She ran some checks on Canadian and US banks and looked at Spelt's records at RBC, TD, and Truestone Credit Union in Minneapolis. See the account activity in column six."

Warren frowned. "Minneapolis."

"He's from there," Monroe said. "And his father lives there, in an assisted-living home. He's an emeritus professor, has his own pension—probably not enough to live on—and still spends time at the University of Minnesota."

"This is all good, but I wonder . . ." Monroe paused, thinking of his own shortcuts to get evidence. "Can information captured illegally be used in a court case?"

Meyer shrugged his shoulders. "You'd have to ask a lawyer."

"What is this other sheet?" Warren asked as he pointed to another printout to one side.

"It's partly what you emailed me yesterday. I've correlated Spelt's official travel for university business with his daughter's travel to play as an invited soloist or to attend a master class."

Monroe and Warren leaned over to look more closely. "In a way this makes it even more blatant," Monroe said after studying it. "How did he think he could get away with it?"

Warren smiled. "I didn't expect it to come together so neatly."

Monroe poured more coffee. This has to be the last piece of the puzzle. All in plain view. "The motive to kill Eliot," he said in a low voice. "Meyer, this is dangerous stuff. Send copies of it to Inspector Martino right away and Warren and I will take a printed copy. Meanwhile, why don't you and your wife drive to Kelowna for a few days?"

Meyer started to protest but Monroe cut him short. "You're still on paid leave and something could happen. Just go."

52

In the car, Monroe sat for a minute staring straight ahead. Warren finally broke the silence. "Think he'll go to Kelowna?"

"No."

"Why not?"

"First, he's a stubborn sonofabitch. Second, he's not afraid. His family lived through the war in Germany. His grandparents probably told him what it was like to live under the Nazis. And in the end, they might even have felt complicit in war crimes."

Warren fiddled with his seatbelt. "And maybe things aren't going so well with his wife. You know . . . the thing with Mildred."

"That, too. He could be worried about her." Monroe started the car, drove two blocks, and turned left on Anderson Crescent. He stopped beside a large Douglas fir.

"What are you doing?"

"I'm getting out. Need to think and walking helps. Drive yourself home and I'll get the car later."

Monroe took Meyer's spreadsheets and stepped from the car. With a wave he started up Anderson Crescent as if to circle toward Acacia Park. As soon as the car was out of sight, though, he turned around and headed toward Stevens Avenue. He walked along Stevens until he came to Dogwood Lane.

At 935 Dogwood he saw a blue SUV in the driveway. He looked at the house for a few minutes and was about to approach it when the front door opened and Mrs. Spelt stepped out. She seemed to be dressed for yoga and had a purple mat tucked under one arm.

She backed the SUV out quickly and roared away. Monroe pressed the record button on his cell and slipped it into an inner pocket before he crossed the street and rang the doorbell. After an interval, the door swung open and Spelt, looking disheveled as if he hadn't slept well, squinted out at him, his face twisted into a frown. "What are *you* doing here?"

Monroe smiled. "I was in the neighbourhood. It shouldn't take too long."

Spelt sighed. "I suppose this is about your suspension. You're wasting my time. My Saturday." With a flick of his hand, Spelt gestured for Monroe to enter.

Monroe could hear the mellow tones of a cello somewhere in the house. "Could we do this in your office?" he asked.

"Damn right," Spelt muttered. He gestured down a hallway. "Straight ahead past the stairs and the door to the left."

Spelt stationed himself behind his desk and, using the same flick of the hand, gestured toward a chair in front. The wall behind was covered with framed photos, mostly of Chiara with her cello or with other musicians—another one with Yo-Yo Ma—and others apparently friends of Spelt and his wife, second- or third-level local celebrities, including Chancellor Davis. A thick curtain rod leaned against one side of the desk, apparently ready to be placed over a row of windows at one side.

Spelt leaned forward, elbows down, chin in hands. "I thought I made it clear that your suspension's in the hands of the ethics committee. I know you don't like it, old fellow, but you have to take one for the team. The chancellor has to protect the public persona of the university: a place of orderly processes that are judicious and fair. Everyone knows that you sometime say things without thinking them through. That one about Eliot was over the top though."

"Except I didn't say it. I think you made it up just as you pushed for my suspension. Chancellor Davis told me so himself. But I'm not here to talk about my suspension. That little put-up job you organized with Turner and Renwick will be clarified as soon as he recovers from a little bike accident and talks to the police. Renwick will explain how you masterminded it, maybe with a little push by Fred Turner."

"Wait a min—"

Monroe interrupted. "Don't be surprised, Renwick's OK. Yes, you clipped him and he went over the embankment, but some shrubbery gave him a soft landing. But there's more." Monroe patted the sheets that Meyer had printed out. "You charged your personal travel—to Chiara's concerts and master classes—to the university."

Spelt froze in his chair, his face red. "Get out of my house. Leave Chiara out of this."

Monroe leaned forward and spoke in a soft voice. "Oh, but this isn't about Chiara; it's about *you*." Monroe slid one of the sheets across the desk. "For starters, take a look at this. This summarizes your embezzlement of funds from the Dean's Research Fund. In August, Eliot told you he would be investigating the file of complaints assembled by Bancroft. When he brought Meyer in you realized it was serious and you couldn't let him succeed. You sent Aziz to destroy Eliot's EpiPen—decked out as a carpet cleaner doing an estimate—to make sure Eliot had no defense against the anaphylactic shock that would come from switching his muffin. It all started with your embezzlement scheme."

Spelt said nothing but then smiled. "Nice try, Monroe, but you've got it wrong. This is something Eliot would have cooked up with the help of that German in Financial Services." There was contempt in his voice. "They both hated me; they were trying to frame me, they were jealous of my record as dean and the vision I would have brought to the presidency in partnership with our chancellor. And on a personal level, they resented my daughter's growing international reputation. I could have lived with Eliot, you know. Given him a term as president if that's what the minister wanted. But he overstepped the way we do things. Me, a dean, a tenured professor, a respected scholar. He tried to humiliate me.

Old Bancroft knew the rules, trusted his deans and the way we manage our domains. You and I, Monroe, we're colleagues. We're on the same team, man. Come on, some cooked-up sheets by the German accountant? It can't be serious. OK, I timed some of my university travel to correlate—an important word, Monroe, *correlate*—with Chiara's travel, but, believe me, these trips were about university business. The timing was fortuitous."

Monroe said nothing.

"Look, Monroe, Eliot was a fool and an outsider. I was patient until he started cooking up conspiracies and coming after me. The man was paranoid. Too bad he died, but I'm not sorry he's gone. He wasn't a real academic. Imagine, no doctorate, no teaching experience. He wasn't one of us. A fish out of water. We have advanced degrees, we understand universities. I don't mind telling you that I have plans to jump you into the position of vice-president academic, where your vision and intelligence can play a proper role in bringing Northlake to its potential."

Monroe sat back in his chair. "Don't make me laugh. You don't care about Northlake. You care about Evan Spelt. You're ambitious for yourself, to prove something to your father who overshadows you, to support your daughter, a gifted musician. None of this is wrong in itself except that it scaled out of control. Monroe reached over and tapped one of the spreadsheets. "The motive, Evan. This is it. Hans Meyer did some good work by tracking down the fake grants. He correlated the amounts withdrawn from the fund with dates and amounts that you deposited into your bank accounts. Facts.

All those ghost recipients, by the way, have been contacted by the police and will be making statements. This is fraud, theft, breach of trust. The prosecutors will figure out what to call it. But you knew you couldn't let it come to light, destroy your career, send you to jail, disgrace you, and perhaps taint your daughter's reputation. That's why you organized the bombing of Meyer's van. He had become dangerous when Eliot got him to look closely at your handling of the Dean's Research Fund, but you probably didn't know how much he had found out. And that's also why you organized my suspension: because you didn't like me poking around trying to figure out who killed Eliot. So far then we have theft, murder, and attempted murder."

Spelt was clenching and unclenching his jaw. A manic laugh escaped him. "I tell you, this is crazy, a put-up job. I'll get a lawyer—Sarah McKenzie, the best—and she will show all this is fantasy and circumstantial. You'll look like a fool."

The sounds of the cello had stopped and it seemed eerily quiet. Chiara's playing had been seeping into the study from a nearby room, a passage from Bach's first cello suite, the only one Monroe could recognize for sure.

"Look, Evan, I know you needed money. What with the new house, expensive cars, expenses for Chiara's training and your father's care. But you lost your bearings, whatever ethical bearings you once had. I've got a witness who saw you switch the killer muffin in the corridor the day Eliot died. Police forensics will find the crumbs from Eliot's muffin in the pocket of your raincoat.

"I guess you're not aware that Aziz wrote down all the dirty tricks he did for you—if you want to call them that—in exchange for your promise to get his family out of Iraq. He put them into a safety deposit box and then warned you that he was going to talk to Chancellor Davis, whom he thought was in on the plan to sponsor his family." Monroe lowered his voice. "You couldn't let that happen, so you killed Aziz. The police now have access to Aziz's safety deposit box. They will know how, to pay for your daughter's new cello, he fenced the violin you stole after stranding the Japanese woman to die on Grouse Mountain. That's yet another death to your credit."

"Aziz was an intemperate man," Spelt said with indifference. "A piece of flotsam that washed up on our shores. He was dangerous. He threatened me. A Muslim, for god's sake. What I did was for the greater good. Look, Monroe, I cut a couple corners, but we're all in a better place now because of it."

Monroe was pretty sure, missing some details, that his version of events was true, but he knew it didn't amount to something a judge would buy. He had to keep Spelt talking.

He turned his head and noticed that an adjoining door had opened a crack.

"You're rushing to judgment, Monroe. Taking things out of context. Yes, I had some extra expenses and borrowed some funds from the Dean's Research Fund. Borrowed, you hear? I was going to pay them back. Eliot was a hothead, out to get me. Setting up an investigation of a dean is an insult. He had no real understanding of collegiality. I switched his muffin, I'll admit, but it was meant as a warning and a kind of joke. I acted for the greater good of Northlake University. Can't you see that? He wasn't one of us. You should be thanking me."

"Thanking you? Are you crazy? You've harmed all of us by killing that good man, a far better man than you, a man of integrity, good faith, and vision. You've harmed Chiara by stealing that violin and leaving Mrs. Tanaka to die on the mountain." Monroe glanced to one side again as the door moved slightly.

Before he could turn back, a book slammed into the side of his head, knocking him off his chair. A sharp pain knifed into his temple, but he had the presence of mind to wonder what had hit him. With bleary eyesight, he recognized *The Concise Oxford Dictionary* on the floor next to him with a trickle of his blood pooling next to it. *A small weapon*, he thought, *but proof of the power of words.*

Monroe felt groggy and his vision was blurred. Spelt kicked Monroe in the head and then recoiled in pain, for he was wearing soft slippers. The blow nevertheless hurt like hell and Monroe felt that his left eye had begun to close from the blow of the dictionary.

Spelt, meanwhile, recovered from the pain in his foot. Monroe didn't see that Spelt had snatched the curtain rod until it was too late. He swung it toward his head. At the last moment, Monroe rolled partly under the desk and the rod hit the floor with a loud whack.

Before Spelt could strike again, Monroe grabbed the end of it with one hand and reached out and pulled Spelt's ankle as hard as he could toward the desk. Spelt went down but managed to pull the rod away. By now, Monroe had crawled through to the other side of the desk and pulled himself to his knees. He grabbed Spelt's desk lamp and threw it as hard as he could. Spelt blocked it partly with curtain rod and then managed to hit Monroe again on the head.

Monroe went down and, like a cat, Spelt was on him, pressing the rod into his throat. Through a fog Monroe heard him, his face close and his breath foul. "You're finished, Monroe. It's your own fault. We could've worked together. Bloody minded is what you are, and a traitor. This too is for the greater good."

Monroe couldn't breathe, and was trying to push up to loosen the rod jammed against his throat. An attempt to kick Spelt was ineffective and he felt himself losing consciousness.

As if in the distance, he then heard a scream. "Daddy, no!" It seemed that Chiara had run into the room. Her cry distracted Spelt enough that he turned toward her, thus shifting the rod enough for Monroe to get a breath. But then Spelt pressed down harder than ever and the pain was terrible. Monroe blacked out just after Chiara screamed again. He was vaguely aware of a crashing noise. Miraculously, the pressure on his throat was gone.

Later, he learned that Chiara had charged into Spelt with her cello, using the instrument's endpin as a lance. She pronged him hard enough to topple him and he lay groaning on the floor, clutching his ribs. Coming to, Monroe managed to roll to one side, crawl over to Spelt, and jab his knees into him.

Pulling Spelt's arms back into a hammerlock, Monroe just sat for a while, enjoying the sweet intake of air. *So much for my judo lessons*, he thought. Chiara spoke calmly, perhaps still in shock about what she had just done. "Are you OK, Professor Monroe? I can't believe what I just heard."

"I think so," Monroe said although he wasn't yet sure. "Do you have a roll of duct tape in the house? And if you wouldn't mind, could you bring me a glass of water?"

"Tape's in the basement," she said. "I'll get it first."

Monroe pulled on Spelt and got him into a chair. "Looks like she gave you quite a spearing," he said. "Lucky for me, you bastard. And lucky for you that the cello has that rubber tip on it."

"Pain," he said. "Hurts to breathe."

Chiara returned with the duct tape and ran toward the kitchen to get the water. Monroe wrapped Spelt's wrists and ankles together and secured his torso to the back of his chair. "Spelt, you're a violent man who has killed three people and tried to kill two others."

"You have no proof. It is circumstantial. I'm president of a university. I want a lawyer. And I can see someone—Meyer, I suppose—hacked into my bank records to prepare this garbage. Violation of my privacy. It won't stand up in court."

Monroe nodded. "Why don't you make it easy for yourself? Come clean. I can see why you did all this. You were doing it for Chiara. She was the greater good you keep talking about, right? And then it got out of control."

"Greater good?" Chiara shouted in a near-hysterical voice. She had been standing at the doorway with the glass of water. "How could killing people be for the greater good?"

"Explain yourself," Monroe said. "She needs to know. She needs to know why Mrs. Tanaka had to die so you could steal her violin and buy this beautiful cello."

Chiara leaned over as if she had been punched. "I'm not your greater good," she said, her voice raspy and breaking up.

Spelt looked at her as if waking up to what he had done. "It was the only way, darling. Your career, talent, legacy of your sister. You needed a new instrument—"

Chiara interrupted him, her voice now a shriek. "This instrument?" She grabbed the cello by the neck with both hands, lifted it over her head, and smashed it on Spelt's desk. Spelt's involuntary "no" escaped his mouth. She then lifted it again and was about to hit Spelt with it, but Monroe caught her by one arm. "He deserves it, but from now on the courts and the prison system will take care of things." Chiara threw the cello down and left the room, slamming the door behind her.

"So much for that crap about a greater good," Monroe said. "Maybe you really believed it. A lot of people talk themselves into such things and then, step by step, turn themselves into monsters."

Spelt looked defeated. "It started small," he said in a soft voice. "Claiming the trips with Chiara as university business. That evolved into the scheme to borrow from the research fund." He nodded toward the spreadsheet. "Actually, this sums it up pretty well. I thought I would be able to make it up when I became president, but the minister parachuted Eliot into the job . . . a job I needed, deserved, and earned, which would have given me the salary and perks to make it all good."

"Eliot was a decent man," Monroe said. "He did his homework and wanted to make the place better. No one forced him to review those old files that Bolton left behind. Not a bad president, Bolton. He wasn't evil or anything but he ran out of gas. Eliot looked at those files and right away smelled a rat. That's you, Spelt, a rat using a public trust for private gain. Spare me the victim argument. It was ambition and greed."

Monroe pulled out his cell, stopped the recording, and punched in a number. "Hey, Jim. Monroe here. I'm at 935 Dogwood. Can you send a car right away to pick up Mr. Spelt?"

240

53

Monroe arrived at the campus early. It was Tuesday, October 26, overcast with rain forecast for later in the day. As he locked his bike in a rack next to Stirling Hall, he thought of Eliot, murdered exactly four weeks ago. *Back to normal. No, there's no such thing. Eliot's gone. There's aftermath, change. At least Spelt's gone.* He glanced across the quad and saw Fred Turner walking briskly toward The Buzz. They made eye contact and Turner looked away. Perhaps he didn't know yet that Renwick's statement would put him in the picture for that stupid Norwester caper. Not exactly a confirmation of integrity for someone who hoped to head an institute.

The phone call from Mrs. Kerr yesterday had caught him by surprise. A unanimous vote for immediate reinstatement, and an apology for his suspension by the board of governors, who'd had a special meeting on Sunday. *On Sunday.* How did that happen? And Jim had phoned to scold him for confronting Spelt alone, calling him a loose cannon again. *But a damn effective one.* The recording and Spelt's statement, he said, should lock him away for a long time. He would be collecting Aziz's documents from the metal box with a search warrant later in the day.

At the entrance to Stirling, Jean-Michel spotted him. He rushed over and gave him a hug, sloshing some coffee he'd been holding onto the floor and splattering Monroe's shoes. "Well done, Bruce. I heard you were back and Spelt's under arrest. It was in the news yester—" Jean-Michel stopped and did a double take. "Hey . . . your eye? And neck? Looks nasty."

Monroe laughed and tugged at his collar to pull it as high as possible. "It'll get better."

"Apparently, Spelt brought Davis down. He wasn't involved, so he claims, but he *should* have been more vigilant. That's what the minister of higher ed said."

"Yes, the two of them were tied together pretty closely. I don't know why. Davis isn't such a bad guy. I kind of liked him; he's a good supporter of the university. There was some talk that Davis and Spelt's wife had something going. If true, that might have been a reason not to monitor Spelt too closely. I don't want to know."

Jean-Michel puffed out his cheeks and blew his breath out slowly. "Me neither. I've had enough."

"By the way, have you heard who the acting chancellor is?"

"You bet. It's Mrs. Kerr. And she's been busy. Sent me a message that she had contacted a couple of Murphy experts—the curator emeritus at Yale where Murphy's papers are and also one of his paintings and Deborah Rothschild, who organized a huge exhibition of the Murphys and their friends at Williams College."

"She's been busy. She phoned me Sunday to tell me I was reinstated. Meyer, too, after a pro forma physical today. And I got an email last night from Luce Drummond. The board has asked her to sit as acting president until a new search can be done. That's Kerr again." Monroe paused and smiled. "Luce said she's thinking about it, but apparently she already has an offer from Mt. Holyoke."

Jean-Michel frowned. "A tremendous compliment. I'll bet she takes Holyoke. So *you* could be next in line."

Monroe laughed. "Are you kidding? I'm just trying to get my book done. And teach my classes. I hope Luce bails us out. You know Mrs. Kerr can be pretty persuasive." Monroe patted Jean-Michel on the shoulder and hurried off. He had to stop at his office before his class, which would be starting in a few minutes.

A message was taped to the door: *SPCA called: The beagle you rescued has recovered and can be adopted after Wednesday.* Monroe smiled as he tucked the note into his pocket. Then he stepped to his desk, grabbed a folder, and hurried out the door.

As he neared the lecture room, his phone dinged and he saw it was a message from Jim: *Breaking news. Got Aziz's papers from a Royal Bank safety deposit box. Everything getting locked down. Renwick able to give a statement later today. Paint on Mildred's car matches the bike, hit and run if not attempted homicide. Probably won't use the raincoat. Thanks, anyway. Cactus Club tomorrow night?*

Monroe entered the lecture room, trying to look nonchalant as he stepped to the podium. Students were looking down at their notebooks. Monroe took a deep breath and began. "Before our interruption, we were thinking about how Stephen Greenblatt takes an ordinary occasion—Thomas More's memory of eminent men at table sharing a meal—as a reflection of the broader culture. Let's carry on—"

The class erupted, clapping and cheering, and pulling out several banners from hiding spots: *Welcome Back, Professor M! Good Riddance to Spelt. A Fresh Start.* Monroe just stood there, pleased to be part of it. Yet it was also bigger. A celebration of inquiry, interchange, critical thinking, dialogue. Maybe just something that starts slowly when students arrive and then builds by showing up again and again.

That dog on Cypress for some reason flashed into his mind, his joyful dash to make contact, an innocent recklessness that nearly did Peter in. Peter saw his goodness, liked it, and imagined a *next time. Sometimes, we do get one.*

Acknowledgments

The university, a place of bright ideas and big egos, became the setting for my stories when I joined a writers' group at the West Vancouver Community Centre. Caron Penhall, our facilitator, encouraged me to keep them coming. My writing mates—patient, smart, critical—tolerated and then became interested in the comings and goings of Professor Monroe.

Monroe's world, and mine, became more complicated when he began to investigate a death on campus and I somehow slipped into the facilitator's chair.

A lot of people helped. Jane Richardson, at work on her own novel, exchanged chapters with me, which led to a flurry of comments and ideas at the beginning.

Eric Brown edited a bulked-up first draft and told me to cut the throat clearings, stoppages, and sideshows. Take out the scissors; start rewriting.

First readers tackled it. David Barnhill read it twice and engaged me with countless conversations. Josette Salles, with eagle eye and busy pencil, spotted inconsistencies, weaknesses in structure, and slips in detail. Yikes, quite a few. Peter Keith reads slowly, doesn't miss a thing, takes time to mull things over, and engages with a spirit of inquiry. He gave Monroe and his world a thorough vetting. Nancy Keith treated the manuscript as a book at bedtime and it didn't put her to sleep. Pure encouragement.

Erin Parker worked through the manuscript twice with the skills and thoroughness of a professional editor. Her detailed reports gave me suggestions to tighten the plot, improve pacing, and deepen the characters and their connections.

The Salles family are creative. Charlotte, my niece, drafted a early version of the cover. Later, Josette, my wife, developed a collage that served as the basis for the design developed by Helen Eady.

Jim Boothroyd, a serious writer with published fiction and a manuscript or two simmering in the slow cooker of his desk drawer read the manuscript at a late stage when he was busy with his day job. He gave wise suggestions for all aspects of the project, even from his garden while tending his basil and tomato plants. Or while looking for Sophie, the family's charming but slyly mischievous dog, on a caper again in the neighbourhood.

Amanda Vaill's portrait of the Murphys and their friends, *Everybody was so Young,* became the ground for my treatment of the lost Murphy sketch in the Northlake gallery.

Howard Jones knows about finances. He answered questions about the way illicit funds slide through banks and off-shore repositories for nefarious ends.

My sons, their friends, and many others over the years tossed in a friendly "how's the book going?" Surely perplexed it was taking so long to write the darn thing. Each time it was a small encouragement. And now—*maybe just one more rewrite?*—I let it go. You, the reader, will have to decide if it was ready.

To my sons, Nick, Thomas, and Christophe, and to my wife, Josette Salles, *Murder 101* is dedicated. They sustained the project by sustaining me. I'm grateful to them as always.

Printed in Canada